Onus on Truths

An Agents's

Journal

Hamilton Spiers

Copyright @ 2022 Hamilton Spiers
All rights reserved
This is a work of fiction. Names, characters, businesses, places, events, and incidents are either the product of the author's imagination or used in a fictitious manner. Any resemblance to actual persons, living or dead, or actual events, is purely coincidental. Real names and locations have only been used in cases of known historical fact, supported by independent, publicly available material.

Chapter 26 Operation 'Spud u like' 122

Chapter 27 Moonlight Flit 124

Chapter 28 Billy: Breaking News 133

Chapter 29 Everyone is suspect 136

Chapter 30 Mary: Suspicion Calls 139

Chapter 31 Loyalist feud 141

Chapter 32 Micky: Tout Rumours 144

Chapter 33 Liam: Close watch 148

Chapter 34 Bridget and Frankie 152

Chapter 35 The Guilty Four 155

Chapter 36 Interrogation 158

Chapter 37 Mary & Bridget 162

Chapter 38 Liam's Recovery 166

Chapter 39 A Spy in the House 169

Chapter 40 Frankie, I Want Names 172

Chapter 41 Bridget: The damage is done 178

Chapter 42 A Guilty Conscience 180

Chapter 43 Micky Comes Clean 183

Chapter 44 Bridget 186

Chapter 45 Verdict Needed 191

Chapter 46 Parlour visit 196

Chapter 47 Safety Measures 198

Chapter 48 Knock Knock, Who's There? 202

Chapter 49 Caught Out 210

Chapter 50 Burning Ash: No regrets 212

Chapter 51 Time to Act 215

Chapter 52 The aftermath 227

Chapter 53 Post Op reaction 228

Chapter 54 24 hours earlier 229

Chapter 55 Fake News 230

Chapter 56 The Detachment 233

Chapter 57 Mary's Rise in status 236

Chapter 58 Girls Reunited 245

Chapter 59 Operation Transfer 247

Chapter 60 Wakey Wakey 249

Death Rattle Epilogue 252

References 255

Chapter 1

Turn Coat

1996

Billy peered out through the rain-stained windscreen of the firm's totally non-descript, ten-year-old silver VW Estate and waited for the call. It was what the detachment called SOPs, or Standard Operating Practice. The handler stayed off the route until he got confirmation from the cover team.

The Ormeau Road was busy, but that wasn't unusual. The same red brick houses that had once belonged to the shipyard workers that built the Titanic clashed uneasily with the fast-food chains that now supplied the only current employment. This area of Belfast was chosen because it did not belong territorially to one side or the other. It was like a cultural no man's land, where you couldn't really tell which religion they belonged to. That was always a good thing. In Belfast city language, it was both diverse and multicultural. Young university students rubbed shoulders uneasily with pensioners while they, in turn, negotiated baby prams being pushed by mothers that looked younger than the students.

CT1 (Cover Team One): "Standby, Standby. Alpha is just passing the pharmacy and wearing black on black and clear."

Billy, the Handler, responded, "Roger, Alpha, black on black and clear, moving in to affect pick up."

CT2 (Cover Team Two): "Roger, that's us in position."

Billy, having been shadowing and avoiding coming onto the route until clearance was received, was now manoeuvring his vehicle onto the Ormeau Road, where he sighted the Agent walking along the footpath. Billy smiled as he watched the Agent dodge his way past a small Asian man with a very large duffle bag perched precariously on his back. As Billy approached, he gave a countdown to the Agent. "200 to Alpha, 100 to Alpha, 50 to Alpha, Alpha now." Billy pulled up alongside the Agent, who was now just passing the Sean Graham bookmaker's shop, and at the same time unlocked the central locking system.

The Agent raised his hand in a friendly gesture, acknowledging the presence of his Handler. He looked in both directions along the street like a child before crossing the road, then opened the passenger door and got in. Billy could hear the cover teams making their calls of progress over the radio through his bean-sized covert earpiece in his right ear as he started to pull away from the curb.

The Agent's smile faded as soon as he sat in the passenger seat. He appeared to be a ball of nerves. A handler gets to know his Agents after a while, and Billy's spider sense clicked in.

Expect the unexpected.

Those words sprang from his subconscious, one of the many maxims learned from his training at the Specialist Intelligence Wing.

"You OK, mate? Put your seat belt on or you will get us pulled by the peelers."

The only reply was "Sorry Billy" as the man reached into his jacket pocket.

Billy could just make out the dark, hard, shape of a 9mm pistol as the Agent tried to point it towards him and reacted as trained. The Handler's left elbow arched over to the passenger side and smashed into his temple and eye socket as the Agent's head cannoned against the door pillar and he screamed. Billy's mobile rang, much to his annoyance, as it was yet another distraction whilst dealing with a life and death situation. Billy frantically groped into the door side pocket, releasing his own pistol from the door holster. He swung towards the assailant and whipped the pistol against his head. The Agent was knocked unconscious. Billy was shocked by the Agent's actions and tried desperately to comprehend why he would want him dead. It was the Agent who had requested this emergency meeting, stating he had vital and lifesaving information to pass.

The impact of a ford transit van smashing into the driver's side of the car snapped Billy out of his self-analysis of the Agent's actions. Billy was momentarily winded by the impact of the collision, and his body was thrust forward, with his head striking the rear-view mirror. He was also halted in his struggle to retrieve the pistol from the Agent's Jacket. The van hit the front right side of the car, forcing it back into the side of the road and up tight against the curb. Billy's initial thought was that he had caused the accident by not paying attention to the road whilst dealing with the Agent, but it soon became apparent that he was being deliberately rammed, with the van intentionally stopping alongside the vehicle, ensuring there was no escape for Billy through the driver's door.

Billy managed to press his covert radio pressel and convey the words, "Contact, Contact."

All hell broke loose. CT1, having completed the trigger and clearance of the Agent, had just managed to get back into a position to provide close support when the Ford Transit van passed them at speed. It overtook the line of traffic between Billy and CT1's car. The team witnessed as the van rammed into the Handler's car, forcing it back toward the curb, almost simultaneously receiving the 'Contact' report from Billy.

Both cover teams rapidly manoeuvred their vehicles through the traffic, totally unaware of the struggle between Billy and the Agent. But in accordance with their operational orders, the priority was to protect the Handler and Agent.

CT2 had just reached the bridge which crossed the Stranmillis embankment when they heard the 'Contact' call. The team completed a handbrake turn on the bridge, narrowly avoiding oncoming traffic. The sound of blaring vehicle horns and the smell of burning rubber filled the air. A cyclist was thrown from his bike, landing in a heap on the footpath in his attempt to avoid a head on collision with the cover team's car. This was no drill, but the teams had practiced this type of scenario a thousand times on the ranges of Ballykinler. This was going to be a hard extraction, under fire and in a heavily populated area against a determined PIRA (Provisional Irish Republican Army) ASU (Active Service Unit).

It was a reckless attack by thoughtless, despicable people who showed a total disregard for human life, and in particular, the many civilians who could be caught up in the crossfire of their actions. The two cover cars very quickly forced their way through the traffic to get into a position to engage the threat.

The two occupants in the front of the van exited via their respective doors. One man armed with an AK-47 got out of the driver's door. The passenger appeared to be leaning out of the door, facing in the direction of Billy's car. He was holding a 9mm pistol in his right hand whilst holding onto the side of the cab with his left.

CT2 came to a halt twenty-five meters short of the transit van.

Shoppers and passers-by seemed transfixed with what was happening before the realisation that a sinister and deadly attack was taking place. It was then that panic set in. People started running for cover in all directions to get out of the line of fire. What was a very busy road had suddenly become a lot less so as the road and the footpaths started to clear of civilians.

CT2 exited their vehicle, taking up firing positions behind the open armoured doors of their car. CT1, who were forced to stop short to the rear of the van and dismount, were making progress on foot through traffic toward Billy and the van. They were screaming, "ARMY! Stay in your vehicles!" at the shocked occupants of the trapped vehicles as they passed.

Two further terrorists were attempting to exit the rear of the transit van armed with AK-47's. All four individuals were dressed in dark boiler suits, wearing balaclavas and leather gloves.

Billy, although trapped in the vehicle, was able to force his seat back, dropping his back rest so he was almost horizontal. This enabled him to raise his pistol in both hands whilst aligning it in the centre of his body. He pointed it toward the front windscreen in anticipation for a target to appear. He knew he couldn't escape out his side, as the van was blocking his exit. His unconscious passenger was also preventing his escape on the near side.

The driver of the van exited and moved round toward the front of the vehicle with the intention of supporting his passenger. On seeing this, CT2 shouted, "Army! Stop, or I will fire."

The terrorist turned in the direction of the cover team and fired a burst of shots in their direction. Several shots managed to hit the front of the vehicle, but they were sporadic and inaccurate. By now, the terrorist had reached the front of the van.

Both operators opened fire, hitting the terrorist multiple times with the front of the vehicle, taking the additional impact of the missed shots. This reduced the risk to the remaining members of the public, who may have been on either side of the street and trying desperately to escape the firefight. The terrorist was propelled back against the van by the impact of the rounds hitting his chest and head, before eventually sliding down in a crumbled heap on the road. The windscreen of the van was covered in blood and brain matter.

CT2 turned their attention to the passenger, who was only partially sighted to them as the open door of the van obscured any possible engagement. The passenger terrorist appeared to be standing on a foot bar and gripping the doorframe with his left hand for balance.

CT2 knew the arc of fire which they had would only endanger the occupants of the car, along with the civilians on that side of the road. Even engaging through the van door would potentially endanger Billy in the trapped car. It was a risk they didn't want to take, but there was still the threat of the obscured target.

John, a member of CT2, was in the process of moving closer to try and get a better view of the target when he received the call to remain on the western side of the street to avoid being in the line of fire from CT1.

The terrorist holding the pistol in his right-hand opened fire through the windscreen, emptying his 8-round magazine toward the interior of the car. Billy could see the passenger leaning out of the van, but only had a partial view of the terrorist as the side of the van protruded beyond the cab. However, there was enough of the target to engage. Billy fired well-aimed shots in the direction of the terrorist, hitting him on the upper right side of his chest and face. The bullet exited up through the top of his head, killing him instantly. The passenger fell forward onto the bonnet of Billy's car, his twisted body lying in a heap, with wide, lifeless eyes looking at Billy.

CT1 were closing in fast on the target vehicle. The rear sliding steel shutter was pulled up as the two terrorists tried to exit the van. The first of the two men managed to jump to the ground armed with an AK-47 but both terrorists were caught off guard, as they were not ready for the two fast-moving, armed men in civilian clothes bearing down on them. Both operators had been manoeuvring up either side of the line of traffic. It was Davy who reacted first to the terrorist. Having screamed a warning, he took cover by the front of a stationary car to engage his target. He fired two well aimed shots with his pistol, as he believed the risk of firing his MP5K submachine gun could endanger Billy and the Agent due to the reduced arc of fire he had. He knew the pistol would ensure more accuracy. The shots hit the terrorist squarely in the chest, neutralising him.

Mac, the CT1 commander, engaged the second terrorist, who had just finished raising the sliding steel shutter but was in the process of reaching down for the AK-47 which was slung across his body. Mac, firing his Heckler Koch HK53 assault rifle, hit the terrorist, lifting him off his feet and thrusting him deep into the rear of the van. Unfortunately, the terrorist involuntarily squeezed the trigger, which was on automatic mode, shooting sporadically, rounds ricocheting through the side of the van, but fortunately, above the roof level of Billy's vehicle. The buildings nearest the incident got sprayed by the bullets, the large front window of one of the shops splattering into a tiny million diamond pieces of glass, much to the horror of the several civilians sheltering behind it.

Billy could see he had found and hit his target through the bullet ridden fragmented, laminated windscreen. He observed the lifeless body and the bloody mass on the side of the van's cab, his only view being through the small bullet hole apertures created by the exchange of gunfire between the terrorist and himself. The deafening sound of gunfire and concussive noise subsided to become almost a cocoon of total silence. It was like he was sitting in a soundproof room or someone had turned the volume down.

He glanced over his left shoulder and could see the Agent slumped in the seat, his eyes closed and his head rested on his right shoulder. He had a large red bump on his forehead from the impact of Billy's pistol. Billy realized he was still unconscious and therefore totally oblivious to the whole incident taking place.

Billy wasn't sure if he was in a state of shock or whether the adrenaline rush, he had just experienced during the terrifying ordeal was simply easing off. Regardless, he felt a strange calmness come over him. It was as if he was having a lucid dream. He had the awareness and clarity that something wasn't quite right, yet he felt a level of calm and contentment that he had survived an ambush attempt on him. He started to feel somewhat lightheaded and faint, with his body feeling clammy, as if in a cold sweat. His breathing had become more laboured. He looked down toward his chest and stomach and could see that blood was seeping through his clothing. The realisation that he had been shot hit him. Despite the wearing of covert body armour under his shirt, a round had ricocheted and struck him between the front and back ballistic plates, entering the side of his chest. The space around him seemed to close in like a veil of darkness starting to descend upon him. His struggle for breath becoming more profound.

Billy now realised his condition was serious, as his medical training told him he was dry land drowning. His lungs were unable to extract oxygen from the air. He recognised he had a puncture wound to the torso causing a persistence of laryngospasm in his throat, which was affecting his ability to get a breath. In cases of dry land drowning, very little fluid is aspirated into the lungs. It was something he had experienced on his RtoI course (Resistance to Interrogation). It was one of the effects of waterboarding. Billy was fighting for his last breaths as he knew the gurgling noise, he was experiencing was the 'Death Rattle'.

His thoughts were now of his wife and two sons. the realisation he would never see them again. Everything seemed to be in slow motion, he could just about make out voices as they approached the vehicle, but they just sounded like a distant whisper getting further away. He felt detached, yet completely peaceful. He was without pain, feeling nothing but a sense of complete wellbeing. A darkness descended on him, as well as a complete silence, before closing his eyes.

Both cover teams had closed in on the scene with their pistols drawn and their assault rifles slung by their sides. A Renault Espace people carrier driven at speed exited University Avenue onto the Ormeau Road before coming to a temporary halt short of the contact scene. The driver, on seeing the carnage in front of him and no sign of any terrorists running in his direction needing extraction, decided on discretion rather than valour. He struggled desperately to find reverse gear, only to cause loud screeching noises of the gearbox in his endeavour to escape. He eventually found a gear but the vehicle catapulted forward in the direction of CT2.

John from CT2, who was directly in line of the car, fired two shots through the windscreen, hitting the driver of the vehicle. The driver lost control and smashed into a stationary vehicle. The driver lay hunched and motionless over the steering wheel.

Mac and Davy from CT1 were the first to reach Billy's vehicle as CT2 continued to secure the scene. They now needed to wait for the QRF (Quick Reaction Force) to arrive. Each member of the team had already donned their Army hats to avoid a friendly-on-friendly situation occurring when the QRF turned up. As all the operators were in civilian clothes, it was important the QRF could recognize friend from foe. Mac gained access to the car whilst Davy supplied close support to him.

CT2 gathered up the terrorist weapons before checking on the terrorists' vital signs, declaring all four terrorists in and around the van dead.

Mac encountered two lifeless bodies still in their seats. Both men had been shot several times, and the blood-stained clothing showed evidence of severe blood loss. Mac ripped open the shirt of Billy to examine his body for injuries and found two gunshot wounds to the right side of his chest. He then ran his hands down the spine and back, seeking any sign of exit wounds.

The sirens of the approaching emergency services could be heard, along with the mutterings of the crowds as they tried to gather for a better view of the macabre incident that had taken place. Mac continued to examine both bodies. After a minute or so, he shouted from the interior of the vehicle,

"I've got a pulse."

Chapter 2

Liam Murray

September 1973

Liam Murray, a fresh-faced, slim-built, 17-year-old from the Ardoyne area of West Belfast had entered through the rear gates of Palace Barracks, an Army Camp on the outskirts of Belfast and close to the village of Holywood. Having initially arrived at the main gate to be greeted by a cordon of soldiers and a team from the EOD (Explosive Ordnance Disposal Specialists) dealing with a suspect vehicle which had been abandoned directly facing the main gate, Liam was directed away from the entrance and sent to the rear gates of the camp, where he was checked in at the security post by a member of the camp's security. Liam was held briefly at the guardroom until the security alert was over. The suspect vehicle was declared a hoax—the third such incident that week.

Following the security alert, Liam was escorted to Sande's café to await processing for his interview. Sande's was a Christian-run Café where support and fellowship were provided to the military community as well as somewhere you could get great snacks. It was a bright clear day, and as he was being escorted down to the Café, he could see from the elevated site of the camp right across Belfast lough, as far right as Carrickfergus and left to the Belfast Shipyard, which set against the backdrop of Divis Mountain and the magnificent cranes of Harland & Wolff, home of HMS Titanic.

Onus on Truths

Liam was told to wait in the café and that a member of the Army recruiting team would be along to escort him for his interview to join the Army. There were several potential recruits in the Café waiting their turn. Soldiers in uniform were playing snooker on the two tables that dominated one portion of the room. The sight of soldiers relaxing was a strange experience for Liam, as he was so used to seeing these same men dressed in body armour, steel helmets with rifles at the ready, crouched in doorways or street corners providing protection for their fellow comrades patrolling through his part of town. They appeared much more threatening on the streets. These lads didn't seem much older than himself and yet were out in the streets of Belfast and beyond, providing security whilst being abused, spat on, and shot at. Liam had a sudden empathy for these lads, and knew he was doing the right thing by joining. Although it was mainly for adventure and to see the world, not patrolling the Ardoyne.

Liam remembered how it was the soldiers who helped him and his family move when they were evicted from their home by loyalists. His house in Conway Street was attacked with petrol bombs and bricks, and he recalled how he, his mother, and father had to be escorted by the soldiers for their own safety. It was a frightening time, but it was also happening to Loyalists living in similar districts. The family had lost most of their possessions because of the expulsion. He recalled how it was shortly after the tragic events in Londonderry, during a civil rights march where 13 civilians were shot following disturbances and rioting by members of the Parachute Regiment.

Liam turned his attention back to the room and the uncomfortable-looking recruits in their Sunday best attire as they sat at the small wooden tables, deep in their own thoughts. Liam wondered what their motivation was for being there. No doubt, he thought some were considering their various Regimental options, whilst others knew that the Army or juvenile detention centres were the limited choices to be had. Liam couldn't determine if anyone else in the place was from his side of town. There was a distinct lack of football shirts being worn that would distinguish whether the lads in the café were protestant or catholic. No Rangers or Celtic shirts, which was a good tell-tale sign when you walked through the city centre.

A soldier dressed in a smart barrack dress uniform with highly polished boots and trousers starched so severely the creases could have cut butter, entered the café and called out the name of the next potential recruit. "Bennett." Not having got a response he repeated the call, "Bennett… Billy Bennett," before one of the lads at the table responded and followed the soldier out.

Liam had just joined the small queue for refreshments when a lad in front of him noticed the crucifix on his neck and rounded on him, getting extremely aggressive and right into his face.

"What's a Fenian Bastard doing in here?"

Although meant as an insult and received as such, he was only giving him a backhanded compliment, as Fenian referred to a member of a secret 19th century organization dedicated to the overthrow of British rule in Ireland. Liam could feel the spray of spit from the lad's mouth against his face as he swore at him. A fight broke out between the two, and it was a Sergeant by the name of Norman McAteer who had seen the altercation and intervened to break up the fight.

Norman was known in the camp as 'Gentleman Norm' because of his dapper attire and officer-like appearance. He worked in the Intelligence Cell for 7/10 UDR (Ulster Defence Regiment) and was also known as the oracle when it came to the Intelligence scene in the city of Belfast.

Having separated the lads and determined the circumstances surrounding the incident, he had the foul-mouthed youth ejected from the camp and his interview cancelled, but not before pointing out, "I'm a catholic and my soldier buddies never worried about what religion I was when needing me to provide covering fire as they ran down streets being shot at or vice versa. In the Army, we are all brothers together, and the Army doesn't need or want your type."

Norman took Liam to the side and after a brief chat he obtained several interesting facts concerning Liam's background. He immediately recognised the family name along with other close associates that were still currently active in the republican movement.

Liam's initial interview took place later in the morning, and following an aptitude test, he was told that once certain security checks had been concluded, he would be invited back for a further interview. It was Liam's desire to join the Royal Irish Rangers, as this was the sister Regiment his uncle had served in during the fifties as a member of the Royal Ulster Rifles, the latter merging along with the Royal Enniskillen Fusiliers and the Royal Irish Rifles to form two battalions of the Royal Irish Rangers in 1969. Ironically, this was the same time civil unrest had come to the streets of Belfast, along with the sight of the first British soldiers patrolling the interfaces.

Norman had maintained good liaison with members of the British Military Intelligence in the form of MRF (Military Reaction Force), who were co-located in Palace Barracks. MRF was a small, covert Intelligence gathering and counter insurgency unit whose members were handpicked from throughout the British Army. The Unit was described by some as a legalised death squad. It was set up exclusively to defeat PIRA, or as they were more commonly referred to, 'The Provos.'

On completion of Liam's interview, it became clear that the security clearance would not be granted, as he was deemed to be a security risk due to his affiliation with several PIRA members. As Norman was the AIO (Assistant Intelligence Officer), he was informed of the decision by the recruiters but saw an opportunity to exploit the situation further. Not many Catholic lads joined the Army, and particularly not from west Belfast. The recruiting team were consulted, and it was agreed that a follow up interview would take place, but it would be down to the intelligence cell to conduct it, in the hope of gaining additional exploitable information from Liam.

Norman mentioned the potential opportunity which had presented itself to a MRF member and good friend, Davy Davis, affectionately known as 'Desperate Dan' because of his huge frame and square jawline. Davy requested a seat at the interview with Liam Murray to make his own assessment. It was important to ascertain the true intentions of Liam or at least determine whether this was an attempt by the Provos to infiltrate the military with one of their own. Either way, it was a golden opportunity to have a one on one with someone with such good connections.

A further interview was arranged for Liam, but Norman was requested to stand down, with two members of the MRF replacing the original interviewers. It was a deliberate ploy by the MRF to distance anyone associated with Liam thus far to ensure total privacy and help them facilitate their own agenda for the chat. It would be a standard interview to probe into his lifestyle and obtain as much additional information as possible before breaking the unwelcome news of his unsuccessful application to join the Armed Forces.

Another prospect of work for Her Majesties Government which was potentially on offer was that of a CASCON (Casual Contact). Someone with Liam's pedigree could be used to infiltrate the IRA and provide much needed intelligence to enable MRF to conduct pre-emptive strikes against the terrorist cells and kill the main players.

As a lad still in his teens hanging around street corners with his mates was probably the best he could hope for. As deprivation was ripe in the area, low employment opportunities, was causing sectarian tensions, and resentment amongst the catholic population. There had been widespread discrimination festering, which eventually erupted into violence. Liam had already experienced both protestant and catholic families being burnt out of their homes and made to move into areas populated by their own religion. Liam just wanted away from the hatred and bigotry. He was a talented young footballer who loved Manchester United and idolised his footballing hero, George Best, despite George being from a protestant background and from the Loyalist east Belfast.

The government, through an organisation called NICRC (Northern Ireland Community Relations Commission) brought together children from both protestant and catholic traditions and sent them on holidays together to the mainland. Liam had attended one of these holidays and enjoyed the experience, even making good friends with some of the protestant boys. Unfortunately, although these holidays were well intended, they did not really achieve what was hoped for by the organisation. This was because the institutionalisation of violence in Northern Ireland had become so endemic that, for kids like Liam, when the holiday was over, it was back to his republican enclave were the bigotry was commonplace and he would never expect to see the protestant lads again. Liam believed he was too young for it to have had the desired, hoped-for effect.

It was difficult growing up in such a toxic environment, but being regaled by stories from his uncle, 'Rifleman Seamus Murray' about his overseas adventures, as well as those of his grandfather who had fought at the Battle of the Somme, kept a desire burning inside him of wanting to follow in their footsteps. He knew that he needed to get away from his mates and their bigoted ways. Already, some had fallen into the trap of believing that the fight for a United Ireland would only be achieved through the bomb and the gun. The rise of paramilitarism, bullying, extortion, and intimidation was mainly being carried out on their own community, yet the younger lads were gravitating to this new form of excitement. Liam had already lost a good friend Pat to the Troubles.

Pat was 16 when a riot took place at the interface between the protestant Shankill Road and the catholic Falls Road. It was at a time when internment without trial in the early 1970's had taken place, with 342 republicans incarcerated from the city on suspicion of being involved with PIRA. The result was riots on the streets. Pat was keeping a safe distance but was watching events unfold. It was exciting, and he had tried in vain to get Liam to go down and watch. He was standing near the end of a gable wall when a man dressed in a balaclava and bomber jacket ran round the corner and smashed into him. The fact the man had a petrol bomb already ignited and was in the process of throwing it meant it hit Pat squarely on the back before dropping to the ground, smashing at his feet and engulfing him in petrol and flames. The bomber, a known paramilitary, fell backwards, avoiding the flames which resulted in Pat receiving 85% burns to his body and eventually dying in the Mater hospital by a slow and agonising death. This tragic event and many of the senseless beatings conducted by the paramilitaries caused Liam to resent them and especially the petrol bomber, who showed no remorse, having been heard to mock Pat by stating, "The idiot got in my way." A statement that angered Liam so much.

Liam's desire to join the Army had remained a secret. He had the presence of mind not to let anyone know of his Army ambitions for fear of recriminations. He had it all worked out in his head: He would tell everyone he had secured a building job in London and was moving over in search of a better life. He believed he was growing up in a hopeless place.

Chapter 3

Flirty Mary

1995

Mary Sweeney, a curvaceous and attractive lady in her late 30's with shoulder-length, fair hair, was someone who could still turn heads. A secret agent working for British Intelligence for over two decades, and a divorcee with no children, she enjoyed her clandestine work. She lived alone following the death of her mother in the parental, three-bedroom, semi-detached home in the Ardoyne. Mary had been a neighbour of Sean and Bridget Pearse for over twenty years, and it was fair to say she knew everything there was to know about the couple, including the infidelity by both Bridget and Sean.

She had always been a shoulder to cry on for Bridget when Sean was imprisoned for his part in various terrorist activities. She had acted as a custodian for weapons when Sean's house was being raided by the Army and the knuckle dragging HMSU (Headquarters Mobile Support Unit) of the RUC (Royal Ulster Constabulary). She also recalled the numerous times she'd witnessed Sean being arrested and questioned over his republican involvement. Sean was the self-proclaimed hardman and member of West Belfast Brigade PIRA.

Both INLA (Irish National and Liberation Army) and PIRA were in direct competition with each other, but although INLA were considered dangerous, they were also deemed an ineffective grouping by the security forces mainly due to their unpredictable and careless approach to mounting operations. Areas within the city were fought over by these rival republicans for control, with PIRA being the more successful and dominant force of the two. However, INLA were still difficult to infiltrate, though it was believed that one well-placed Agent could probably bring down the whole grouping. PIRA, on the other hand, worked in much smaller cells and was therefore harder to get beyond the periphery of the organisation.

Sean was a ruthless thug, who Mary disliked immensely; she found him repulsive, a letch, and would often catch him leering at her when she happened to be in his and Bridget's company at social events. She did have a sexual experience with him, but it was a long time ago and when she was at a low point in her life. She had just separated from her husband of seventeen months and was drunk, vulnerable, and he had taken advantage of the situation. It was a frustrated sex act but nothing more than that, rough and quick on the bonnet of his car. The next morning, she could make out the bum and handprints that were still present on the frost-covered bonnet, and it made her feel physically sick. Sean had tried it on with her on numerous other occasions, but she would always remind him of her friendship with Bridget and a loyalty she had already betrayed, an act she would not do again. It didn't stop Mary from having many other relationships but they were always short lived or simply one-night stands.

One such relationship occurred when she was just a young girl of 17 back in the early 1970s with a young Scottish lad by the name of Jason. She met him in the Pig & Chicken nightclub in Templepatrick on the outskirts of Belfast.

It was a place that had live bands most weekends and was very popular with young people.

Jason was a soldier stationed at the RAF Base at Aldergrove, which was situated to the rear of Belfast International Airport. He told Mary he was working on construction sites in Antrim. She had no reason to disbelieve him, but she knew better. Whenever they met, it was always in the city centre and he would never leave her home, but only ever walked her round to the taxi rank. There was always some excuse, like needing to catch the last train back to Antrim or being on site early the next morning.

One night, whilst in town with Mary, Jason bumped into a few lads from camp, despite trying hard to avoid them. One lad shouted across the bar toward him. He ignored the shouts, but Mary immediately picked up on the act and asked, "How do you know those boys?" She continued by stating, "Those boys are Brit soldiers." Jason denied knowing them and said, "You must have been mistaken, I don't know them," before trying to change the subject. He suggested they leave the bar. On the way to the taxi rank, Jason asked "Why do you think those lads are soldiers?"

Mary laughed and said, "Because they look like you," then continued by stating, "You all look alike, and there is a way in which you hold yourselves, you're so straight and upright for goodness' sake and you practically march when you walk."

Jason tried to interject by protesting that he was not, but again Mary laughed and said, "Look, for a navvy, your hands are too soft, something my dad never had, and he worked his whole life on building sites."

Mary stated, "I knew straight away you were a soldier that night at the Pig & Chicken. You and your mates stood out like sore thumbs. I know that's why you don't leave me home and I wouldn't want you to."

She explained that her mum was dying to know who her new fella was, but it was too dangerous for both of them. "I know what these people are like, you and I would end up shot and in the same dustbin. I hate everything about them and what they stand for. I have seen the torment my Mum and the family went through because of the Provos and how they destroy lives."

Mary explained, "Look I'm having fun, and I know that one day soon, you will leave Northern Ireland and I will be left behind, but that's ok because there would be other nights at the Pig & Chicken and life will go on."

Mary told Jason about her older brother Tommy, who had been involved with PIRA and was now serving ten years in the Maze prison, or as the Provos call it 'H Block' for his part in attempting to place a UVIED (Under Vehicle Improvised Explosive Device) under a policeman's car. She did not agree with what he was doing but partly blamed the people he was with, as Tommy was only the driver of the vehicle and wasn't told what or who the target was.

She explained that Tommy had driven the car along with two others, Paddy Devlin and Finbar Greer. Paddy directed him to the area of Marlborough Park, an affluent part of the city. He was told to wait in the car as the two men went to conduct a walk pass of the targets house and ensure the policeman's car was parked as expected. They were armed with two pistols, having left an AK-47 assault rifle and an UVIED in the car.

As they entered the street of rich, red brick, double bay, Victorian houses with their wrap-around gardens set back from the tree-lined avenue, it was unnervingly quiet, with fewer cars parked on the street than when they conducted the initial recce of the target's address. Paddy noticed a dark-coloured Ford Sedan parked at the side of the street, and the hairs on his neck instantly stood on end. He sensed something was wrong. His mouth went dry, and as he went to speak to Finbar, he had no voice, with only a dry husky sound escaping, unable to form any words. He noticed the light above the front door of the target's house was off. This was something else that was out of place.

Lights suddenly appeared from both directions in the form of the headlights from the dark-coloured Sedan parked at the end of the street and a further vehicle which had been backed into a driveway of an adjacent property. Both men were trapped like rabbits in the headlights. It was as if the whole street had burst into life, the curtain going up in the opera house.

Suddenly, there was a shout of "Police! Stand still!" Paddy, as if by instinct, reached for his pistol as Finbar tried to turn and run, but both men's movements were met by bursts of gunfire.

Paddy was hit twice in the chest and was thrown backwards, only being stopped by a garden wall which he slid down, slumped with his chin resting on his chest. Finbar was hit in the shoulder blade, the bullet entering and ricocheting up before exiting through the top of his head. Another round went through his cheekbone before embedding itself within his skull.

Tommy could hear the commotion and the gunshots and immediately sought self-preservation and the need to get as far away from the incident as quickly as possible. As soon as he pulled away from the curb, two police wagons blocked off his escape route, and suddenly there were armed police surrounding the car. Tommy offered no resistance and was arrested at the scene, then taken to Castlereagh, the police interrogation centre. Recovered from the car was an UVIED and an AK-47 in the backseat. Tommy was charged with possession of arms and ammunition, with intent to endanger life, and received fourteen years, expected to serve at least ten.

Chapter 4

The Interview

October 1973

Liam turned up for his second interview at Palace barracks full of optimism and looking forward to hearing he had been successful with his application. He had it all figured out, although he was dating a girl from the Ardoyne, he was not worried about breaking it off if he was to go away to train. He liked her a lot, but he didn't love her. The relationship was more a casual affair and the Army would come first. He had plenty of time for serious relationships.

It was agreed that Norman would meet Liam and take him to the interview room but would then leave the guys from MRF to conduct their business. It was important Liam see a familiar face, at least initially, and Norman had already built a degree of rapport with the lad, making him the obvious choice. The interview room was in the main offices of the Army recruitment building, which had been comfortably furnished and inviting. Soft chairs had replaced the poly prop ones and a sideboard had been furnished with an assortment of snacks and soft drinks. All very cosy and convenient. It was important Liam should feel relaxed and comfortable in the setting.

Two men from the MRF were already in situ and primed. Davy was accompanied by an intelligence analyst who worked on the Belfast desk and was considered the best person to confirm or deny any information that Liam may divulge during the interview. Davy knew Liam would be devastated by the news of his failure to enlist.

There would be an even harder decision to make that would invariably change his life forever as he knew it.

Subject to the progress made on the interview, Liam would be offered a vastly different contract—one to work for a large and powerful organisation, namely British Military Intelligence. A contract which he could never divulge to anyone, not friends or family. A secret covert mission and not one to be celebrated with his closest friends; rather, he would be totally on his own. Davy thought long and hard over what buttons needed to be pushed regarding Liam and what incentives would be needed to entice or motivate him to work. The fact he wanted to join the military in the first instance was a plus, but it needed to be determined what would motivate him to take on such a contract knowing if caught would result in certain death. The Provos did not do slaps on the wrists. The consequences of caught informers would be a bullet to the back of the head, then dumped on an isolated country road at the border with the Republic of Ireland.

Research by the analyst highlighted that Liam had the right access and connections to make him a viable target for recruitment by MRF. However, additional work was still needed to determine if he would be capable of carrying out his covert work. A matter they hoped the interview could establish.

Liam's current girlfriend, Roslyn Connolly, was the sister of Frankie Connolly, an active member of the Belfast Brigade PIRA, and they knew her house was visited by other Provo members.

Davy hoped this could be the start of a long and fruitful arrangement between himself and Liam, by getting him to infiltrate the terrorist groupings. The further up the chain Liam could get, the better the intelligence gleaned. Davy would explain his intention to Liam by referring to this as the onion ring effect. Simply put, he would explain an onion is made up of several layers, so if Liam considered the centre of the onion as being the heart of the organisation, and the outer layers being the periphery, Liam would be deemed as being on the periphery. For example, someone on the periphery like Liam who could be tasked to stand on a street corner and give a signal when he sees police or army coming into an area. He would not know what is planned or by who. So, his information would be of limited use, but a better placed ASU member would be much more informed and would know who was involved and what the target was, which meant he would be much more valuable in terms of intelligence. He would therefore be closer to the inner layers of the onion.

Davy would be considering Liam's level of access; although he may be on the outer fringes of the onion now, with good direction he could be developed and progress through the layers toward the centre of the ring. All of this would be considered, but at the end of the day, Liam would need to consent to becoming an Agent. It would be the most difficult decision he could ever make.

The term 'Tout' is used to describe an informant/agent. Young girls have been tarred and feathered for just being seen talking to police or soldiers, but Touts would always be killed. Davy knew the decision Liam would be undertaking, and if he decided to accept, it was one he would not be taking lightly.

Norman met Liam at the gate and brought him to the interview room. The conversation between the two men was cordial, with Liam seemingly in good form. He was clearly excited by his prospects of joining. Norman escorted Liam along the corridor of the recruitment building to the interview room. He wished Liam good luck before knocking on the door which was answered by the analyst. The analyst greeted Liam with a friendly handshake and words of welcome. Norman was thanked and walked back along the corridor toward the exit.

Liam was shown into the room and offered a seat. Davy stood up to greet Liam and in doing so seemed to block out any natural light that was coming in through the window behind him. Liam looked up at the bulk of a man in front of him. All of six feet three inches tall and almost as wide, he made for an impressive but imposing figure. Taking Liam's hand in his to shake, he totally dwarfed it, making Liam seem small and vulnerable. Off course this wasn't his intention, as he was just a dominant character.

The interview was conducted with the analyst taking notes. They discussed the security details of the clearance process and the connections Liam had that were a potential impediment to his success in application. Already it was starting to look bleak for Liam. It was as if Davy was knocking him down only to build him back up again when it came to other options on offer. It was pointed out that despite not having had any previous convictions himself, he did have a friend killed by a petrol bomb during rioting in Belfast, and therefore was guilty by association. Notwithstanding the fact Pat was not involved but rather an innocent bystander and victim, but the nail in the coffin was the girlfriend Roslyn, and her brother Frankie Connolly.

Liam was confused and bewildered about how much they knew about his background and particularly the people he talked to and hung around with. There was the question of two cousins from his late mother's side who had terrorist convictions and had both served time at her majesties pleasure. It was so much to take in. It was put to Liam that all was not lost, as other opportunities were potentially on offer. Liam was devastated, and he could see Davy was still talking, but he was not getting any audio, as he was in a state of shock. It was as if he was watching this unfold from afar, not even in the room, but more like in a distant haze.

"Liam…Liam… LIAM." His name was being called, and eventually the room came back into focus. He just wanted to get up and leave the room. He wanted to get out of the camp and get himself back across the city and into familiar grounds.

Davy wanted to drive on and build a better picture for Liam. Having established the secrecy behind his application and how he intended to cover his absence for training, he'd proved he could establish a cover story and therefore had the ability to be inconspicuous, which met another of Davy's strict criteria. Surprisingly, the interview continued, and Liam seemed less anxious, starting to open up about his family connections but mainly in an attempt to distance himself from their activities and lifestyle. He spoke about his father's connection with the military and why he was so keen to join. Mainly, he wanted adventure and to get to see the world.

Davy was more philosophical about the current situation in Northern Ireland. He discussed the need to find a way to obtain peace and solutions to getting the two communities to live together, and if not live together, at least to a place where they were not killing each other. It was going well, and he was slowly making progress and finding common ground. The realisation that he wasn't getting to enlist was lessening, but the question of what other opportunities there might be was not yet clear. Davy eventually asked Liam if he would be interested in meeting with him from time to time on a casual basis just to chat about things in general. The penny dropped, with Liam going weak at the knees as the realisation and magnitude of the statement hit him. Liam looked up at Davy and stated, "Bloody hell, you want me to be a TOUT."

"That's not how I would term it, I just feel you could help us bring some of these thugs to justice, like the one who killed your friend Pat."

Liam looked surprised.

"We know who was responsible for his death, it was Finbar Greer, but he met his end along with his pal trying to kill a police officer shortly after the riot. There are many more like him out there, and they are like parasites living on the backs of good, law-abiding citizens. The world would be a much better place without them in it. Paramilitaries are not your protectors, Liam, but rather your controllers, and we need to flush them all out."

Liam was at least listening and stated, "I don't know what good I could be."

He was told he just needed to go about his normal business but keep his eyes and ears open, then, when he and Davy met up, report on those observations, for which he would be well paid. He was told not to worry too much about it now but take the number Davy would give him and phone him whenever he had something he felt was worthy of reporting, then they would arrange to meet somewhere secure and away from his area. He was told it would be kept simple for now, but they could discuss it more when they next met up. The only thing he was advised on was the need to make a second call immediately after he phoned Davy, so it could be verified, if challenged.

It couldn't have gone better, and they believed a successful recruitment of a CASCON (Casual Contact) was established by the name of Liam Murray—Codenamed: 'Weeping Willow'.

Chapter 5

Disclosures:

1974

Jason was shocked by Mary's revelations and knew he must report any contact with the local population to his Unit so the Intelligence Cell could conduct security checks on them.

Every soldier was warned about the Provos and how they had used a method of abduction called 'Honey Traps.' It was a constant fear that young soldiers could be set up by young women. Jason was told how such an event had occurred only the previous year when three young Scottish soldiers were enticed away from a Belfast city centre bar and into a car on the pretence of going to a party with the girls. They were later shot dead by PIRA members at an isolated area known as White Brae in north Belfast. This was a sickening and barbaric act and there was a constant threat and fear that it could happen again. It had caused revulsion and lost PIRA a lot of support at the time.

Considering Mary's links, her brothers' involvement, and his subsequent incarceration, he knew he was left with no choice. Had it only been a one-night stand, then it wouldn't have mattered, but it was more than that; he liked the girl.

The duty orderly Intelligence NCO (Non-Commissioned Officer) informed the IO (Intelligence Officer) about Private Jason McCandless and Mary Sweeney's liaisons. McCandless was reprimanded for not reporting his liaison sooner and was told that he should cut off all links with Mary immediately. Jason was gutted, as he wanted to continue to see her.

Considering the information provided and further enhanced checks carried out on Mary, her name was passed over to MRF for exploitation.

Davy was once again the main point of contact between the Units. The IO briefed him and immediately Davy could see the advantages of Mary, her fondness of soldiers, and how this could be exploited. He requested that Private Jason McCandless be ordered to attend an interview with himself at the IO's office. MRF members always visited the resident Battalions early in their tour of duty to explain the benefits of 'Talent Spotting' by patrolling soldiers. It was encouraged for these patrols to report back on any contact which they had with the general public, particularly where the engagement was positive and helpful to their mission.

The interview, or rather the debrief, would be much more formal than the one held with Liam Murray. For one, this was a young soldier, and he would do as he was told. The debrief would be thorough, with everything that was known about Mary and her relationship with Jason being extracted. Jason had already stated Mary had other soldier boyfriends prior to him and that she preferred them over the boys in the Ardoyne because they were deemed to be more mature. It was a case of orchestrating a way of getting someone else alongside Mary in the hope of recruiting her.

It wasn't just her relationships with soldiers that made her an ideal target for recruitment, but also the relationships and connections she had within her own neighbourhood.

Chapter 6

Liam: Reverse Contact

Liam had not been in touch with Davy since agreeing to help him. Four weeks had passed, and Liam had gotten himself a job working as a sales representative in a sports shop within the city centre. Davy was worried that he had gotten cold feet and was just ignoring him by getting on with his life. It was decided to pay him a visit at the shop. As a result of numerous bombings in the city and the threat to life and property, a security barrier had been built around the city centre. It meant people entering the centre could only do so through four designated gates where they had their personal belongings and body searched by Police or Army personnel. Once through the gates, shoppers could move about freely and feel more secure.

The operation was planned, and a four-man team deployed to the city centre. Three members of the team provided cover out on the street, whilst Davy entered the shop and identified Liam, who was helping a customer picking out a pair Gola football boots. Davy casually looked around the shop. Liam noticed Davy loitering and it made him feel anxious and shocked that he would show up there. He remained concentrated on the task at hand whilst giving the odd nervous glance toward Davy.

Davy was approached by another member of staff but stated he was only browsing for now and was left alone to continue his unsolicited intimidation of Liam. Once the customer left with his new plastic Gola boots, Davy pretended to be interested in a baseball bat on display. He informed Liam that it was ironic to think that sports shops in Northern Ireland sold more baseball bats than anywhere else within the United Kingdom. What was more interesting was the fact that there wasn't a single baseball team in the country. It was clearly a favourite tool for paramilitary punishment beatings.

Whether Liam saw this as some poetic statement of intent by Davy is not certain. However, he certainly got the message. He hadn't been in touch, and if he wasn't prepared to contact Davy, then Davy was quite prepared to meet him on his own doorstep. Whilst pretending to discuss the merchandise, Davy managed to convey that a telephone call was expected and he was keen to have a follow up meeting.

Liam agreed to phone at six that evening on completion of his work.

Davy left the shop, minus the baseball bat, but thanked Liam for his assistance.

At six o'clock, Liam did call Davy on the designated telephone line and immediately confronted him on his presence in the shop. Davy turned the conversation to his advantage by stating that it was a natural encounter with absolutely no compromise to either party. It was deemed a natural coming together of shop assistant and customer.

Once Liam calmed down, it was decided that a meeting should take place between them. A route was given to Liam to walk, and it was kept quite simple, with him being given a reason for being on that route in case he was seen by anyone from his area. It was explained that, at some point along that route, he would be picked up by Davy and taken somewhere private for a chat. He was also told if he wasn't happy for any reason, he should carry a newspaper in his right hand and no pickup would take place. Liam was further ensured that numerous other members of Davy's team would be deployed on the ground to guarantee his safety.

Although concerned, Liam was intrigued, and if he was honest with himself, excited by the clandestine nature of the task.

The meeting was arranged for the following day, with Liam instructed to leave his place of work and told to walk to Botanic Train

Hamilton Spiers

Station, then cut through the student area known as the Holylands of South Belfast. He was reminded of the actions to be carried out should he feel compromised or became suspicious of anyone.

Chapter 7

Frankie Connolly

1974

Frankie was several years older than his sister Roslyn. He was in his late twenties, medium build with a dark, oily complexion and a mop of black, shoulder-length hair with long but neatly trimmed sideburns. At 5' 8" tall, he was not an intimidating figure but was known to be ruthless and revered in the community—a reputation gained from his father, Patrick Connolly.

His father was a bare-knuckle street fighter, who was taught to fight by the world-renowned Alexander 'Buck Alec' Robinson: the Belfast Street fighter, Loyalist Paramilitary, and a member of the Ulster Special Constabulary. Buck Alec gained notoriety for being a gangster, his fighting, and for being an owner of a pet lion, which he walked around the streets of Belfast. He was always seen shouting at people who would be running across roads and streets to avoid encountering the man and his lion, that the lion had no teeth and wouldn't harm them.

Pat had died when Frankie was still in his teens. He had just won one of his underground fights against a gypsy who had travelled up from Dublin for the match up, but having collected his winnings for the bout, he was set upon by the gypsy's brothers and beaten to death, his body dumped at the side of the road on the outskirts of Belfast.

Frankie was a half decent boxer himself at amateur level, who fought out of the Holy Family boxing club. He treated everyone with suspicion and had no real friends to speak of, and despite Liam going out with his sister, treated him with indifference.

Whenever Liam would visit Roslyn at home, Frankie would always be asking questions about his mates and their allegiances to the republican cause. He always made Liam feel uncomfortable with his lack of friendly interaction and piercing stare. On several occasions when Liam was present, men would turn up at the door and hold discrete conversations with Frankie. This would normally be followed with Frankie grabbing his coat from the hall pegs and leaving the house to a waiting car. His departure was always without explanation or farewells. These visits always seemed to be followed by local gossip of knee capping's (bullets to the back of the knees) or worse, a black & decker drill through the leg, bursting out the knee cap. These punishments were brutal and savage in their administration but were methods of the paramilitaries to maintain control over the community and instil fear. It was always justified as punishment for anti-social behaviour.

Liam believed it was no coincidence, believing Frankie was very much part of the internal security of the Provos. Either way, he was clearly feared in the community.

It wasn't only Liam who was suspicious of Frankie; the MRF had known for quite some time of his involvement within PIRA. Other Intelligence Agents had provided information on his steady rise within the republican movement. Many a recipient of his beatings and torture were also only too happy to report his activities when interviewed by Police following their treatment. Several of his punishment recipients had described receiving what Frankie called a 'Six Pack,' meaning two bullets to the knees, ankles, and elbows.

Chapter 8

The Meeting

The area of Shaws Bridge was picked by Davy for the meeting because of its seclusiveness. It was also an area that could be easily defended. 'Shaws Bridge' is an area of historical interest, as the stone bridge was built in 1665 for the purpose of Oliver Cromwell's troops to cross the river Lagan to crush the Irish revolt of the time. Although it was now considered a romantic landmark, which was popular for walkers and picnic-goers.

Liam was picked up by Davy as he walked his route. Davy and the team joked over their radios as they reported his progress, stating Liam was being a little overzealous in his actions. His cautiousness made him stand out from the crowd, an action which could have drawn attention to himself. The constant looking back over his shoulder, the quickening of his pace as he reached junctions only to slow down again in his attempt to anticipate where or when he would be picked up. It appeared he was constantly checking if he was being followed. A point Davy realised needed to be addressed once he was picked up and secure.

The meeting at shaws bridge was used by Davy to make Liam aware of the importance of his relationship with Roslyn. It was explained how the relationship was a good thing and enabled a good degree of access to Frankie and his activities. It was further explained that it was people like Frankie who caused the death of his good friend, Pat, as it was the Provos who had orchestrated the riots which resulted in his death. It was important to motivate Liam, and by pushing all the right buttons, to ensure he would work freely and feel compelled to do the right thing. Even at this early stage, the MRF believed Liam met most of the required criteria to be a fully accredited Agent.

Liam had already shown a secretive characteristic when applying for the Army by ensuring it remained a secret from his loved ones and friends alike. He showed a contempt for the perpetrators of violence and a sense of duty to do the right thing. He already had a degree of access to Frankie and the organisation by means of his relationship with Roslyn, an area the MRF were determined to exploit further. The relationship between the two was essential, otherwise Liam would lose the access he already had. It was still difficult for Liam to comprehend what use he could be to the MRF. However, he liked the covert nature of his actions, even if he was being chastised by Davy for his poor situational awareness displayed thus far. The feeling of belonging to a large and powerful organisation and being part of a special covert military team was exciting.

By way of demonstrating Liam's importance to the MRF, Davy asked for detailed descriptions of the individuals who had called at the house, or better still if Liam knew these men by sight or name. He was asked if he recognised the car or remembered the registration. He was informed that no matter how small or insignificant he thought the information was, it might be of interest to his new intelligence friends.

The meeting was thorough, with a working relationship being established. A reporting procedure for future passage of information and his personal security was discussed in detail. Davy asked if Liam had anything he thought might be of interest to his new friends at this early stage of proceedings.

Liam mentioned a failed recruitment attempt by SB (Special Branch) was being widely reported. The individual had held a meeting with PIRA, who in turn had reported to the Ardoyne Echo Newspaper. Of course, the paper took great delight in publishing it in full, explicit detail. PIRA had issued a warning about the consequences for dealing with the Crown Forces. They even painted the telephone number given to the targeted man on a gable wall with the caption 'TOUT LINE.' However, they deliberately changed the last digit of the number. Liam was reassured that the MRF were not as reckless as the RUC, and he had nothing to fear if he followed their instructions, training, and security advice. Liam was dropped off in the city centre and instructed to fulfil his cover story before returning home to ensure, if seen, he had an alibi for being where he was and why.

Following the meeting with Liam, Davy reported the failed recruitment pitch and explained the effort by PIRA to discredit the SB by painting the number on the wall.

It was decided that a marketing operation was required to rectify such a failure, so Davy and his four-man team deployed to the Falls Road under the cover of darkness. Dressed in a dirty trench coat, which was concealing his body armour and pistol, he was dropped off on the Falls Road. Carrying a half-empty bottle of Bushmills whiskey, Davy made his way along the Falls Road, acting a drunken bum whilst being covered by his mobile callsigns on the ground. He eventually arrived at the graffitied wall and sat down under the slogan. Several people walking along the road deliberately crossed the street to avoid the gibbering, incoherent drunk. When the coast was clear, Davy produced a jam jar of paint and paint brush from under his coat and proceeded to correct the intentional error by inserting the correct digit into the number.

A good friend in the Special Branch later informed Davy that several calls were received following the correction. Davy took great delight in knowing that PIRA had assisted the recruiting cause of the Crown Forces they so intently and desperately despised.

Chapter 9

Private Jason McCandless

"McCandless get your backside in here," was the command of the RSM (Regimental Sergeant Major). McCandless sprang to attention and marched into the office. "Close the door and sit-down son, this Gentleman wants to have a word with you." The RSM made his excuses and left the room.

McCandless was left staring at a mountain of a man in front of him who smiled and introduced himself only as Davy. "I believe you can't keep it in your pants and are going out with a wee lass from the Ardoyne."

McCandless tried to explain by stating, "It's not like that, I like the girl but I just wasn't aware of her background when I started dating her."

"Isn't that why we have procedures in place so you can get background checks done by reporting your extra-curricular activities to the Intelligence Cell, lad?" Davy went on to explain, "I have reason to suspect Mary is more involved in the republican movement than you know, she isn't just a lass from the Ardoyne. She has a brother locked up in the Maze prison and she pays regular visits to him. Considering three of your own countrymen had been abducted and murdered the previous year, should have made you more security conscious. This relationship needs to be terminated, but I have decided that a joint enterprise be undertaken to get Mary to mutual venue for my team to get alongside her."

A dinner dance in the La Mon Hotel and Country Club was chosen as the venue. It was a unique, award-winning, four-star hotel, conveniently located fifteen minutes from Belfast city centre and

Onus on Truths

nestled in the picturesque countryside of County Down. McCandless had little option but to go along with the arrangements.

A plan was set for the following Thursday evening. Davy briefed the team on their roles and responsibilities for the cultivation operation. A set of orders was produced, covering all eventualities that could go wrong. Chuck, a young Intelligence Corps collator was chosen to be the eye candy and intermediary to ensure a smooth transition from one party to another, or at least establish contact between the two parties for future exploitation.

On the evening, Jason and Mary arrived at the venue, with Mary feeling slightly overwhelmed by the opulence of the place. She also felt slightly underdressed as she watched men in lounge suits and ladies in cocktail dresses stroll pass them arm in arm as they entered the reception area. Mary was fascinated by the large chandelier which dominated the ceiling as it showered the room with its magical dazzling display of light. Mary turned to Jason as if it was a Cinderella moment and one, she never wanted to end and said, "This is definitely a step up from the Pig & Chicken and the bars I'm used to."

Jason smiled back at her taking her arm and said, "Shall we my Lady," as he led her to the large function room and their table.

Jason and Mary were conveniently seated at a table with Chuck and a female operative from the team using the pseudonym of Jill. Introductions were easily achieved, with good interaction between the parties. A satisfactory level of rapport was built over the course of the evening. So much so, promises of meeting up for drinks were agreed to by the end of the night. Mary was totally relaxed in the company of her new friends and accepted offers of further nights out without hesitation. This was achieved despite Jill and Chuck being English and claiming to work at the Belfast International Airport. Unlike the standout soldiers at the Pig and Chicken, Mary never suspected anything other than what she was told. These people were different from the soldiers she had dated and known.

It was important Jason be somehow distanced from the operation, so having got Mary up for a slow romantic dance, he held her close and said, "Mary, I have to attend a course back in England soon and when I go it is unlikely, I will return to Northern Ireland." Mary was disappointed by his revelation but had always been of the mind that one day he would go, so she was resigned to the inevitable. The disappointment was clear to see. Mary tightened her grip and for the first time that evening she had a feeling of sadness. "When will you go?" "Soon" he replied. They held their embrace and she whispered in his ear, "I will miss you," "Ditto."

The successful contact was achieved with Jill, and over a period of several weeks, Jill and Mary met for drinks with introductions of lads including Chuck, who she claimed all worked with her at the Airport. Mary seemed to get over Jason quite quickly, focusing her attention on the tall, dark, good-looking Chuck.

During the courtship by Jill, Mary was invited to a party which she believed was to be held at the Airport. On her arrival, she was met by Jill and several friends. Instead of going to a private lounge as expected, she was transferred into a minibus which took her and the group across the airfield into RAF Aldergrove. Mary was confused but not overly alarmed, as she was with all her recently acquired new friends and reassured, she was in safe hands. Mary felt it was probably fitting for the airport staff to have access to other Brits and the RAF base.

The minibus passed through military checkpoints without being checked and eventually arrived at a large, corrugated compound. The gate to the compound was opened by a tall man in his thirties, with long dark hair, wearing blue jeans and a tee shirt. It was obvious to Mary he worked out due to the skin-tight tee-shirt and large biceps. He had a pistol still holstered on his hip. Jill noticed the anxious look on Mary's face and smiled at her, giving Mary a reassuring look.

Jill showed Mary into a small but lavishly decorated living room in the building where she was met by Davy. She was offered a drink, which she took graciously but downed a little too quickly. Once her glass was replenished, she became a little more relaxed. Davy informed Mary about the operation conducted to get her to this point and the deliberate actions by Jill and the team. Mary asked the obvious question of, "Why me."

Davy responded by stating, "Because of your contempt for the perpetrators of violence and having the moral courage to do something about it. You have already displayed an excellent degree of astuteness by dating soldiers and maintaining a discrete relationship knowing the consequences if found out."

Mary was totally taken in by the whole recruitment and was equally astonished by the revelation that Jill worked for British Military Intelligence. The whole natural cover operation from its inception at the LA Mon Hotel and Country Club and the numerous outings with Jill left her flabbergasted. Mary looked at Jill and smiled whilst shaking her head in disbelief, realising that although Jill always stated she worked at the Airport, she'd just lied about what part. A successful recruitment was achieved of Mary Sweeney Codenamed: 'Wee Fern.'

The La Mon House Hotel was subjected to an incendiary bombing some years later than depicted. It was described as one of the worst atrocities of the Troubles when, in 1978, 12 people were killed, with 30 more being severely injured. The IRA only gave a 9-minute telephone warning, which was totally inadequate to evacuate over 450 diners and members of staff. Robert Murphy was charged and received 12 life sentences, only to be released on licence after having only served 14 years.

Chapter 10

Operation COMM 1983

Mary had been working very successfully for the MRF as an eyes and ears Agent for some time. She had produced some excellent intelligence on several known PIRA members and in particular her neighbour, Sean Pearse. She continued to make visits to her brother Tommy in prison. She would get on the republican prisoner's minibus at the Ardoyne shops for the thirty-minute journey to the Maze on the outskirts of Lisburn or as it was better known, Long Kesh or the H-Block. At the prison, she would spend an hour with her brother Tommy. Things had changed at the prison following the disaster of the hunger strikes by republican prisoners.

The protest which began as the blanket protest when the British government withdrew Special Category Status (criminal rather than prisoner of war status) for convicted paramilitary prisoners. A second hunger strike took place in 1981 and was a showdown between the prisoners and the Prime Minister, Margaret Thatcher. One hunger striker, Bobby Sands, had been elected as a member of parliament during the strike.

The hunger strike was the driving force behind Irish nationalist politics and enabled Sinn Féin to become a mainstream political party.

The day was an extremely busy one for Mary, which started when she was awakened by someone banging on her front door. Still half asleep, she wrapped a flimsy dressing gown around her body to try and fend off the cold September morning air. The embers were all but out in the fire grate, and she could see her own breath escaping as she breathed out through her laboured yawn.

As she opened the door, she could feel the wind rush in through the small gap between body and doorframe. Standing on her step was

Sean Pearce, who was leering at her, looking her up and down. He made her skin crawl, so she pulled tighter on her dressing gown but doing so only added to his pleasure, as her nipples could be seen protruding through the material as the cold took hold of her body. "What do you want?" she asked.

Raising his eyes to look at her above shoulder level for the first time, he retorted "I have a message you need to deliver to your Tommy for Frankie."

"Frankie who?" she asked but wasn't given an answer.

Sean handed Mary a small piece of paper wrapped in clingfilm no larger than a small thumb nail. He said, "It's a COMM. Don't tamper with it in any way, as they will know, and make sure to conceal it somewhere where it wouldn't be found going into the H-Block." He looked down toward her crotch and smiled.

Mary took the COMM (Covert Communication) and returned inside, slamming the door behind her. Mary had helped Sean out on several occasions in the past and this was no different. It was an act always encouraged by her handling team. It was Bridget who had told her about a previous weapon hide Sean had constructed in his own coal shed during a drunken girl's night out. Information Mary passed on, and which resulted in Sean doing four years at her majesty's pleasure.

Mary telephoned her Handler, and a meeting was hastily arranged to get Mary in and to gain access to the COMM. Mary had continued to make steady progress, providing valuable information on many PIRA personalities over that time and even managing to bed a few.

Mary's original Handlers of Davy and Jill had long since gone, only to be replaced by new Handlers; Marty was her third such Handler since she had been recruited. However, she did manage to see Jill again some years later when Jill unexpectedly turned up at one of her more relaxed socials debriefs conducted over in London during a luxury spa break, courtesy of Her Majesty's Government. Jill had been promoted and was now working for MI5 at Thames House London in their Northern Ireland Section.

Davy, who had returned to his own Unit, 22 SAS, was killed in the Falklands when the helicopter he was travelling in crashed on route into Goose Green.

Shortly after Mary was recruited, the MRF was disbanded, following the compromise of two of their fake cover companies. One was the Four-Leaf Laundry service, which entailed a van traveling around Belfast picking up laundry belonging to PIRA members for cleaning and taking the dirty clothes for forensic analysis in the process. The practice could also determine if different size shirts or trousers were being washed, which was a tell-tale sign that more than one man was staying in a property, potentially highlighting it as a safe house.

The laundry service was compromised, resulting in the laundry van being ambushed as it was about to leave the Ardoyne. Davy was one of the lucky ones to escape the carnage, taking out three armed terrorists as he escaped. The driver of the van wasn't so lucky, along with a female operative who was shot and killed as she approached the van with a bundle of clothes she had just collected.

The other company was a Massage Parlour which had been extremely successful in gaining forensic evidence from clothing as the men were being massaged. As the building was bugged, there was also the obvious pillow talk between hostess and client to be gleaned from the PIRA members who frequented the place. Conversations were captured whilst relaxing over a beer either before or after the oils were applied.

Although the two companies were compromised, a dozen or more continued without hinderance.

The Unit was eventually disbanded, with 14 Intelligence Company taking its place. This Unit conducted undercover surveillance operations against suspected members of the loyalist and republican terrorist groupings.

Onus on Truths

There was still a gap in intelligence gathering and therefore the FRU (Force Research Unit), which was an Intelligence Corps Unit took on the responsibility. Marty, a Royal Marine Commando seconded to the Unit, was now responsible as the primary Handler for Mary.

Mary presented the COMM to Marty, who was ready with Mike, an expert in dealing with such communications. It was carefully opened, with every action documented and photographed to ensure the reconstruction back to its original state would not be compromised. The COMM was written on a small sheet of cigarette rolling paper and was probably constructed under a large magnifying glass to ensure as much information as possible could be contained on it. It was tightly squeezed and wrapped in clingfilm before having a security mark made on it, Mike found a small bird seed placed between the layers of clingfilm. Others that Mike had worked on had small cigarette burns on the edges. It was returned to Mary, and she was delighted to see it didn't look like it had been tampered with.

The information contained on the COMM was a reference to a planned breakout of republican prisoners from the H-Block. The details highlighted logistical arrangements following the mass escape. Although cryptic, it was clear a large operation was being planned.

Tommy was to pass the relevant instruction to the OC (Officer Commanding) of the republican wing, a man called Barry McGinn. Mary was confused by Tommy taking such a risk when he was due to be released soon, although no date had been set for his release. Mary believed he must have been institutionalised whilst in the H-Block, because if not, then he had been more involved than he had previously stated concerning the attempt on the police officer's life. He appeared to be fully committed to the republican cause.

Mary was keen to know what the COMM had said, but even she knew it was better not to know for her own safety. It was returned to her and she made it back in suitable time for her transport to the prison.

Hamilton Spiers

Several weeks following her visit, Mary and the whole world became aware of the major break out of the Maze prison. 38 republican prisoners managed to escape H-Block (H7). In their pursuit to escape, they shot two prison officers with handguns that had been smuggled into the prison. One prison officer died from a heart attack and over twenty others were injured.

Tommy was a model prisoner, who never attempted to escape and was released on licence two weeks following the exodus of his cell mates. It was clearly decided he would not escape so close to his release date, otherwise he would have to spend at least the remainder of his sentence, which was four years, in prison, if recaptured. A good decision by Tommy. On his release from prison, he moved into Mary's house, although it had been the family home before their mother had passed away. Mary blamed Tommy in part, as their mother was devastated and heartbroken when Tommy was sent down. This was something Mary believed contributed to her death, as she never got over his incarceration. Mary had taken over the rent book and therefore ownership of the property.

A party was held in the Shamrock Arms to welcome Tommy home. Several members of the local PIRA were in attendance, and even a few of the OTR's, (On the Runs) from the prison break made an appearance. Mary was in attendance and would be reporting the activities to her Handlers in due course. Mary was introduced to Frankie, the man who asked, or more accurately demanded she take the COMM to Tommy at the Maze. Mary took an instant dislike to Frankie, she thought he had dead eyes and was a bit shifty.

Mary recognised several of the Provo boys including Jerry Cosgrove, John Fee, and even an old school friend Roslyn Connolly, although she had no idea that Frankie was her brother. Sean and Bridget were also in attendance, with Sean being his usual lecherous self. Several others were in attendance who Tommy said were the Derry boys.

One of the Derry boys was a fella by the name of Gilmour, who would later become known for his part in the CPS (Crown Prosecution Service) charging 38 republicans with terrorist related charges. However, the court case collapsed, with the Judge declaring Gilmour as an unreliable witness and all charges against the 38 were dropped. Gilmour, known as the supergrass, was whisked away to be resettled in England and given a new identity by the RUC.

The party was a roaring success, with traditional Irish ballads being sung into the early hours, accompanied with some good old fashion republican tunes. Songs like 'The men behind the wire' earned rapturous laughter, as so many were no longer behind the wire following the massive breakout.

Chapter 11

Liam's Progress 1985

Liam had worked successfully for the FRU as an eyes and ears Agent for several years. Following his marriage to his long-term girlfriend Roslyn Connolly and because of his change in employment status, he became more accepted by Frankie. A development which was appreciated by the FRU. Liam was now a self-employed taxi driver, a position helped by his Handlers in providing the much-needed funding to purchase a car. The Unit was covering the cost of his car payments, which was their way of having some measure of control over his affairs. If he was to stop working, then so would his payments. He had received several bonus payments over the years whenever he provided good, exploitable intelligence. This he saved in a secret account and was deemed by him as his retirement pension pot. Liam was a confident and diligent Agent, who had been instrumental in the prevention of many attempted attacks on off duty police and prison officers.

One such incident occurred whilst he was conducting his taxi business. Having just dropped a fare on the Malone Road in south Belfast and as he was starting to return to the city, he noticed a familiar ford escort parked at the bottom of Malone Avenue. Manoeuvring his vehicle, he came back on himself but along an adjacent street. He saw his cousin Jerry walking along with another republican by the name of Shane McNabb. Both men were walking slowly in the direction of the Lisburn Road. It didn't seem right to Liam, as they were walking away from their vehicle within an affluent residential area, which was considered neither loyalist nor republican.

Both men were dressed in dark clothing, but it was obvious to Liam they were up to no good.

It was later collaborated by police sources that there had been targeting of a police officer living in the street. Once again, thanks to Liam, a member of the security forces life may have been saved due to his actions.

Frankie and his henchmen were from time to time taken to various meetings by Liam in his taxi or to certain addresses within West Belfast. A popular and frequently visited destination was Divis Flats. Divis Flats consisted of twelve 8-story blocks of terraces and flats, named after the nearby Divis Mountain. Liam would not normally get to go inside, but on one occasion, he had been waiting in the car for what seemed like an age. So, he decided to venture into the open doorway of a flat. As he entered, he could hear a male's voice pleading for the people in the room to stop. The sounds were clearly of a male in distress and being tortured. Immediately inside the front entrance was the bathroom on one side of the hall with the kitchen on the other. The bathroom door was open, and the white plastic shower curtain was neatly laid out on the floor adjacent to the bath, which was full to the brim with water. Liam shivered at the thought of someone being interrogated and made a hasty retreat to the car.

Frankie eventually returned to the car, looking dishevelled, with Liam noticing both of his sleeves were soaking wet. Frankie lit a cigarette and stood smoking with a perverse, wicked look of satisfaction on his face. He discarded his butt before climbing into the passenger seat. He turned to Liam and said, "Home James, and don't spare the horses." Liam always reported these excursions to his handling team, believing that yet another punishment, beating, or interrogation had taken place.

Chapter 12

Billy Bennett

1992

The Government took a political decision to change the name of FRU to JSG (Joint Support Group) following revelations concerning the loyalist paramilitary, Brian Nelson, and the alleged reports of collusion between the paramilitaries and the FRU. Nothing changed in the process of recruitment and running of agents. There was greater scrutiny of procedures and the introduction of trained legal advisors who were brought in to advise and have oversight of all operations and ensure the rule of law was adhered to, but for all intents and purposes, it was business as usual.

Both Liam and Mary continued their invaluable work, and the continuity of the cases was attained.

Billy had arrived at the Unit having completed his arduous Agent Handling course at the School of Service Intelligence in Ashford Kent. Of the fifty students who started the course, only six made it to the Unit, such was the intensely challenging nature of it. Billy was a married man in his prime and a senior NCO from the Royal Irish Rangers. A keen marathon runner and light weight amateur boxer who fought out of the east Belfast club, Ledley Hall. As a young man, Billy gave up the opportunity to turn professional, opting to join the Army.

Billy's upbringing was not that dissimilar to Liam. They were of similar age and grew up a few streets apart in Belfast during the 1960's and early 1970's and like Liam, Billy too was burnt out of his home at the height of the Troubles. His family moved to the east of the city, relocating to the Newtownards Road, a predominately protestant area. Although it still had an interface with the catholic enclave of Short Strand. Nightly battles between the two communities were commonplace.

Billy's uncle and namesake had been attacked as he walked past the interface one night. He was pulled into a side street and beaten by a gang of youths with Hurley sticks. As a result, he suffered a severe head injury and finally, unable to recover, succumbed to his injuries and died a few years later. The tensions between the communities were not caused by some theological differences but more based on reasons of culture identity. The gerrymandering ensured elections were just a ploy to manipulate the boundaries to disadvantage minority population of electoral districts and give power to rich unionists—this being just one of the reasons for the outbreak of violence in 1969. Despite these difficult times, Billy had a happy childhood with his seven brothers. It was often remarked that his mother must have been trying for a football team. She was a small woman but a formidable one, who was extremely protective over her boys. Billy's father had gained a reputation in the community as a hard man and someone well known to the local police. He was tough on his sons and whenever any of them took a beating or was deemed to have lost a fight, the remainder of the brothers were lined up in the hallway of the house with the next eldest sent out to get retribution for his sibling. This would continue along the line until justice had been achieved.

From a very early age, Billy always aspired to join the Army, having been regaled by stories from his grandfather who served during World War II and hearing stories about his great-uncle William who was underage when he enlisted and subsequently died in foreign lands at the battle of Gallipoli. Billy would have queued in the very same queue within Sande's Cafe at the same time as Liam back in 1973, yet both boys were totally oblivious to each other's presence, ultimately taking two very different career paths but with the same objective. Their lives were aligned in some strange way. Billy's options were not 'Jail or Army' as was the case for lots of youths in the early seventies. He was there out of choice and desire. Although many of his school friends did choose a very different path, which ended in paramilitary involvement and subsequent imprisonment.

Handlers were hand-picked individuals from all three services, as was the case with their predecessors in the MRF and FRU. However, this wasn't a Gerald Seymour novel. Recruits weren't taken to some remote country mansion, taught how to speak with Irish accents, and parachuted into west Belfast. The SAS instructors ensured Handlers had the highest possible level of training to enable them to recruit, train, manage and protect their Agents. Each Handler was put through several phases or packages, such as an extensive CQB (Close Quarter Battle) combat package with non-conventional specialist weapons and a RtoI (Resistance to Interrogation) phase.

Three months of long hours conducting covert mechanics and Agent handling meetings, combined with numerous hours on the rifle ranges of Lydd and Hyde, ensured highly prolific operators graduated out of the SIW (Specialist Intelligence Wing).

When someone graduated from the school, they were under no illusions of the mammoth task they would be undertaking as an Agent Handler. What was different about Billy, however, was the fact he was a native of Northern Ireland, which was rare. At the time of arriving in the Unit, there was only one other indigenous operator. As a result, Billy was used extensively, particularly when it involved direct contact with the local populace on both covert and overt (Natural Cover) recruitment operations.

Billy's aspirations of joining such a specialist Unit first came about after having spent months stationed in a Patrol Base (PB) on the Fermanagh-Monaghan border, watching specialist troops arrive from the FRU, heavily armed and dressed in civilian clothing at the PB. They would park their cars in the base and take over the operation of the base by controlling all access in and out of the border crossing point whilst conducting their own targeting operations of the civilian population traveling through it. They would also disappear into the night on some covert mission only to return in time for breakfast.

There was always a real threat of being targeted by PIRA whilst manning the PB's along the border. Attacks were commonplace, and the risk to life was a real possibility. Being stationed in Roslea PB in Southwest Fermanagh on the border with Monaghan had its fair share of terrorists' attacks during the Troubles. Most of these attacks were conducted from across the Irish border or from within Northern Ireland, only for the terrorists to flee back across the border into the relevant safety of the Irish Republic.

One morning, having just completed a clearance patrol around the base, Billy put his equipment away and retired to the rest room of the base for a well-earned, over-stewed cup of tea. As he entered the room, the other members of the base were all transfixed by the large, wall-mounted television displaying images of two Army Corporals being dragged from a car on the Andersonstown Road in Belfast and subsequently murdered by republican terrorists.

Billy remembered feeling sick to the core and thinking how barbaric it was. It was on the 19th of March 1988. It was a week of cosmic proportion. Corporals Derek Wood and David Howes were killed by the IRA when they were caught up in a funeral cortege in Belfast—one of the most notorious incidents of the Troubles. The TV showed crystal-clear images taken by the specialist camera of the surveillance helicopter that had been covering the funeral of IRA volunteer Kevin Brady and two other people.

Three days previously, during the funerals of three IRA volunteers shot dead by British Special forces in Gibraltar, loyalist gunman Michael Stone, had launched a gun and grenade attack at the funerals in Milltown cemetery. Three people had been killed, including Kevin Brady. The events of those two previous weeks had produced some of the tensest moments of the troubles. Northern Ireland at the time was a powder keg waiting to explode.

The funeral cortege was shown moving down the Andersonstown Road in West Belfast towards Milltown cemetery. PIRA volunteers were mingling with the mourners. The security forces were noticeably absent, giving the area a wide birth to reduce tensions. In the images shown, a silver VW Passat could be seen approaching the cortege, stopped by the funeral stewards, and directed to turn around and move away.

For reasons not quite clear, the vehicle reversed at speed and mounted the pavement. Panic set in amongst those in the cortege. They must have wondered if this was yet another Loyalist attack.

Derek Woods and David Howes were both members of the British Army's Royal Corps of Signals. The vehicle was quickly surrounded with black taxis boxing it in from the front and rear. As the crowd attacked the vehicle, Wood drew his 9mm browning pistol and fired one shot into the air. For an instant, the crowd panicked and withdrew back a little, but then converged on in the same way an army of ants aggressively and predatorily attack their prey in vast numbers. The vehicle's windows were smashed, with both men being abruptly dragged from the vehicle and taken to the rear of nearby Casement Park, where they were strip-searched and beaten further. The men were then thrown over a wall and bundled into taxis before being taken a couple of hundred metres away to waste ground near Penny Lane. The beatings and then stabbings continued until both men were eventually shot multiple times at point-blank range as they lay on the ground.

The incident was all that Billy needed to motivate him to volunteer for Special Duties. The perpetrators of such heinous crimes should not go unpunished.

On his arrival at the detachment, Billy was assigned to the cases of both Liam and Mary. They were easy cases to be involved in, as both agents, or CHIS (Covert Human Intelligence Source) were extremely proficient in their duties. With his continued oversight, each CHIS progressed steadily, gaining better access to top republican figures over the years. Liam was now driving Frankie and reporting on his movements and contacts. Mary was a known custodian with direct links to several active members of PIRA.

Both agents were closely aligned and able to provide collaboration of intelligence, despite not being aware of each other's involvement. When reading the files of the Agents, Billy became aware that both his and Liam Murray's paths had indeed crossed back in 1973 when both were in Sandes Café within Palace Barracks the day Billy took his country's shilling and enlisted on the roll.

Chapter 13

Operation Special delivery

The banging at the back door startled Mary. She could feel her heart thumping against her chest. Mary's instinct was to switch on the kitchen light as she entered to see what the commotion was. As she went closer to the door to answer it, she was filled with trepidation of who or what could be causing such a racket this late at night. As she reached for the handle, the voice on the other side screamed at her, "Turn the bloody light off and open the dammed door."

She immediately recognised the voice as that of Sean Pearce, her neighbour. She did as she was told, turned off the light, and unlocked the door. The force of Sean entering the kitchen knocked Mary off her feet, landing on her backside on the cold linoleum kitchen floor. Sean was in a state of shock and his face was as white as a sheet.

"Jesus Sean, you look like you have just seen a ghost."

"Jesus Mary, John's dead and Jerry's in a bad way. If they get me, I'll go away for a long time. The peelers could be up here any minute, so I need you to hide this."

He took a pistol wrapped in a flimsy piece of cloth out of his pocket.

"Mary, I think I've just killed a Brit."

Mary felt sick, for she knew that it was her who had told her Handler, Billy, when Sean had left the house that evening along with two others. She was previously made aware that something was in the works and it was important she noted all of Sean's movements over the coming days, particularly if John Fee turned up. John did appear that day. It was just before teatime, but he left again with Sean and

Jerry just after six. It was 9:00 pm now and Sean was back, but alone and in a terrible state.

Mary was still in a state of shock as she looked at the small bundle still in her hands. She just froze.

Sean said, "Hide it for a couple of days, just till things blow over and I will get it back off you." With that, he was gone back out the door and away.

Mary did a circuit of the kitchen, not knowing where to go, moving back and forward from cupboard to cupboard before realizing the door was still open and the wintry night air was attacking her. She locked the door and eventually settled for placing the pistol behind her bath panel for safe keeping. Still shaking, she went out into the back yard and could see Sean's bathroom light on. She knew he was already stripped, in the bath, and getting rid of any forensic evidence on his body. No doubt, Bridget was busy washing his clothes in the washing machine for the same reason.

Once she had gathered her thoughts and composure, Mary left the house and walked far enough away from the area to find a telephone box from which she could make the call to Billy. She reported Sean's return and the fact she had a suspected murder weapon in her possession.

Billy wasn't in the office, but the duty operator confirmed that an incident had taken place, and she needed to phone back in 30 minutes to receive further instructions. She was congratulated for the excellent work she was doing and told that the boss and Billy would be delighted by her efforts.

Mary hung up and made a second call to a female friend to arrange a girl's night out for the weekend. This was done in accordance with her security protocol, remembering the call should be checkable.

Following the call, Mary went to the pub, knowing she would be seen there, which would enhance her cover story. If she was questioned later, she would state with a degree of confidence she had to get out of the house in case it was searched following Sean's return.

To Mary, it was plausible. Mary made the call again and was told that the ten o'clock news had run with a story of a shootout at a VCP (Vehicle Check Point), in which a soldier had been wounded but not fatally. However, an unidentified armed terrorist was shot and killed at the scene.

It was emphasised to Mary that the weapon which she had, could indeed be the one used by an escaped terrorist who was responsible for shooting a soldier. Mary had been told that it was unlikely Sean would return for the weapon any time soon. So, it was essential to recover it from her in order to carry out forensic and ballistic tests. Mary was instructed to place the gun in the top of her rubbish bin just inside her yard before she went to bed and leave off the latch to the back gate. Although hesitant, she was assured it would be back before first light the next morning when she could retrieve it.

Billy and the team then set a plan in motion to retrieve the pistol. Billy forewarned the team it was going to be a long night. Orders were produced at the OP's Room with all the detachment personnel in attendance.

A team from WIS (Weapon Intelligence Specialists) arrived at the detachment to carry out their magic. On completion of their work the pistol would be rendered useless and there would be no tell-tale signs that it had been tampered with. The same applied to the ammunition contained within the magazine. The pistol would be further Jarked, so that any future movement of the device could be monitored by the men from 14 Int.

Jarked is military slang to modify weaponry to disadvantage, and especially to attach and use a tracking device to covertly monitor its location.

It would only be a matter of time before Sean Pearce would be behind bars again, and it would all be thanks to Mary.

Mary carried out her instructions by leaving the pistol in the bin just after midnight. She was careful not to make any noise or draw attention to herself. Her brother Tommy had turned up just after 11pm, a little worse for wear, and was slurring his words. He was ranting about the news and how a member of an ASU had been killed on active duty. He wasn't making much sense but eventually took himself off to the spare room and bed.

It didn't take him long before he went back to mixing with all the undesirables from PIRA, Mary thought.

The news at ten o'clock did report the incident. The information was superficial, only stating that a vehicle had failed to stop at an Army checkpoint on the Ballylesson Road on the outskirts of Lisburn. During the incident, a soldier had been shot and injured but not fatally. However, the driver of the vehicle was killed during an exchange of fire. The name of the individual had yet to be released.

It later transpired that PIRA had sent a death squad to kill a part time UDR soldier, John Spence, who was the owner of a post office in the small village of Drumbeg.

Drumbeg had a population of around 900 inhabitants and was a tight knit and predominately protestant community. Several members of the RUC and Army also lived in the area.

It was the intention of PIRA to kill Spence as he was about to close the shop. It wasn't as the news report had indicated concerning an Army checkpoint incident but rather an Intelligence-led operation by the security forces to deny the enemy the killing opportunity by stepping up patrolling in the area.

An OP (Observation Post) had been set up with over watch of the village main street. They observed the car arriving, but it wasn't until the two men got out, that they paid any particular attention to it.

The car driven by Jerry Cosgrove, accompanied by Sean Pearse and John Fee had pulled up in a side street just short of the Post Office. Jerry Cosgrove remained in the car whilst Sean and John got out, armed with a pistol each and walked the short distance toward the Post Office. It was just starting to get dark, and although it was a cold, crisp night, at least it was dry, which the men were grateful for. It was the intention of Sean and John to enter the premises with both men opening fire with both weapons, ensuring maximum carnage and certain death of the part time soldier.

The soldiers in the OP noticed two darkly dressed figures as they approached the shop. Both appeared to have bubble hats on. It was only as they reached the corner of the Post Office that both men pulled the hats down over their faces, exposing only their eyes through Balaclavas.

The OP operators radioed the QRF and updated them on the happenings at the shop. The QRF had been satelliting the area and were only a minute away from the main street. Intelligence had indicated an attack was imminent in the area, but no specific target had been identified.

John Fee opened the door to the shop, but the part time soldier had seen the two would-be killers on his CCTV camera system and so had positioned himself in the corner of the shop, out of sight to the terrorists. Before either terrorist could react, the soldier, using his PPW (Personal Protection Weapon), fired two shots, hitting John Fee in the chest. Fee was dead before he hit the floor. Sean, who was protected by Fee's body positioning when the shots were fired, hadn't even made it into the shop, but decided valour was not in his interest, so turned and ran back in the direction of the car.

The Soldier ran out into the street and fired another round in the direction of the fleeing terrorist but missed his fast-moving target.

Jerry, hearing the shots and having already turned the car in the direction of the Ballylesson road, started to accelerate out of the side street to pick up his comrades.

Sean reached the car just as the QRF arrived at the junction of the Ballylesson Road. The soldiers alighted from the vehicle, taking up fire positions to the side of the vehicle and the nearest hedgerow. Sean screamed for Jerry to drive and raised the gun, firing shots toward the troop carrier. In doing so, he heard a scream and a thud as a soldier fell backwards into the side of the vehicle.

A volley of shots rang out from the soldiers' rifles and the windscreen of the car shattered but remained intact, with tiny starburst shapes appearing where the bullets had penetrated the windscreen.

Onus on Truths

The car managed to get through the blockade, but once clear, and with the adrenalin pumping, Sean started trembling uncontrollably whilst swearing and repeating the name John over and over again as he looked back over his shoulder in the direction of the Army, the Post Office, and his dead comrade.

Jerry, who had become very quiet, appeared to be driving on auto pilot, his breathing becoming shallower by the second. Sean looked across at his driver and realised he had been shot in the chest. They had managed to reach the end of the Ballylesson Road, arriving at the Belfast fever hospital grounds at Purdysburn.

Jerry was by now in and out of consciousness, with his breathing becoming just a laboured gurgling sound from his throat.

Sean abandoned the car and ran on foot, leaving Jerry, but not before placing Jerry's head against the horn, ensuring it was blaring as he ran. He believed someone would come out and help his friend. Sean managed to get to a phone box and phoned Frankie.

Frankie just happened to have arrived home when the house phone rang. He picked up the handset, listened intently to the caller, and was heard to say, "Listen, relax, stay put and we will come and get you."

Liam, who had been in the house, overheard Frankie but didn't know who he was talking too. Liam had taken Roslyn over to see her Mum and was comfortably seated in front of the TV, content to spend the evening relaxed and in his wife's company.

After a brief conversation, Frankie hung up the phone, then turned to Liam and stated he needed him to pick up Sean Pearse, who was somewhere along Ballynahatty Road near the Giants Ring—a prehistoric rock formation built in 2700 BC—and get him home.

"What's he doing out there?" asked Liam, only to be told, "Mind your own business. Just do it."

Frankie accompanied Liam as they travelled out to the area looking for Sean. As the car left the main A55 Road and entered the Ballynahatty Road, visibility was restricted by the lack of streetlamps in this less populated countryside. With heavy clouds, the sky was shrouded in darkness, and both men were transfixed on the road ahead, the headlights the only illumination. They continued slowly along the dark, dreary road as they searched hedgerows and the fields ahead. They eventually found Sean perched up against a gate post to an open field. He had been waiting about 30 minutes and had been contemplating hijacking the first vehicle that he came across. However, not a single vehicle had passed him on the quiet country road in that period.

Once in the Taxi, Sean started to recite his tale of utter failure but was immediately halted by Frankie, who cast a stare in his direction before glancing sideways in Liam's direction. This was enough to shut him up. Sean got the unspoken message and sat back in the rear seat.

He was dropped off at the rear of the houses in Jamaica Street, with the only words from Frankie being,

"Use the girl for that thing."

With that, Liam drove away, taking Frankie back home.

Chapter 14

Operation WIS

On the way to drop Frankie off, Liam was instructed to stop by the phone box whilst Frankie made a call. Liam noted Frankie appeared to make a few calls before returning to the car. He then took Frankie home, picked up Roslyn and went back to his own house. Once he got Roslyn home, he told her he needed to go out and refuel the car for the next days' work, as he had a taxi fare to the Airport early in the morning.

Whilst out, Liam made a call to his Handler, informing him of the night's activities, and stated that he had heard on the car radio that a shooting had taken place on the Ballylesson Road and that he'd picked up Sean Pearse in a terrible state in the area in question.

This was excellent news for the handling team, as they not only had Liam reporting on the incident but Mary with the weapon in her possession. This was top grade intelligence with collaboration of the facts.

A meeting was arranged to fully debrief Liam the following day but, in the meantime, the JSG detachment had a weapon to be recovered before anything else.

The team deployed to the Ardoyne just after midnight for the retrieval of the pistol. The cover teams travelled along the Crumlin Road, dropping Billy and Mac, the co-Handler, on Edna Drive. One cover car remained on Edna Drive whilst another went to the rear of Jamaica Street to provide close support. The streets were quiet, with only the odd taxi transiting through, bringing back the late-night revellers from the city centre bars.

On completion of the drop off, Billy and Mac used an entry cut-through, which brought them onto Jamaica street. Jamacia street was a dead end, with a small cul-de-sac at the bottom, which meant the cover teams were limited in the time spent in the street for fear of detection.

Billy and Mac moved as quickly as they could along the rear of the houses until they were directly outside the rear entrance of Mary's house. Mary had complied with her instructions and the gate to the rear yard was off the latch. This made the entry a quieter and less complicated operation. She had also placed a drawing pin on the wooden gate post, which was a sign to the handling team she had carried out her instructions.

Suddenly, a neighbouring bathroom light went on, partially illuminating the back of the house. Both men stood still in the shadows of the yard until the light was extinguished again. Billy reached into the bin and had to rummage through the upper layers of the contents in search of the weapon. As he went to move a cereal box to the side, he realised it was too heavy just to be an empty box. Mary had placed the weapon inside the carton. He quickly took it out of the box and placed it inside his jacket before replacing the lid and exiting out the gate. He removed the drawing pin from the gate post, which was his tell-tale sign to Mary that he had completed the task. They moved stealthily back along the alleyway to the end of the row of houses. Only once he was clear of the houses did he dare break radio silence and convey to the team the retrieval was successful.

Both men returned out onto Edna Drive and were picked up by the cover teams. It was a textbook operation, and all that remained was to get the weapon back for the forensic and technical teams to do their part.

Chapter 15

A small piece of Justice

1992

Because Sinn Fein had become a major political party and with the other political parties declaring them to be explicitly linked to PIRA, it was decided it would be advantageous for Mary to be directed toward becoming a volunteer at one of the many offices in the city. One of the first tasks Mary was given by Sinn Fein was canvasing on Sinn Fein's behalf by distributing electoral leaflets to members of the public. At the same time, as Mary was canvasing on behalf of Sinn Fein, Billy was conducting a targeting operation of a well-known PIRA member from the Lower Falls area.

The operation was taking place outside the unemployment/Job centre on the Falls Road. A two-man team consisting of Billy and Mac had been positioned outside the building in an attempt to obtain a pattern of life study on the well-known republican. As they were waiting for said individual to exit the centre to conduct surveillance on him. Mary appeared along with her boss, Seamus Andrews. They were handing out leaflets for the upcoming elections. Mary saw Billy, and she had a questioning look on her face but calmly approached, smirked, handed over a leaflet to him, and stated, "I hope we can count on your vote," before walking on.

In April 1992, the General Election was held, with Sinn Fein (SF) gaining over 78,000 votes, yet they were still well behind the SDLP (Socialist Democratic Labour Party) who were by far the largest nationalist party, with over 23% of the vote. However, SF was growing in popularity, despite the belief by many that they were still dealing in the armed struggle through both the bomb and the ballot box. Seamus Andrews contested the seat of Belfast West against the immensely popular Eamon Rankin of the SDLP. Mary had reported to Billy how she couldn't understand how so many dead people had managed to cast their votes during the election, and it was all because of fictional polling cards.

The operation to return the weapon to Mary had gone to plan, with everything back on site as promised and without incident. Mary opened her rear gate and removed the drawing pin before retrieving the pistol and placing it back into its hidey-hole, waiting for the next episode to be played out.

The police arrested Sean Pearce later that morning and took him in for questioning. He was held for 48 hours but released pending further inquiries. It was a deliberate act by the police. His house was searched, but nothing was found and nothing was expected to be.

John Fee's body was removed from the Post Office. The car and the body of Jerry Cosgrove were also retrieved. Although help did come to his aid, it had been in vain, and he died in the car. Forensic tests were still being carried out on the vehicle, and police were waiting the results.

Although Liam had reported Sean's location to his Handlers, which put Sean near the incident, the case required more for a conviction. No prints were found on the weapon, so it was hoped any subsequent movement of the weapon would clinch the case.

The funeral of the two terrorists took place the day after Sean's release from Castlereagh. Sean attended and was seen in a heated debate with Kieran O'Kane. Kieran was suspected of being the OC Belfast Brigade PIRA. Several thousand people had turned up for the funeral, as they were buried in the republican plot in Milltown Cemetery.

Onus on Truths

Liam was in attendance, as Jerry Cosgrove was his cousin. Although putting up a front of acting remorseful, he wasn't a bit phased by his cousin's death and believed he got what he deserved.

It was a major blow to PIRA that two of their men had died during the murderous attempt on the part time soldier. Following the funeral, Sean attempted to retrieve the weapon from Mary, but as instructed by Billy, Mary delayed the return, stating she had taken it somewhere away from the house and needed time to get it back. This was a deliberate act to ensure a timeframe was built in to exploit the situation.

A team from 14 Int and the police C4, HMSU were already on standby should the weapon move from its current location. It would also be monitored by the tracking device.

Mary telephoned Billy, and arrangements were made and time agreed for the weapon release to Sean. At four o'clock the following afternoon, Mary handed the weapon over to Sean, who went directly to a car that had been waiting for him outside his house. A close associate of Frankie Connolly, a man known as Patrick McCartney, was driving the car and who was believed to be part of the IRA's inner circle. The car departed Jamacia Street and was immediately tailed by four surveillance cars from 14 Int.

Mary telephoned Billy, who thanked her and told her to note the time of his return and phone through once he returned.

The car travelled out of the Ardoyne and headed west along the Glen Road, closely monitored by the teams. The car continued to the Colin Glen Forest Park. On arrival at the carpark, a male/female 14 Int surveillance team entered and took up a position with overwatch of McCartney's car. For several minutes, there was no movement; both men just sat with the car engine ticking over.

The HMSU team alighted from their vehicles and moved into the woods, taking up positions, covering the main transit routes and pathways in the densely populated forest. The forest provided excellent cover from view for the teams. The team leader was getting concerned and wondering if this was to be another attack on someone, so soon after the terrorists last failure. Was there someone who used the forest for exercise or walking their dog? All sorts of scenarios were going through his head. Suddenly, the courting couple team reported movement at the vehicle.

McCartney got out of the driver's door, made his way to the rear of the vehicle, and opened the boot.

"Standby Standby," came the call from the surveillance team covering the car. "Target two at rear of vehicle and is black on blue."

The target took out a small holdall and, placing it over his shoulder, walked round to the passenger side.

Sean Pearse then got out of the vehicle and stood next to McCartney.

"Target one now out of the vehicle," came the next call.

Both men entered the forest, monitored by the surveillance teams. There were only a few cars in the carpark, so the number of civilians in the forest was expected to be minimal. The two men walked deep into the forest to a clearing which had a small forestry commission hut, no larger than a large garden shed. Still being kept under stringent surveillance, McCartney stopped at the entrance of the hut and proceeded to take a set of keys out of his pocket, opening the large, oversized mortise lock hanging on the bar and bolt.

The team on the ground moved closer to the hut, but still maintained a discrete distance to avoid any possible compromise.

McCartney entered the hut, with Sean remaining at the entrance, watching the surrounding pathways for signs of trouble. McCartney could be heard moving something heavy inside. It was believed at this point it must have been a weapon hide and therefore the opportunity of retrieval was too good to miss. The team was instructed to apprehend both men at the scene and recover whatever weapons were present.

A cry of "Police, stand still!" rang out, and total pandemonium ensued.

Sean turned sharply, reaching inside his jacket to retrieve his pistol, which was still wrapped in the flimsy cloth. He was fumbling to gain some sort of control on the weapon's handle when he was cut short by a volley of shots that struck him in both legs. He collapsed to his knees before falling flat on his face in the dirt track at the front of the hut.

McCartney, still in the inner sanctum of the hut, opened fire through the door with a 9mm pistol at shadows before being cut down by the hard-hitting response from several G3 automatic rifles. McCartney died instantly, but Sean was treated at the scene before being transferred to the city hospital for treatment.

Sean was lucky, as he was in full view of the HMSU teams, or more sporadic firing would have been used to neutralise the target. A follow up search was conducted of the shed, which was found to contain a large plastic oil drum hidden under the floor which had a quantity of weapons ranging from Pistols, AK-47's, G3 Rifles, hundreds of rounds of ammunition, and Semtex explosives.

Sean was still in possession of the pistol when he was shot, but because of the excellent work carried out by the WIS team, even if he had managed to retrieve it and attempted to fire it, the pistol wouldn't have functioned anyway.

The evidence against Sean was overwhelming and following his continued recovery from being shot in both legs, it was going to be a long rehabilitation. But then, the 20-year prison sentence he received for the attempted murder of the part-time soldier would give him all the time he needed to recover. He would have a permanent limp and would need to use a walking aid for the remainder of his days.

McCartney was the QM (Quartermaster) of the Belfast Brigade, and his death sent even more shock waves through the PIRA ranks.

Questions were being asked as to how Sean Pearce had managed to escape the attempt on the UDR man's life and yet two volunteers were killed. Now with the discovery of the hide, and the death of McCartney, suspicion was growing within the ranks and the finger was being firmly pointed in the direction of Sean Pearse as being a tout.

Frankie questioned whether Sean had been recruited during his time in Castlereagh interrogation centre or if had he been a Police informant all along. These were all questions which needed answering.

Frankie visited Sean in prison to put the allegations of suspicion to him. Sean was told that an internal investigation was underway, and he would be informed of the decision following its completion. Sean pleaded his case stating, "I have given everything for the republican cause, not to mention being made a virtual cripple into the bargain."

Frankie was totally unsympathetic to his pleas stating, "I will get to the bottom of it, but in the meantime word in the H-Block is for no action or recrimination to be administered without my say so. "You are safe for now, but don't think I can't get my hands on you should we prove you're a tout. You will be nutted son."

The meeting with Sean ended with Frankie returning to Belfast to start his investigation.

Mary was shocked when Frankie turned up at her door and asked to speak with her. He wanted to know if Sean had been acting suspiciously leading up to his shooting and subsequent arrest. Frankie had already spoken with Bridget and she was, in Frankie's words, "Flippen furious that Sean was suspected of being a tout." More importantly, she stated, "He has just been sentenced for twenty years doing RA business."

Mary, knowing she had been instrumental in Sean's incarceration, was extremely calm and responded to Frankie's questions, giving nothing away and certainly not incriminating Sean any more than he already was. Mary felt guilty about Sean, even though he was a letch and she always felt uncomfortable in his presence but knew she had done the right thing and believed Bridget would be better off without him.

He was a thug, and Bridget had the bruises to prove it. Whenever he had too much drink, he was always abusive to her, and many a night, Mary had to play chaperon as Bridget took refuge in Mary's house following such altercations. Mary's only concern was the fact that she may have been implicated because she was privy to the weapon and was the last person to see Sean on the day he was shot, having just handed over the weapon to him.

Frankie appeared satisfied with Mary's answers and thanked her for her cooperation but stated he may be in touch later. Mary was uncomfortable by that remark but just smiled and stated she was only pleased to be of help.

A meeting with Billy the following day allowed Mary to be reassured that her suspicions were unfounded. A large period of the meeting was taken up dealing with her insecurities and building her confidence. She was told that Billy would know from other Agents if she was ever under suspicion and not to worry, as he had her security as his number one priority.

As a result of her excellent endeavours over the past few months, she was in line for a bonus, with the prospect of another London trip for a luxury break and the potential of meeting up with Jill again. It needed time to organise and a chance for her to feed the idea to those close to her, so that it came across as a natural weekend break to get away from the tedious life she lived. At least, that's how it would be portrayed because her life was anything but tedious.

Several weeks after Frankie's last visit, he made another unexpected call to Mary. This time he was accompanied by another PIRA member, Jimmy Rice, and asked to speak with Tommy, her brother.

Mary was relieved it wasn't her they wanted, but at the same time, concerned as to why they wanted Tommy.

"What do you want with him?" she asked.

"Woman, this is men's business so there is no need to concern yourself."

"Don't patronise me you son of a bitch," she retorted.

"I'm sorry love, I didn't mean..." That was as far as he got before she interrupted him again, stating, "Its my house and don't dare call me love."

Tommy appeared in the doorway and said, "For God's sake, Mary, just give us a minute, will you."

Mary went into the kitchen and tried desperately to overhear the men's conversation but wasn't successful in her attempts. It wasn't until the men had departed that Mary was able to ask Tommy what the conversation was about.

Tommy stated that it was down to him to construct a weapon's hide for the RA. Apparently, because she had previously been hiding weapons for Sean, they thought it would be prudent for a proper hide to be constructed in their house.

Mary went ballistic. "My house Tommy, it's my house, not yours!"

Tommy had to grip her by the arms. "That's why Jimmy and Frankie asked me not to tell you. They knew you wouldn't agree, despite all that you had done for Sean."

Mary continued by stating, "A hide is bigger than hiding a pistol in my pants, Tommy, for Christ's sake."

Tommy stated it would entail a bit of work to be conducted in the house, and in particular, the kitchen. It was suggested that they could move the cooker and a hole would be dug and lined, deep enough to hold weapons both short and long. He assured her when the cooker was replaced, the hole would be invisible.

Mary's mind was racing, thinking whether Billy could still protect her if it all blew up in her face or if he would encourage such an opportunity. She needed to talk with him to get clarity. She loved her brother and he was her only surviving relative but this was profoundly serious. He or both could be jailed for a very long time. Despite her protests, Tommy was adamant it was going to be done.

Mary did talk to Billy, and it was deemed a calculated risk that could be managed if she kept the detachment informed of any activity relating to the hide.

The hide was expected to be constructed over several days and evenings, with Tommy digging down into the foundations of the kitchen floor. At one stage, a jack hammer had to be used to get through the concrete foundation before reaching a more pliable surface. A cover was made of plywood and covered with lino matching the remainder of the kitchen surface. The cover fit perfectly into its recess. It was a few inches narrower than the cooker, ensuring the cooker could move freely without causing any weight-bearing on the cover.

Mary had been given a disposable camera by Billy and asked to photograph the hide, then bring the camera to her next meeting. Mary complied and produced some excellent photos of the hide.

Chapter 16

Liam: Green Booked

1993

Liam had been green booked (recruited) by PIRA, with Frankie being one of the conducting members at the induction ceremony.

The Green book is a training and induction manual issued by the Irish Republican Army to new volunteers.

Liam was now deemed trustworthy by Frankie. This was a huge step forward for Liam's access and something which his handling team was delighted to hear as it had taken a long time to get that level of trust and acceptance from Frankie.

On several occasions, Liam was requested by Frankie to collect individuals from various parts of the city and transport them to certain, so-called, safe houses. Frankie would always be at these properties to await the arrival of these individuals.

Liam was now under no illusions as to the nature of these meetings and the subsequent punishment being administered. It always amazed Liam how calm these individuals were, or at least how they appeared calm, knowingly and willingly complying with their instruction to attend a meeting because of their anti-social behaviour. Some lads were even accompanied by family members to plead their case for clemency in the hope of getting downgraded from a 'Six Pack' to just to a knee capping.

Unfortunately, Liam was seldom given notice but was expected to deliver these individuals within a quick time frame. The meetings were always quick affairs, with the individuals being told the level of punishment to be administered and a location to go to for the implementation of that ruling. Liam would always, at the earliest convenience, relay this information to Billy. However, the punishments were always so quick in their execution, making it difficult to do anything reactive to combat it.

Frankie confided in Liam concerning the growing fear within PIRA that there was a tout within their ranks, and he was determined to seek out whoever it was and "Nutt" them. He told Liam that recent losses had caused sincere concern, and as a result everyone was under suspicion now. He asked if Liam would drive him down to Armagh later that afternoon, as he had business to do with a certain individual, and his guys were out of town at the minute.

The guys he was referring too were known to Liam as Pinkie and Perky. They were twin brothers and well-known henchmen for Frankie. Padraic and Padar Conway were small, stumpy, bald men with curled-up noses, hence the appropriate nicknames, but they were ruthless when inflicting summary justice on behalf of the RA. They were two people you didn't want to get on the wrong side of. These were the same individuals that would turn up at Roslyn's Mum's house looking for Frankie when Liam was still dating her and whom he'd informed Billy about.

Liam informed Billy of the intended trip to Armagh but stated he wasn't given a location by Frankie, only a time to be picked up.

Liam arrived at Frankie's just after five in the evening but didn't go into the house; instead, he sat in the car, waiting for Frankie to exit. Frankie acknowledged Liam through the window, only raising his hand to confirm his existence. Several minutes later, Frankie exited the house wearing a paddy cap, brown Barbour jacket, and blue jeans, carrying a small plastic bag. Frankie got into the car and placed the bag into his footwell between his feet. He then asked Liam to stop at the corner shop, as he needed cigarettes. When Frankie was out of the car, Liam looked in the plastic bag and was bewildered by the presence of a Trophy CR20 tape recorder machine and several cassettes.

Once out on the M1 motorway, Frankie told Liam to head in the direction of the A1, and after twenty miles or so, told him to take the exit to Jonesborough. At no stage was Liam given any other instructions, despite asking where he was going. Frankie stated he would find out soon enough and just to keep driving.

Billy had told Liam to keep him informed as to who Frankie was meeting and where possible, to check in with the office. Liam was starting to get worried now, and considering all the previous revelations concerning the theory of a tout in their mist, he now felt he had cause for concern.

Frankie smoked a few cigarettes during the journey, despite Liam requesting he not smoke in his car. What made it worse was the fact he smoked Camel, a non-filtered cigarette with a pungent odour.

As they approached Jonesborough, Frankie asked Liam to pull over into the entrance of the chapel just short of the Village.

"I need to make a call," said Frankie.

Again, Liam was confused, as there wasn't a telephone box nearby. Frankie got out of the car and took out a large black Nokia mobile phone from his inner jacket pocket and punched in a number. Mobiles had only been launched earlier that year and were relevantly new and rare. Liam turned off the engine to enable him to eavesdrop and could hear Frankie speaking to someone on the other end of the phone.

Liam heard Frankie say, "Spud, that's us at the village now." Frankie seemed to listen and then said, "OK see you shortly."

Frankie got back into the car and gave Liam directions to a garage just west of Jonesborough Village. Liam could just make out the lights of the village behind him. The country road was dark and uninviting as the darkness engulfed the landscape. They waited at the garage for several minutes, with Liam's anxiety levels starting to reach fever pitch.

A dark Range Rover appeared from the darkness. Liam noted that the Rover had come from just over the border with the Irish Republic. The Rover never stopped in the garage but crossed the front of Liam's car, with Frankie instructing Liam to follow it.

They travelled deep into the countryside and what seemed far from civilisation before arriving at a secluded, single-story cottage with two small outbuildings.

Pinkie's combi van was parked in the yard of the cottage, and this only added to Liam's anxiety. It was not good if Pinkie, Perky, and Frankie were all in the same place at the same time. It was a coming together or reunion that could only spell trouble. When Liam's car was parked up, Frankie said, "Liam go into the cottage and wait in the kitchen for me."

He then retrieved the plastic bag from the footwell and walked in the direction of an outbuilding.

The cottage was old and dated, as if an elderly person or persons lived there. There was no one else in the kitchen, but Liam could hear weak or low voices from a room to the rear of the property. Liam's mouth was dry and he felt clammy; he put his hand out straight in front of his body and it was shaking. He went over to the sink to get a glass of water, unsure of what lay ahead of him. As he was filling the glass, he continued to take in his surroundings. He could see empty sandwich packaging and a flask on the table, but his eyes were drawn to the top of the cooker. Liam thought he was looking at charred pieces of food stuck to the rings but what was odd, he could see writing, that was barely visible on one small, charred piece. As he looked closer, he could just make out what he thought were the letters L O V.

Liam dropped his glass and fell backwards, just managing to retain his balance by grabbing the edge of the kitchen table. He realised, he was looking at burnt skin and what must have been part of someone's tattoo.

He thought, *Christ, someone was being tortured here and Frankie and Co are the masters of ceremony.*

Liam felt sick to the pit of his stomach, but the sudden realisation that at least it wasn't him who was being viciously abused was almost comforting. Liam wanted none of it and desperately wanted to get as far away from the cottage as possible but Frankie would never allow him to leave now. He wasn't even sure he could find his way back out to the main roads. If only he could make a call to the office and let Billy know what was happening but then he knew he would be mixed up in whatever dirty and treacherous deed was being carried out at the cottage.

Christ, how could I even let Billy know where I am when I don't know himself.

Being in the Republic of Ireland further complicated the situation. Even if it had been Liam being tortured, the British Army and Billy couldn't have turned up.

Liam searched the kitchen for any signs of evidence as to the location of the cottage. On the wall next to a larder cupboard was a letter rack. The rack had a small calendar with a religious picture of the virgin Mary cradling a baby. The small rack contained a set of keys and a series of envelopes. The address of the cottage was on an unopened letter from Electric I.E, the Republics main energy supplier. There was no number but rather the name Donnelly, the cottage name, 'O' Morn Cottage', and the townland Faughart, Dundalk.

The name wasn't lost on Liam as he remembered John Wayne and Maureen O'Hara in the "Quiet Man" and the cottage which had the same name.

Frankie entered the outbuilding along with Spud and was greeted by Pinkie and Perky, who were in the process of dragging a male in his 30's onto a stool. The man was already in a terrible state, both physically and mentally. He was stripped down to his badly stained underwear, which were covered in wet urine stains and mud. He had horrendous burns to his legs and backside. One of his eyes was completely closed shut, with dark swelling around it. His left forearm looked like a piece of raw meat.

The man was finished, he had nothing left to give as his body and spirit were brutally broken. His dark hair was badly matted with congealed blood.

Frankie walked to a small table and placed down the tape recorder. He then lifted a cheese slice, which had a large piece of skin still attached to it and walked over to the man, dangling it in front of his face.

"Malachy, do you know what this is? It's that pretty tattoo you had on your arm. I am going to send it in an envelope to your Ma and Da, you fucking tout."

The man just moaned and pleaded through broken teeth with his torturers, "Please stop, I've confessed already, I just want it to stop."

Frankie stated, "That's why I'm here, I need you to repeat all that you had told Spud about your work with Special Branch." Frankie then retrieved the tape recorder and Malachy told his story to Frankie for the benefit of the tape.

Liam tiptoed along the corridor to the rear of the cottage before pausing outside the room he believed the voices were coming from. It sounded like two people talking in low voices in the hope of not being overheard. Liam opened the door slightly and peered inside and could see an elderly man and woman sitting on the side of the bed with their backs to the door. Liam quietly closed the door and retreated to the kitchen. The elderly couple must have been placed in the room and instructed not to move, effectively being held hostage whilst the torture in the outbuildings was being conducted. Liam searched the cottage in the hope of locating a telephone, but there was none at the property, or at least none that Liam could find.

Liam was in the cottage for about an hour before Frankie and his cronies returned inside. After a brief conversation between Frankie and Spud, they then made their way to the vehicles, with Liam in tow but leaving Pinkie and Perky in situ.

Frankie was in exceedingly high spirits and was extremely talkative on the route back across the border but never mentioned anything about his actions at the cottage.

Liam turned to Frankie and asked, "Who's Spud?"

"Just a bloke from Armagh and someone you should forget," Frankie said and wouldn't be drawn any further on the matter.

Liam only stated that the whole evening had been bizarre, but he was grateful to be heading home.

After dropping off Frankie, Liam went immediately to a phone box and telephoned Billy. The location of the cottage, the people involved, and as much as he could remember was given. Liam stated that he believed a punishment beating or worse was taking place at the cottage and the Conway brothers were still in situ.

Following the call from Liam, Billy contacted his boss and was told to inform the duty watchkeeper at HQNI (Headquarters Northern Ireland) and produce a MISR (Military Intelligence Agent Report) detailing the information gained from Liam.

The report was passed onto the RUC and the Special Branch for the South Armagh Region. The cooperation between the North and South policing bodies was haphazard at best, and since it was in the Garda Siochana jurisdiction, it would be their rescue operation to be conducted.

In the early hours, the Garda ERU (Emergency Response Unit), the equivalent to the British SAS did locate the cottage, but there was no sign of life. On entering the cottage, they did locate the old man and woman, who were sitting in complete darkness on the side of the bed with their backs to the door. Both were in a state of shock and hadn't dared moved from their position in the room.

A clean up of the property had been conducted, with a cooker having its rings cleaned for what was probably the first time in their existence. The outbuildings were forensically searched. Tyre casts and prints were taken, along with a cigarette ending found at the side of the outbuilding. It was a quick response by the Garda but unfortunately didn't produce the desired outcome.

Onus on Truths

The following morning, a body was found on an isolated country road on the border between south Armagh and the Republic. The body was bound, blindfolded, and had two bullet holes to the back of the head. A ten-pound note was placed in the hands of the man. It was his final payment in this life and what he was believed to be worth to the IRA for his information.

The man was later identified as Malachy Tweed, a father of three from the Armagh area.

Liam woke up to the news of the killing and was physically sick. He started to think about self-preservation. He remembered having touched the glass which dropped and broke before placing the pieces in the bin. He also touched the envelope with the address of the cottage.

God almighty, he thought*, the door handle, the table I gripped when losing balance, is there anything I didn't touch? How could I have been so stupid, now I'm implicated in a murder.*

Once again, he telephoned Billy and was brought in for a meeting to help reassure him. He was told he was not in any danger of compromise or incriminated with the murder. Liam was reassured he had done everything in his power to warn his Handler by placing the telephone call.

Malachy Tweed would have still been alive at the time of the call and the Garda were just not quick enough to avoid the subsequent move and murder from the cottage.

"Neither the RUC or the Garda have your prints on file and you have no criminal record, so you needn't worry," stated Billy. "I said we would protect you and that's what we will do. You were there unknowingly as to what was taking place, so you were not able to stop it. The fact that you notified us of its location and the people present enabled us to mount the rescue operation for Malachy in the first place. Everything that could be done was done."

It was explained that Liam must never get actively and knowingly involved in any criminal or terrorist activity resulting in injury or death, because Military Intelligence could not protect him. However, there were many ways in which to still be involved that could merit a level of protection, but he needed to keep his Handler informed at every stage. It was only by doing this that measures of safeguard could be put in place to protect him. Liam left the meeting slightly less anxious than when he went in. Liam still couldn't get his head around how Frankie was so relaxed or unfazed by his actions. A man and a father of three was executed, and Frankie took it all in stride. In Liam's eyes, Frankie really was a callous monster.

Chapter 17

Mary: The Hide

The construction of the hide had been completed, and even Mary was impressed by the engineering work conducted by Tommy. It had taken two weeks to complete, although there had been no placement of weapons yet, which was something that Mary was pleased about. However, it was surely only a matter of time before it would be used.

Mary continued the pass information on leading republican figures to Billy. She continued working at the Sinn Fein office. She was a trusted and valued member of the office and was able to pass on numerous policy documents on the internal structure and workings of Sinn Fein.

She was active whilst secret meetings were taking place between Martin McGuinness and 'Fred', the code name of a senior British Intelligence Agent. These talks were taking place in Londonderry under the guise of inward investment into the city.

The IRA at the time believed the war was over but needed assurances from the government about Loyalist paramilitaries decommissioning of arms. Mary was providing some excellent information and even provided the percentage of decommission the IRA were prepared to accept in any tangible deal. This was vital for the government, because before they even entered negotiations, they had a start point from which to apply pressure. Sinn Fein were serious about the process but needed to bring the rank and file along with them if it was to be successful.

These secret talks continued throughout 1993/4. Mary's information was being read by the highest Northern Ireland officials and even the British Prime Minister.

Mary had become quite a celebrity at the detachment and a prized asset. Over the years she had worked, she had Sean Pearce imprisoned twice and two members of the Ballylesson death squad killed, along with the Quartermaster Belfast Brigade, in addition to the recovery of copious quantities of arms and ammunition. Now, she was seated at the tables of Sinn Fein, divulging secrets which were invaluable to the British government and the peace process.

Tommy had moved out of the house and moved in with Fey, a single mother of two from the Twinbrooke, a move Mary was delighted with. Although Tommy had constructed the hide, it was always the intention of Jimmy Rice for Mary to be the main custodian. Tommy moving out was a good thing, as he was a well-known republican and would be on the radar of the security services. It was thought he would have drawn undue attention to the house. As far as the IRA were concerned, it was the perfect scenario. Tommy was only gone a matter of months when he was caught trying to hold up a Spar shop in Dunmurry.

Mary always said he wasn't the sharpest pencil in the box, and now he has been sent down again, this time for four years. He would be reacquainted with his old H- Block cell mate, Barry McGinn, well at least for a brief time until Barry's release a few years later.

Following the secret talks, the IRA declared a complete cessation of military operations. The CLMC (Combined Loyalist Military Command), an umbrella group for Loyalist Paramilitaries, said it would also cease all operational hostilities.

Mary questioned Billy during one of their routine meetings back at one of the OCP's (Official Clandestine Premises) the detachment had scattered about the province as to the ending of the 'Troubles' and subsequent future work for British Military Intelligence.

Billy assured her that the IRA hadn't gone away.

It was a comment Gerry Adams would make at a rally outside the Belfast city hall in 1995.

Evidence that they hadn't gone away soon presented itself when Jimmy Rice arrived at her house late one evening carrying a bundle wrapped in plastic into the kitchen. Inside the plastic sheet were three AK-47's and a Walther 9mm Pistol. The wait was finally over, as Billy received a telephone call from Mary informing him of a weapons cache now securely located within her kitchen floor. Although it was impossible to know when the IRA would be back to remove them, it was decided to wait for a period as not to put Mary under any further pressure or risk. If she kept Billy informed, then no action would take place to remove or inspect them. A cooling off period was decided upon, of which Mary was delighted. Several months had passed and despite numerous attacks and punishment beatings, no one called to Mary's house for the cache.

One day, when Mary was in the city centre, she bumped into Roslyn Murray. The two girls had a coffee together and a bit of a catch-up, reminiscing about the good old days. Roslyn had a young son and a husband who she never saw, not, as she pointed out, because they were having marriage problems but rather because he was always out of the house and with her evil, rotten brother, Frankie. Roslyn stated that she knew so many people who had suffered under Frankie's hands and that he was responsible for so much pain and suffering in the community.

"He's going to get my Liam tied up in his dodginess. The last thing I need is to be traveling up and down to the Maze to visit my husband."

Mary didn't want to probe too deep but was interested in what involvement Roslyn was talking about. She had seen Liam on various occasions in the company of Frankie, but she'd never had any direct involvement with him. However, she did assume, rightly, that he must be involved to some degree to be in Frankie's company in the first place. Mary was interested in getting to know more, particularly about Frankie, so she agreed for the girls to meet up more regularly for coffee and have good old fashion girlie talks. Roslyn agreed and the girls' exchanged numbers, then went their separate ways for the time being.

Mary had one of her routine meetings with Billy the following day and during their conversation Mary said, "I have someone who I think you might be interested in."

She stated the name as Liam Murray and that he was the brother-in-law of Frankie Connolly. "I think he is involved with the RA."

Billy stated he was grateful for the information and would investigate the matter but thanked her for her due diligence.

Mary was given lessons on recognition of various weapon types to assist her in identifying those she currently held within her hide. Time was also taken to go over Mary's security procedures and to remind her of how important it was to remain safe, considering all that she was involved in.

Mary was still providing invaluable information directly out of the Sinn Fein offices. What she did produce and witnessed left her in no doubt that PIRA and Sinn Fein were inextricably linked. She believed PIRA members who frequently visited the offices were planning operations. The targeting of Police, Army, and Prison Service personnel was still very much on the agenda. Mary had found a list of home service Royal Irish soldiers which had dropped out of a folder Kieran was carrying whilst visiting the Sinn Fein offices, complete with names and addresses. This, Mary copied and handed to Billy. The relevant authorities were made aware so that the soldiers in question could step up their own personal security procedures.

Gerry Adams was right,

"They haven't gone away you know."

Chapter 18

Frankie's Tout Hunt

Frankie asked Liam if he could take him up to the Maze, as he wanted a wee chat with Sean Pearce. Frankie had spent a long time going over the events surrounding operations that had gone wrong. As part of his investigations, he concluded that since Sean had been inside, no further compromises or death of volunteers had occurred. Frankie was sure that Sean was the common denominator.

Frankie had been back to Bridget and Mary to follow up on his inquiries but found there was nothing further to glean. Frankie was satisfied but now needed a confession from Sean, otherwise the PAC (Provisional Army Council) of the IRA would not sanction his execution.

Sean continued to protest his innocence. Frankie continued pushing the argument, stating. "The part-time soldier never shot at you in the shop yet managed to put two rounds in John's chest and then missed you as you ran away. The Army patrol shot Gerry, but still you managed to escape unharmed. Then, McCartney gets wasted by the Brits at Colin Glen Forest and yet again you only got shot in the legs. What the fuck are you? A cat with nine lives?"

Frankie was getting nowhere and told Sean, "Unless you confess, something terrible will happen in prison and it will be out of my hands, as the boys are restless and Barry McGinn wants action." Sean's time in prison had already been extremely difficult. Because of Frankie's investigation and the suspicion surrounding all the failed operations, it was not going to get any easier for him.

Whenever Bridget travelled up to visit Sean in prison, she was shunned by the other republican wives on the transport. Even Bridget was starting to doubt Sean's claims of innocence and begged him to tell the truth, otherwise her life wouldn't be worth living.

Sean was furious at Bridget and stated, "What chance do I have if my own wife doesn't believe me? I might as well confess and be done with it." He further stated, "My whole life had been dedicated to the republican cause. "

The wives of republican prisoners were normally well looked after whilst their men folk were incarcerated, but Bridget was starting to feel isolated, with less frequent visits by the support group. She told Sean that could only be because of the suspicion directed at him. It wasn't one of Bridget's more productive visits. She left the prison depressed, in tears, and fearing the worse for Sean, as she could tell he was worried by the allegations against him.

Three days following the visit to Sean by Bridget, Sean received a visitor to his Cell in the form of one of the trustees. Sean was told that an urgent telephone call had been received for him and he was to escort Sean to the control room. Trustees are normally as the word suggests, trusted inmates with impeccable prison records or low crime equating to low-risk inmates.

Sean was not concerned, as calls were received all the time and the procedure was the same for all the other recipients of such calls.

The control room was situated in the cross bar of the H-Block. Each block had four wings, with each wing meeting at the cross section of the H. As Sean approached the cross section, he could see the control room but noticed the prison guard (or Screw) had his back to the gate. This was a controlled entrance into the secure area. No other Screws were present, but the gate was locked, and he noticed Barry McGinn and another republican, Lips O'Hare, standing to either side of the entrance to the last cell.

As Sean stood at the gated door, waiting for the Screw to unlock it, he noticed the trustee had backed away, leaving Sean looking toward the Screw but getting no response or access to the secure area.

Barry came up to the back of Sean and spoke quietly into his ear. "Sean, I need a private word." Then, he pointed to the cell door.

This was not good, and Sean knew he was in trouble. He considered using his walking aid to try to fight his way out of the situation, but Barry was a formidable character, and Lips would be another daunting handful to take on. He tightened his grip on the stick and looked again toward the control room, but no help was forthcoming.

Sean was still unsteady on his feet and still recovering from the damage caused by the shooting in Colin Glen Forest. The conspicuous absence of prison guards was unquestionably unwelcome news.

As Sean entered the cell, he could see another member of the block, Tommy Sweeney, lurking in the back of the cell. Sean decided he was not going out without a fight and turned, sharply swinging the stick at Lips's head, but only catching him on the upper arm, whilst at the same time calling out for help.

Barry punched Sean on the back of the head, and he fell headfirst through the entrance of the cell onto the floor.

Sean was attacked by Tommy and Barry whilst Lips was still recovering from the pain of the blow to his arm.

Once restrained, Sean was set on the toilet bowl with both Tommy and Lips holding him. Barry landed several punches to Sean's head and body before saying, "Confess you tout bastard."

Sean pleaded his innocence as more punches rained down on him.

Tommy pulled Sean's arm back flush against the cell wall as Barry smashed the stick against Sean's clenched fist. Sean screamed out in pain but continued to plead his innocence. The beatings and the torture continued for the next twenty minutes, with Sean left on the floor in a pool of blood and semi-conscious.

Through broken teeth and swollen lips, Sean forced out the words, "Not fucking guilty."

A solid, ten-pound block of concrete on a large, thick brush shaft normally used for polishing the floor of the cell block, referred to as a bumper, was lifted by Lips O'Hare and dropped onto the head of

Sean. His head opened like a raw egg being dropped from height. Barry rounded on Lips, calling him a stupid fucker, as he wanted a written confession from Sean.

The three men then fabricated a story for Sean's confession. There was now the little matter of the dead body in the cell, but closed ranks would ensure the inquiry would never get anywhere, and the authorities wouldn't get too excited over the death of an IRA terrorist anyway.

Chapter 19

Jamie O'Connor

Numerous attempts were made to get Mary to bring out the cache from the hide, but there was always one reason or another preventing its extraction.

Mary was now in a relationship with the barman from the Shamrock Arms by the name of Jamie O'Connor. It wasn't serious, but Mary would joke when meeting with Billy that it was good sex and something she had missed for a few years.

She reported that Bridget wasn't exactly in mourning following the death of Sean. Although it had been several months since his murder with, as expected, no conviction, she was already back playing the field. This never surprised Mary, as she was aware of her previous infidelity whilst still married to a living Sean.

Mary felt somewhat to blame, as she was the one who encouraged Bridget to get out, as both girls were regulars at the Shamrock Arms. It was there that Mary had met Jamie.

Jamie had been a long-term barman in the Shamrock. A small but wiry man who wasn't afraid to dump boys on their backsides when it came to kicking out time. He was known for having a small aikido bat which he kept behind the counter, which he called "The Tamer." His softer side came out on karaoke nights, as the man had a terrific voice and was always giving renditions of Elvis Presley numbers. The punters loved it, and he was always called out from behind the bar for his solo performances.

One night in the bar, Mary and Bridget joined Roslyn and Liam Murray's company. They had a good evening, with Mary having a good interaction with Liam for the first time, and she was keen to learn more about him for Billy. However, as the evening went on, with more drinks being consumed, Bridget got very upset when a lad came round with a collection tin for the 'Men behind the wire.' She threw a tantrum and traded insults with the lad, who was trying to say the prisoners had made the ultimate sacrifice for the republican cause.

The lad was clearly not aware who Bridget was, or more importantly, who she had been married to. Bridget threw her glass of beer over the lad and told him to fuck off. Liam was first to react, getting between Bridget and the lad before he could punch her out, which was exactly what he was about to do. However, 'The Tamer' in the hands of Jamie was over to the table like lightning to ensure peace was restored.

Liam led the lad away and informed him as to the identity of Bridget and why she was so upset. The lad calmed down, enabling Liam for the first time to release his grip of the lads tensed up arms. The whole bar was silent and watching as the event unfolded, but as Liam was walking back toward the table, the lad shouted, "Tout bastard."

For an instant, Liam froze, the hairs on his neck standing on edge before realising the words were directed at Bridget and her deceased husband.

Mary also felt the shockwave of the comment but turned her attention back to Bridget, who was frantic and screaming, "They killed an innocent man!"

Jamie didn't need 'The Tamer' but did ask Bridget to leave the bar.

Mary lost the opportunity to astutely pump Liam on his relationship with his brother-in-law, Frankie Connolly. Bridget was very upset but was left home by Mary.

Mary reflected on the evening's events and the way in which the lad had shouted the word 'tout'. There was a realisation that everyone in the bar were totally impassive to the whole affair. No offer of comfort or condolences were offered; the engrossed audience just stared at Bridget with a total lack of empathy.

Mary thought, *what a sad people we are, regardless of the circumstances,* Sean was still a human being, and to be brutely murdered the way he was, gave Mary justification for doing what she did.

Although she did feel a little guilty, as she was the one who'd put him in jail in the first place.

The following morning, Mary paid Bridget a visit and was shown through into the kitchen for a much-needed cup of tea. Once in the kitchen, Mary could smell what she could only describe as a potent odour, a strong smell of stale tobacco.

Mary knew Bridget didn't smoke, so someone else had been in the house. Mary didn't want to pry, but her curiosity got the better of her and asked, "Have you got a visitor Bridget?"

Bridget showed a degree of awkwardness before responding with a very direct, "No" before attempting to change the subject.

Mary knew better but decided to leave the matter alone, at least for now.

Chapter 20

Operation Compromise

A long-term recruitment operation had been conducted against a prominent INLA member, Thomas Fee, from the Oldpark area of Belfast. Thomas was a taxi driver who was hired to conduct several journeys using John, an operator from the Unit, as bait. All these trips were fictitious in nature but consisted of journeys to the Airport for both pickups and drop-offs along with several business meetings in the city.

The aim of the operation was to build rapport with the target and advance it to a point when the recruitment pitch could be affected. It was vital the integrity of the operation was not compromised.

During these trips, a business proposition was put to the target for a venture in the creation of an executive style taxi firm located at Templepatrick, close to the Hilton Hotel and Airport. Although the target appeared extremely enthusiastic to begin with, John had grown suspicious of the target in the last few encounters and had a gut feeling the target was himself growing suspicious of John.

A plan was devised to have the target pick John up at a city centre hotel and take him to Templepatrick for a meeting. It would be here that other bogus business partners were introduced, but instead of a business pitch, it would be an attempt to recruit the target for British Military Intelligence. Regardless of the level of sophistication or complexity that goes into a recruitment scam, it would always come down to a simple question with enormous consequences.

Would they be prepared to work for a large and powerful organization: yes, or no?

Because it was going to be a recruitment attempt of the target, additional manpower was drafted into the team. The local resident battalion's QRF along with the AAC (Army Air Corps) helicopter were used. The helicopter could provide overwatch and downlink cameras that could be monitored from the detachment's operations room. Close support teams would deploy on the ground as mobile callsigns, with the helicopter providing the target's vehicle movements from the city centre out to Templepatrick, along with any subsequent movement following the recruitment attempt.

Operators were pre-positioned in the recruitment venue to provide close support during the pitch.

John was dressed in his business attire but armed with a pistol and covert radio communication, complete with covert earpiece. He also had a briefcase containing his MP5K submachine gun.

The cover teams moved into position and waited for the target to appear.

The target showed up on time, with John leaving the hotel entrance then entering the vehicle.

The cover teams reported John and the target's movements as they departed the city centre hotel. John was able to hear all the radio chatter as they travelled past the Belfast Opera House, closely followed by the cover teams. The target turned left toward Divis Street, away from the most direct and obvious route.

John asked, "Why aren't you going straight out toward the York Street or Shore Road?"

The target stated, "I'm not going to any more of your fucking meetings, you Brit bastard." At the same time, the rear seat of the vehicle dropped down and a man pointing a pistol at John climbed through into the back seat and said, "You're coming with us Brit."

The cover team to the rear of the target's vehicle could see the appearance of the third party and radioed that an attempted abduction was in progress whilst relaying the exact location of the target's car.

John was able to press his pressel and say on open mic, "What's this all about and why the gun?"

This now confirmed to the team it was an armed abduction taking place.

The other cover teams had been satelliting the targets vehicle by moving along parallel routes but had now moved closer to be able to intercept the target. The helicopter was able to guide the vehicles along less busy roads and avenues as they closed in.

John could still hear the progress of the cover teams, and although still trying to convey his innocence, was told to shut up.

Thomas Fee said, "I suspected you from the very start."

It transpired that on the initial airport run and subsequent drop off, the target received a call to pick up another passenger from the same terminal. So, having completed the one-way circuit out of the airport, as he made his second approach for the pickup, he saw John leaving the terminal building and getting into a waiting car.

So much for the business meeting in London John stated he was rushing for, Thomas thought.

The operations room was still desperately trying to determine the safest way to bring the vehicle to a halt as it turned into Albert Street toward St. Peters Close, an area in the Lower Falls. As the car reached the entrance of St. Peters Close, a white VW T4 van pulled out of the junction, with the target's vehicle coming to a halt. The driver of the van remained in the cab, as the passenger and a further individual who had been in the rear jumped out and made their way to the target's vehicle.

The passenger of the van had a pistol, whilst the body from the rear had an AK-47 assault rifle. The passenger of the van pointed the gun at John, telling him to get out of the vehicle.

John opened the door slowly and deliberately, making a feeble attempt at getting out whilst at the same time reaching for his pistol from his waistband.

The rear doors of the van were opened and ready to receive John, but as he was getting out, the first of the covert teams arrived at the rear of the target's car.

John's actions were perfectly timed as the two-man team of Billy and Mac jumped out and immediately moved toward the man closest to John.

Billy engaged the terrorist, shooting him with rounds, hitting him in the stomach and legs.

John pulled out his pistol as he exited the vehicle, turning his attention to the man holding the AK-47, he fired two shots, hitting the man in his chest, neutralising him.

The third party in the car was screaming at Thomas Fee, "Open the fucking child locks," that had been applied in the rear of the car.

The driver of the van tried to accelerate away but, in his haste, crashed into the front of the target's car. John turned and fired another two shots through the rear passenger window at the third party, hitting him in the face and head. The back windscreen was splattered with blood and brains as the man slumped down in the seat.

Thomas Fee remained frozen to the spot, deafened by the gunfire, and made no attempt to move as a second cover team arrived on the scene.

The driver of the van, in his panic, made several more attempts at reversing and forward movements to get clear before being pulled from the cab by Mac and made to lay prone on the floor. The rear of the van had a black boiler suit, plastic cuffs, and assorted ropes laying on the floor.

The intention of the INLA team was clear, John would have been taken somewhere and interrogated before being shot.

The QRF arrived and, after exiting a large blackout transit van, secured the area. The operators could now withdraw from the area and revert to being a covert force again.

The operation was a testament to the arduous and determined training that went into planning and preparations for all operations.

Hard hitting and explosive in nature with well-drilled procedures ensured the teams returned safely to barracks. Although it was a recruitment plan that had gone wrong, it was a success in terms of good operational procedures. A thorough analysis would be undertaken to ensure lessons were learned from it. Three dead terrorists and a further two in police custody was considered a good result.

Chapter 21

A painters Job

1995

In between Agent meetings and CQB range practices, of which there were plenty, Billy would spend several hours during the working week catching up on vital paperwork and reviewing his case files.

He was particularly interested in several CASCON's still on the books but not active. Being casual contacts, it was pretty much left to them to get in touch should they have something worthy of report.

Billy was responsible for three such Agents but had only ever met one out of the three and was keen to conduct a reverse contact procedure to re-evaluate their levels of access. The need for new blood in the fight against the terrorist organisations of both communities was paramount. It was the responsibility of every member of the detachment to conduct their own research in the pursuit of likely potential targets.

Although, kept extremely busy running his two prised assets in Mary and Liam and having the added responsibility for several additional CASCON's, it was difficult to find the time to actively explore fresh blood. Despite the existence of a dedicated targeting team, the current CHIS's were a great basis from where much of the background information on potential targets came.

Since his arrival in the Unit, and in particular, his CHIS cases, Mary had become a top-grade CHIS reporting on political, terrorist, and criminal activities of the IRA.

Liam had been promoted and was now a fully-fledged 'Green Booked' active service member of the IRA and a member of the internal security team.

Mary had always been encouraged by Billy to report on individuals that may be of interest to the detachment. Mary had already passed along Liam's name, to the amusement of Billy. If only she knew! She had also provided several others as suspected IRA members.

One such name that she passed was Micky Crawford, who she stated had been recently stood down by the IRA because of his affair with another IRA member's wife.

Micky Crawford was a member of the Ballymurphy ASU. During one of Mary's routine meetings with Billy, she mentioned that Micky had been in the Shamrock Arms and had been boasting about his part in the ambush of the fake laundry service of the MRF. Micky bragged about being one of the lucky ones to have gotten away. Although, ballistic reports from the time of the incident proved the fatal shots fired that killed the female operative came from one of the dead terrorists' weapons, and all the shots came from the recovered weapons at the scene.

So whatever part Micky Crawford had played in the attack, he wasn't one of the shooters.

This piece of information from Mary was viewed by Billy as worthy of further exploration. He may not be a member any longer, but he would still be able to provide Billy with information on current members and historical operations carried out by the Ballymurphy ASU. Micky would surely be angry at being stood down and, with the right incentives or motivation, could be a good asset if recruited. He could always be reinstated back into the IRA ranks with the right direction and control.

Billy spent much of his time when in the office on researching Micky Crawford's lifestyle and terrorist activities. Several MISR reports had been written, with mention to Micky, but other Agent reports highlighted his addiction to gambling. He was a painter and decorator by trade, who had his own transport. It was all looking quite promising, but a plan of action was required.

A recruitment operation needed to be formed, but first, a cultivation period was needed to establish his motivation and determine a point of contact in which to get alongside him.

Several options were considered, with a natural cover operation being decided upon. An ad would be placed in the local paper, requesting a painter for a large project. A mobile number would be supplied and a name to be contacted. It was hoped that he would see the ad and apply. All other applicants would not be successful in applying, with Micky being offered the chance to meet and tender for the job. Quite simple really. All that was needed now was a project in which he could paint. That was not quite that simple.

Through a network of agencies and friends, a suitable property was found on the outskirts of Antrim. Checks conducted by the UK customs and excise border force highlighted the occupants as being out of the country. The nominated property was a large country house and was used by a retired couple, who spent most of their time in Spain. The property set back off a small country road and had electric controlled gates at the entrance. The wall that ran either side of the gates was five feet tall, with a pebble-dashed exterior painted grey. The house was of the Georgian period, with beautiful inlaid, stained-glass panels on either side of a large period door. It set on several acres of lush, green fields with large conifers lining the long, twisting driveway up to the house.

Billy knew the property was going to be vacant at the time of the scam, so a planning meeting was arranged with the Unit's top brass and a way forward decided.

Micky would be instructed to paint the exterior of the property's boundary wall.

The total length of the wall was roughly 300 meters long and would be painted in the same shade of grey. Access would not be required through the gates. Anyone passing the property would not be suspicious, as the work was genuine and the owner would come home to a freshly painted wall, courtesy of her majesty's government. If compromised by a neighbour or any other third party, then no one would be any the wiser to the person responsible for the job, as nothing would be traceable back to Billy and the Unit.

Billy would be fronting the scam as a fictitious property manager tasked with maintenance and repairs for many properties. If everything went according to plan, then Micky would be offered further jobs to complete. The scope of work could be anything from a large-scale project down to a small domestic job. The concept was only restricted by the imagination of the team.

Once all the various options were considered such as, what if, for example, he goes public, well nothing lost, maybe a bit of bad press like 'Poor, hard-working catholic man targeted by British Agents.' A matter Sinn Fein would take great delight in exploiting. A few hundred pounds for paint and cover expenses would make it a low cost and low risk operation.

As luck would have it, Micky saw the ad and telephoned the number. From the time the ad was placed, it was answered by several applicants within two hours. All enquiries were documented, with these individuals' details going straight to the targeting teams to analyse the information. They would be considered as being other persons of interest and present the office with further opportunities for exploitation.

Micky was invited for a meeting to discuss the work and costs.

The meeting was to be held in a Belfast city café convenient for both parties, or moreover, the target. The operation was considered low risk at this stage, as there was no reason for Micky to be suspicious in any way. However, following the failed recruitment attempt and attempted abduction of John by Thomas Fee, no chances would be taken.

Onus on Truths

A team consisting of a male/female were co-located in the café and in a position to react to any incident that may be directed at the Handler. A further two operators were positioned outside on the street, covering the entrances and exits of the building. A mobile cover team was able to provide overwatch of the target's van, with the intention of conducting surveillance on completion of the meeting. This was a precaution in the event the target got suspicious and decided to pay the Sinn Fein offices a visit.

Billy took up his position within the café, ensuring he was suitably placed with a view of the door and the cover teams but keeping his back to the wall, with a total overview of the room.

It was ten in the morning and the café was relatively quiet when suddenly the covert radio burst into life. The mobile cover team reported the arrival of the target's blue VW Van.

The target was alone and dressed in his white, paint-stained overalls. The cover team described the target as being six feet tall, large build, with black, shoulder length hair which was tied in a ponytail. This matched the description Mary had provided, minus the large Celtic cross tattoo on his neck.

Billy was dressed in a casual but smart attire, jacket, and trousers. Although not on open display, he was wearing covert body armour under his shirt, complete with his covert comms and 9mm pistol tucked into his waistband. He had a briefcase with numerous documents and property details, including pictures of the intended project.

Micky entered the café and immediately looked around in search of his contact. Billy raised his hand to indicate he was the person Micky was to meet. Billy informed Micky that he made a fair assumption he was indeed Micky because of his attire. Micky looked down at his own body and laughed, stating, "Yeah, I guess I'm hard to miss," before he took a seat.

Following a few introductory formalities, Billy gave Micky a brief background on his position and how he was responsible for large numbers of owned and rented properties for executive personnel and corporate clients both here in Northern Ireland and abroad. He further explained he could never have enough tradesmen on his books to carry out the works needed.

The meeting lasted forty minutes, with an element of rapport being established. Micky was always going to get the job, but it had to be seen to be a proper negotiation, and a fair price was agreed upon. This was supported by other quotes obtained by the research team, ensuring Billy had a good starting point to work from. The price was agreed but could only be finalised on an inspection of the wall, in Micky's words, "In case remedial work was needed prior to painting."

A business card was passed to Micky, and a time to visit the property for the following morning was set.

The meeting ended with nothing significant gleaned to further the team's assessment of Micky Crawford as a potential Agent. It was hoped, as time went on and the more the two men met, that an opportunity would present itself to be able to conduct a pitch. Micky was keen to undertake the work and seemed satisfied with what was on offer. Micky left the cafe and returned to his van.

The cover team from the street followed on foot until Micky was secured in the vehicle before going mobile themselves to back up the other mobile team on the surveillance away from the meeting venue.

The two cover teams followed the target back over to the west of the city and to a house which Micky appeared to be working at. This was a positive result, as he never went to Sinn Fein to report the incident. Consideration was given to conduct a cold pitch of the target. This would simply mean at some point during or immediately following the painting of the wall, an attempt to recruit him would take place. To do this, the team would be relying heavily on his rejection by the IRA as the sole motivation to work for British Military Intelligence. It would be a long shot, with the potential of a political fallout from Sinn Fein and the media should it go wrong.

The following morning, Micky turned up at the address and commented on how difficult it was to find. He also had another person with him in the van, something not expected by the team. Although he was triggered to the address by the team members on the ground and loosely followed, which meant Billy was aware prior to his arrival.

The team adjusted accordingly in anticipation of an attack or abduction of Billy. Teams moved and blocked off both directions, with Billy's close support positioned in a hedge row adjacent to the property.

As it transpired, Micky intended to get a colour match and go into Antrim town for the paint, then make an immediate start to the work. The other person with him was a young lad of about seventeen years, who in Micky's words was going to help him and therefore get through the job quicker, reassuring Billy it would be a good job, nonetheless. It was a complication but nothing that couldn't be navigated.

Micky left to get the paint and the teams extracted from the area. It was the intention of Billy to pay visits to the site and have rapport-building conversations during the project.

The project was expected to last five days, with the two men starting at the two furthest points, working their way back to the centre and the entrance gates. This spacing assisted Billy on his visits, as he was always out of ear shot of the young lad.

It transpired work had been slow recently for Micky, and he was therefore grateful for the work given and would welcome any other work offered his way. The week ended with Micky receiving payment and a small bonus for a job well done. There hadn't been any compromise during the project. The men were left alone to complete the work with only one member of the public stopping and asking for contact details concerning hiring him for private work. Further research was needed following the initial phase of the operation to progress the concept, but at least everything to date had gone according to plan.

A further meeting with Mary established that Micky Crawford was in serious debt, and it ran into at least five figures. It was believed this was a result of his gambling addiction.

Billy and the team saw this as a possible avenue that could be explored but it had its risks. To assist with his debt problem with the offer of money may help motivate him to work, but his spending habits could be problematic if he was seen to be spending beyond his means.

Several weeks had passed, and another job was offered to Micky over the phone and a meeting arranged at the site to negotiate a price. He was told it was a bigger project and worth considerably more, but he wouldn't be able to start it the same day. This was done to ensure he came alone without the need for any third party.

Micky was delighted to accept it, despite not even knowing what the job was to entail.

A small industrial Unit in Mullusk on the outskirts of Belfast was designated for the next fictitious project. The site was perfect in its location, as it was isolated and therefore far away from prying eyes. Research suggested the site had been vacant for some time. It was an enclosed site with a twelve-foot, chain-metal fence with two large, metal gates. A shipment container once used as a security hut sat adjacent to the gate. Both the gate and the container had mortise style locks. Under the cover of darkness, the team visited the site and replaced the locks with two new ones, ensuring the team could obtain access and would look completely natural to the target. This was going to be a 'Cold Pitch.' No more time was going to be spent on having complicated operations and scams, but instead a direct approach would be utilized.

The teams were briefed, and members of 14 Int were employed to conduct the surveillance of the target's car following the pitch. It was important to be aware of his actions post operation. The 14 Int team would not be aware of what was taking place but rather have a target to follow until he was housed (meaning he'd reached his destination).

Onus on Truths

The cover teams were positioned near the industrial unit to provide support. Billy was accompanied by Mac for the pitch in the container. A briefcase containing ten thousand pounds was place on a small table, unopened, ready for the big question. As the time drew closer to the target's arrival, Billy could feel the adrenaline pumping through his veins. Although he had conducted many face to face recruitment attempts, the feeling of excitement and the buzz of anticipation was always the same. It was like no other and something you could only experience when working against people who carried out the most nefarious deeds on their fellow human beings. Micky Crawford was one such person who was about to get the shock of his life.

Everything was in place for another operation where, if compromised, total deniability could be achieved and no evidence of it ever having taken place would exist except in the target's own head. Micky arrived, and Mac went to the gate and opened the lock whilst leaving it hanging on its large chain.

The gate was left open to prevent any accusation by Micky of being kidnapped or held against his will. An issue Sinn Fein would exploit should he go public.

Billy was waiting at the entrance of the container and welcomed Micky as he parked up. Mac was introduced as a colleague with an invested interest in this meeting. Mac was no shrinking violet; at just under six feet tall, he had a mass of black hair and huge moustache and would be a match for Micky should he decide to kick off following the revelations he was about to hear.

Several minutes were taken up with small talk and matters surrounding each other's lifestyles. Micky appeared relaxed and happy to chat about social issues and what he described as the deprivation in his area. The conversation was handled or directed to demonstrate the effect the Troubles was having on the younger generation. Micky commented that he could understand why kids got involved in anti-social behaviour and mixed up with paramilitaries but stopped short of denouncing it.

Billy commented on the economic impact and how he believed the paramilitaries were not protecting the community but rather controlling it by fear and suppressing any future development in the country. The impact was on hard-working individuals trying to make a living, like himself.

Mac entered the conversation, stating he had money to invest and was keen to invest it in the right way. He asked Micky if he could be that person.

Micky looked bewildered and said, "I don't get where you are coming from with this."

Mac continued by saying, "Look Micky, you could do something about the people who are destroying these young lads' futures, you could be part of something good here. We know about your involvement and your debt problems."

It was further explained that it was no accident that he'd got the work from Billy.

Mac said, "This is a once in a lifetime offer, a chance to be debt free, earn good money on a regular basis, and get back at the people who dumped you from their ranks."

For such a big man, he looked frightened and appeared dumb struck. He never said anything for what seemed like an age.

Finally, he found his tongue. "You fucking Bastards, this whole thing has been a setup, are you fucking peelers?" he demanded, spitting out the word for police.

Micky was told by Billy he was British Military Intelligence, and he knew everything there was to know about him and his so-called mates in the IRA. He hadn't fled the container or dived over the table at either of the men, so it was a positive sign. They continued to play on the gambling issues and how it could all go away if he decided to work with them.

As soon as he started to ask questions, they knew he was considering the offer. There would still be the realisation once he was away from the container as to the enormity of what was being asked of him, but the opening of the briefcase and the visual impact of the money would help influence his decision.

No paint contract was given, but a guarantee of regular income and the chance to turn his life around was a real possibility.

He left the site tracked by the cover teams and then followed by the 14 Int teams back into the city.

Micky Crawford had much to think about, but he didn't go directly to a solicitor's office or the Sinn Fein offices, and instead, he went home to contemplate his next move.

It took all of 24 hours for Micky to telephone the number on the business card and say he needed certain guarantees and reassurances, but he was interested. Over the next few weeks, several meetings were held with Micky Crawford: codenamed Big Oak.

Chapter 22

Liam's bout of Conscience

During a meeting with Billy, Liam had expressed his concern regarding his commitment, or moreover, his level of involvement with PIRA. Although not having been directly involved in any interrogations with Frankie, he had still been present on several occasions when severe beatings and follow up executions had taken place. It was a level of involvement he wasn't happy about, and he believed sooner or later, he felt he would be inextricably linked to the death of another human being.

In the early days with Davy and the MRF, Liam was only ever used as an eyes and ears Agent, but his involvement had snowballed since those early days. As a married man with a son, he was becoming more philosophical and worried about being exploited by the British Military. Although his ethics hadn't changed, as he still had the desire to do the right thing, there was a lot going on in his life that was giving him reason to revaluate his commitment.

For one, Roslyn was constantly on his back, and if she wasn't accusing him of having an affair, then it was the time he was spending with Frankie that made her mad. Getting a life balance was hard with taxiing, meeting Billy, IRA business and trying to have a stable family life. He believed something had to give.

He was also having Frankie and his team over at the house, something which Roslyn was furious about. Billy could see he was stressed and suggested he needed a little bit of quality time with Roslyn and his son, Shane. Billy highlighted some of Liam's past achievements and the importance he played in the numerous saving of lives over the years. It was explained that he had made a significant difference in the fight against terrorism in Northern Ireland and needed to continue his invaluable work. It was further explained that he was not being exploited but was an integral part of a team working together for the greater good.

Billy expressed a shared empathy with Liam, stating he also had a young family who he rarely saw due to his hectic work pattern. Billy suggested Liam take a short holiday, and he would organise a two week stay in a cottage up in Donegal. This would enable Liam to recharge the batteries and have that much needed quality time with his family. Liam accepted, expressed his gratitude, and agreed some away time might be the answer. Before leaving the meeting, Liam was reminded of the importance of keeping Billy informed of all his activities, because only by knowing could Billy provide the level of protection needed to avoid falling afoul of the law and getting prosecuted.

Chapter 23

Honours and Awards

Mary had been present in the Sinn Fein office during a rather heated exchange of views between Seamus Andrews and the recently released Barry McGinn. The murder of Sean Pearse had caused no end of trouble for Sinn Fein. The head of the Army Council was furious that a murder had taken place without its sign off. Dublin was calling for a full investigation into the murder, and Seamus believed Barry was giving him the run-around. Several members of Sinn Fein and PIRA visited the offices throughout the day, including Kieran O'Kane, Jimmy Rice, and Frankie Connolly. The pointing of fingers was evident, with Barry stating, "The fucker confessed," despite Frankie claiming, "I hadn't give authorisation."

The blame was being shifted from one person to another. Seamus was furious and laboured the point that two years of negotiations and a fragile peace deal were being put in jeopardy by the actions of rogue activities. Seamus stated he didn't give a flying fuck that he was dead, it was the timing and manner of the death that concerned him.

As it happened, the ceasefire only lasted a few more months anyway. It held for seventeen months in total before the IRA announced its end by placing a large lorry bomb, detonating it in the London Docklands, which killed two people and injured over forty more. It caused damage to the area estimated at £150 million.

All of this was reported back to Billy and his team. Mary continued to report on the daily functions and activities from the Sinn Fein offices. Mary had been married early in her spying career but found the pressures of family life and looking after her mother when she was alive too restrictive and had parted ways from her husband after only seventeen months. She joked with Billy that at least her marriage lasted as long as the IRA ceasefire. She had promptly reverted to her family name of Sweeney.

Never once had Mary ever complained or voiced her concern for her clandestine work and admitted she even got such a buzz from it. She was brave but never complacent and knew only too well the consequences should she ever be compromised. It was natural to have an Agent within the terrorist organization but to have one used as a custodian and a fully trusted confidant of the higher echelons of Sinn Fein into the bargain was priceless.

Following a routine weekly debrief of Mary, a planned social event was held at the Unit's detachment bar for her with Chinese food being brought in for the occasion. Mary was enjoying the attention she was receiving by the members of the team and the bit of flattery associated with it. The standout moment had to be the visit from the head of Intelligence, who turned up and presented Mary with a Northern Ireland campaign medal as well as a long service and good conduct medal.

Mary was shocked and delighted all in one. A speech by the commander congratulating her on her covert work and the major contribution it played for the Northern Ireland Office and British Government alike left her speechless, with tears freely flowing down her face. If ever there was a motivator or incentive for doing the work, this ticked all the boxes. The sad thing was, she could only appreciate the medals whenever she was being debriefed at the detachment, because it would be here that the medals would be held. Although not official, as she was a civilian, having worked for over twenty years, she was the longest running CHIS within the Unit, followed closely by Liam Murray. Maybe one day, she would be able to take them home.

Mary's relationship with Jamie was going well, but having been once bitten, she was certainly twice shy and had no intentions of the relationship being anything more than good old-fashioned sex. Jamie would spend the odd evening during the week over at Mary's but had his own place, a flat above the bar he called home. Mary was conscious that she had a cache of weapons under her kitchen floor and Jamie's presence could be awkward if either the IRA or Billy wanted access to it. Equally, she didn't like to leave the house unattended overnight. So apart from the odd night following a lock-in at the Shamrock when she stayed over, her relationship was kept on a very casual basis.

Mary continued to meet with Roslyn for coffees and was becoming quite friendly with the girl. Roslyn had just returned from a family holiday in Malin Head Donegal, the most northernly point of the mainland in Ireland.

She'd spent two weeks in a delightful cottage with breath-taking views of the north Atlantic. Each evening, Roslyn and Liam would be seated by an open fire, listening to the sea waves crashing on the rocks below the cottage whilst playing board games with Shane. Once the teenager had retired to bed, they would just spend the night wrapped up in each other's arms in front of the fire. Mary thought Roslyn had been reinvigorated by the whole experience, as she never stopped talking about it, barely pausing to take a breath. All her negativity from their previous encounter seemed to be gone.

Roslyn did mention the night at the Shamrock when Mary's friend Bridget lost the plot, but understood her actions, as she would probably have reacted the same had that been her Liam who had been murdered. "Did you know Liam had been up to the prison only days before it happened, as he had driven Frankie up to speak with someone?" Roslyn commented

It was a rhetorical question, and she wasn't expecting an answer but wasn't given one anyway.

Mary asked if Roslyn was still concerned about Liam's involvement with her brother. She said, "Liam doesn't talk much about it, but Frankie has him at his beck and call.'

She was still worried, and just couldn't imagine life without him should he be locked up. "I know he is more involved than he is letting on."

Roslyn stated that Liam was tied up somehow with that murder attempt on the part-time soldier in Drumbeg, explaining how she had been in her Ma's house when Frankie got word to go and pick up Sean Pearse later that night. "You know, Jerry Cosgrove died that night and he was Liam's cousin."

"No, I didn't know," said Mary. "That's shocking."

Mary was chuffed with what she was hearing and couldn't wait to pass it on to Billy at her next meeting.

Chapter 24

Special Guest

The knock at the door woke Mary from her sleep. She climbed out of her nice, cosy bed and peeped through the curtains, half-expecting to see the Army or Police outside waiting to conduct a house search and recover the weapons stashed in the kitchen. There were no flashing lights or doors being kicked in but rather a Peugeot 308 estate, which belonged to Liam Murray, parked out front. Pulling on her dressing gown and slippers, she went downstairs and opened the door.

Standing on the doorstep was Jimmy Rice and an unknown male. *Shit,* she thought, the weapons cache, but instead of asking for access Jimmy said, "He's going to stay here for a few days, Mary."

"What….?" said Mary, not believing what she was hearing.

"He needs somewhere safe for a few days, and he won't be in your way. He will only leave his room for the bathroom. You just need to feed him."

Christ, Mary thought, *it sounds like he's giving me some sort of pet.*

With no introductions or how do you do, Jimmy turned and walked back to the Peugeot, and as he opened the door to get in, the interior light illuminated Liam Murray, who was in the driver's seat. Mary was still in a state of shock as she closed the door.

Mary was alone with a stranger, standing and staring at her in the hallway. He asked where his room was and, after being told, went directly upstairs without delay or any other form of communication with his host. He was carrying a small black holdall and was about 30-35 years old, medium build, about 5' 10" tall, dressed in jeans and a blue jumper. He had a very small tattoo of a cross on his left ear lobe.

Onus on Truths

He was good-looking, with sharp features and a dark complexion, with neatly-cut, jet black hair and stubble which looked deliberate rather than because of being unable to shave.

Mary was quite taken by her guest but didn't appreciate the aloofness he was demonstrating. Although uncomfortable with the man's presence, she knew that "Safe houses" were used all the time for members of the IRA who, for one reason or another, went on the run. It would usually only be for one night, with some members of the family not being aware said person was even in the house. They would normally be gone before first light. In Mary's case, she was going to have two, possibly three nights with this individual in her spare bedroom.

The following morning, Mary got up and removed the chair she had placed against her bedroom door for fear she might be visited in the night. She prepared a breakfast consisting of a bacon sandwich and a mug of tea and took it up and placed it outside the door of her guest. She knocked the door and said, "I've placed a sandwich and tea outside. I put two sugars in the tea, because I didn't know if you took any."

"Yeah, thanks," came the response.

Mary retreated across the landing to the bathroom but the bedroom door didn't open immediately.

Maybe he was still in bed, she thought.

She heard the door handle start to turn so she jumped back into her bathroom as he emerged to pick up the tray. Once he was gone back inside, she returned to the door and spoke.

"I've got to go to work now but should be back by two. I will leave a flask of tea and a packet of biscuits outside for you."

"Yeah, thanks," was once again the only response.

When Mary arrived at the Sinn Fein office, she was greeted by Jimmy Rice. He thanked her and asked if her guest was behaving himself.

"Who, the mute?"

Jimmy laughed and stated it was for her own good she had little or no interaction with the man, but he wouldn't step out of line.

"You have my word on that."

"Look Jimmy, I have a fella now and he would normally come over the odd night. Now, I can put him off but just want to let you know because you just turning up like that could have been awkward."

Jimmy acknowledged her point of view and thanked her again. Prior to her arrival at the Sinn Fein office, Mary had stopped at a phone box and informed Billy about her guest with no name. The description she provided was textbook teachings, something she was trained to do during her routine meetings. The details provided immediately sent shivers down Billy's back. This couldn't be anyone other than Declan 'Spud' Swan from South Armagh. Spud was wanted in connection for the murder of Malachy Tweed. Evidence at the scene had implicated him. The old woman at the cottage described a good-looking man with a small, tattooed cross on his left ear and naively questioned how a man with a cross could do such a thing.

Chapter 25

Loyalist Feud

1994

Jim McBurney was having a night out with his wife, Jean, in the Braziers Arms on the Newtownards Road. There was a live band on, and both he and Jean were enjoying the entertainment. His brother, Gary, had just left their company to go home. Jean had excused herself and went to the toilet, but on her way back, she was accosted by a drunk, Bobby Weir. He groped her backside as she passed him. Instinctively, she turned and slapped him in the face. Jim saw this and charged over to his wife's aid whilst swearing and threatening to rip Bobby's head off.

Bobby was quickly joined by his friend, John McCrea, and an altercation ensued. Punches were exchanged, with a full-pitched battle being fought on the dance floor. The two men eventually gained the upper hand. Jean was screaming for them to stop and calling on the motionless bar staff to intervene. Someone in the room shouted, "Stay out of it, it's the UVF!" invoking the name of the Ulster Volunteer Force. Eventually, the fight ended with Jim bloodied and bruised and left lying in a pool of spilled beer and broken glass.

Several days later and still recovering from the incident, a young lad called to Jim's house, telling him,

" You need to report to the Braziers Arms, as Tucker Wright wants to see you." Tucker Wright was the OC East Belfast Brigade UVF. Jim told the lad, "Tell Tucker to fuck off, as it was nothing to do with the UVF but rather two dickheads from the UVF, who I will sort out myself."

That night, four men came to his house, and after forcing their way in, they used baseball bats to carry out summary justice, claiming it was for attacking two UVF members in the Braziers Arms. Jim knew and recognised all four individuals as Bobby Weir, John McCrea, Robbie Martin, and Ian Elwood. Jim McBurney was left unconscious, and because of the beating, he suffered two broken legs and a broken arm.

He was rushed to the Ulster hospital and was found to have swelling on his brain. He was placed in an induced coma for treatment of the swelling. Although he eventually made a full recovery from the fractures, albeit with a bit of a limp, he had a permanent paralysis of the brain which affected his speech and balance.

Gary McBurney went to Tucker and demanded action be taken against the perpetrators, reiterating what Jim had already claimed; it wasn't UVF business. Gary threatened to take it to the RUC to get the four arrested for it.

Tucker threatened the same action would befall him if he did so.

"Fuck you and your wee band of thugs, you're nothing, you claim to be the protectors of loyalism when you don't protect, you just control. You drive your big fancy cars paid for with your drug money, fucking Parasites."

Tucker responded, "What…… and your Jim and his UDA mates are the great protectors? Get the fuck out before we do you some serious damage. Go home to that retard brother of yours."

Gary's passing words were, "You and your lap dogs are going down."

Gary's next port of call was to visit Sammy Carson and the leadership of the UDA. The UDA were reluctant to get involved with Sammy stating, "Jim got himself into that mess, and we don't want to cause an all-out feud with the UVF."

Onus on Truths

Following his failure at either meeting, Gary went immediately to Mountpottinger RUC Station, giving the names of all four assailants and the man who give the order. 'Tucker Wright.'

Chapter 26

Operation 'Spud u like'

The revelations concerning the temporary lodger at the home of Mary Sweeney were received with absolute delight within HQNI. An emergency meeting was held at RUC headquarters to discuss an action plan to deal with a wonderful opportunity of arresting such a high-profile IRA member. The head of TCG (Technical Coordination Group) Chief Superintendent Paul Millar, chaired the meeting, as he would be responsible for all the relevant components that needed to be pulled together. Agencies from the Police and Army would be working in cooperation on this mission.

TCG was set up in the late 1970's to enhance cooperation between the RUC and the Army, Belfast being the first region to avail of this group, but over the years, this increased to Armagh (South) and Londonderry (North).

Paul Millar was keen for a team from the HMSU (Headquarters Mobile Support Unit), whose members were all made up from Special Branch officers to conduct a search and arrest operation on the property. This group of individuals was affectionately known as the door kickers. They were an extremely effective bunch, who took no nonsense when kicking in doors to effect arrests.

Billy attended the meeting along with Mac, his Co-Handler on the case. The Colonel of the Unit, Ed Douglas was also in attendance.

The meeting got quite heated, because in the opinion of the Military Intelligence, under no circumstances should their CHIS be compromised to effect the arrest. Even if Spud was to escape their clutches and go to ground, he would resurface at some point down the line. However, to compromise the CHIS would be unforgivable.

In a pre-discussion with Ed, he had said "It's better to turn up with a solution rather than a problem." Ed suggested E4A (Surveillance Branch) or 14 Int be used to conduct surveillance on the property with HMSU or SAS ready to intercept Spud once he was away from the property. It wouldn't be a long operation, 48 hours at the most, and the likelihood was he would be moving under the hours of darkness.

After much debate, Paul Millar and the HMSU commander, Nick Burns, agreed to the plan but stated they would have primacy and total autonomy, not the SAS. It was to be a Police operation, which got no complaints from the military. Billy was delighted with the outcome and took solace knowing Mary wouldn't be compromised.

Billy, as the Handler, was instructed to ensure Mary (or Wee Fern) telephoned immediately once she knew anything about a possible move by Spud. A two-man team from E4A were inserted into the attic of a derelict house in Ardglen Place with overwatch of the property, with the team from the HMSU being located in Tennent Street RUC Station only a mile or so away.

Chapter 27

Moonlight Flit

Mary returned home at two, as expected, and her guest was still in his room, with no evidence of him having left it except for the toilet seat being left up. Mary tutted to herself thinking, *It's a man thing.* The flask and half-finished packet of biscuits were positioned on the landing directly outside the bedroom.

Mary knocked on the door and asked if he wanted a sandwich and a fresh mug of tea. To Mary's surprise, he answered her by stating, "That would be great, thanks."

Christ, he talks, thought Mary.

Once she made the sandwich and tea, she once again left it outside his door. She informed him that they could have fish & chips later. Mary went about her normal routine and, having tidied up the kitchen, she took some rubbish out the back to the bins. She noticed a drawing pin had been placed on her gate post. This could only mean Billy wanted to speak with her, so she decided that she would contact him when she went out for the fish & chips.

Mary left the house just after five and, on route to the Chip Shop, telephoned the office to speak with Billy. She was told that it was imperative that she kept the office informed of any information regarding the movement of the guest. Mary asked if he knew who it was and was told in the interest of her own security, she was better off not knowing, but investigations were still ongoing as to the identity of her guest.

She was asked if any additional details about him were known from his overnight stay. Mary told Billy the man never spoke to her and was remaining in the spare room. When Mary hung up, she telephoned the Shamrock Arms and spoke with Jamie. She said she wasn't feeling too well but would take a hot bath and go to bed early so there would be no point in him coming over to the house the next few nights. This worked two-fold: for one, she stuck to the security protocol by making a second call, but also ensured Jamie wouldn't come over to the house whilst the guest was present.

Mary returned to the house with the fish & chips. When she entered the house, she shouted up the stairs that she was home and began putting out the dinner. As she was setting out the plates, Mary became startled by the appearance of the man standing in the doorway of the kitchen.

"Christ, you scared the life out of me."

"Do you mind if I eat here? For one, I don't want the bedroom stinking of fish, and two, I'm bored shitless."

He was wearing a white, V-neck tee shirt and blue jeans but wasn't wearing any shoes or socks. Mary told him to take a seat at the kitchen table and poured out the tea, then handed him his plate. Both sat and ate their fish & chips without speaking a word. When they had finished, Mary asked if he wanted anything else.

"No, that was lovely and thanks for this, I mean all this. Its appreciated, but I will be out of your hair soon enough."

Mary could tell his accent was from down south of the country, maybe Portadown or Armagh but couldn't quite pinpoint it. Mary thought, *It's amazing that for such a small country we have such strong regional accents.* Her guest returned upstairs to the room.

Mary tidied up and took the chip papers out to the bin. The evening was cold, and the last of the daylight was quickly disappearing behind Divis & Black Mountain.

Mary pondered what Billy and his team intended to do about her guest. This was his second night, and he could still be leaving, but Jimmy said two or three nights. So, there was the potential he could still be here tomorrow. *Maybe he will get up and leave during the early hours and I won't be any the wiser, it's not like I need to give them access, he's already in the house for God's sake.* It was strange, but there was something about the man she liked, and having him stay wasn't stressing her out.

Finishing her thoughts as the cold started biting at her body, she returned inside and secured the back door. Not expecting him to exit his room again that evening, at least knowingly, Mary made up another flask of tea and placed it outside his room along with the remaining biscuits. By nine o'clock, Mary decided to have a bath and retire as she'd stated to Jamie earlier. As she lay in a hot radox bath, allowing the soothing salts to relax her tired body, she came over all giddy. She found herself thinking about the man only yards from her. Was he a married man? had he a wife and children at home? wherever home was. She knew nothing about the man in her house yet was excited by his presence. She found herself thinking if he found her attractive. She looked down at her firm breasts and thought to herself, not bad, still firm and in the right place.

She allowed herself a slight chuckle. Mary tried to put the thought out of her head and climbed out of the bath. Only having a large hand towel, she placed it over the front of her body, which barely covered her breasts and lower regions. She opened the door of the bathroom with one hand still holding the towel to cover her modesty, only to be confronted by her guest, who was standing directly in front of the door and unintentionally blocking her exit.

Mary was startled by his appearance and held her towel tightly against her chest. She turned to her side, facing him, knowing that her naked body was totally exposed from the rear. She said sorry and edged slowly across the landing toward the room. Spud just stood still and watched as she shimmied toward the room. Spud burst out laughing and pointed to the full-length mirror on the landing wall. Mary had just shimmied across the landing with her backside in full view of her guest. Mary had goosebumps all over her body and simply entered her bedroom with her back still exposed. She had stopped caring and hoped that her guest would take the initiative and follow her into the room.

Mary was not disappointed, as he did indeed enter the room, pushing the door closed behind him. Mary, standing at the foot of the bed, turned to face her guest and dropped her towel as she stood, naked as the day she was born, looking somewhat sheepish and feeling flush with excitement. Her actions weren't lost on her guest, as she could see the bulge in his trousers, it was like a trapped animal trying to escape.

He walked toward her whilst studying her body, which was in great shape and well-proportioned, with a lovely narrow waistline, shapely buttocks, and firm breasts. He caressed her breasts and licked her nipples, then moved his lips slowly down her stomach, and Mary couldn't have cared less if he was married or not, as the sensation was making her weak at the knees. She almost buckled as he kissed her just above her pubic bone, before moving his hand over her inner thigh.

He slipped a finger inside her. Mary gravitated into his hand writhing as she met his fingers. Spud stopped and removed his finger, then lifted Mary under her arm pits and threw her onto the bed. Mary lay flat on her back, pining for him to take her.

Spud removed his tee shirt and dropped his jeans, fighting frantically to release his feet from the trouser legs. He climbed on top of Mary and, using his tongue, he licked her body starting at her neck and traversing her body by navigating her curves down until he reached between her legs. He eventually slithered his manhood deep inside her body. The deeper and faster he went, the louder and longer she moaned. Finally, she collapsed, burying her head into the pillow and coming hard. He came inside of her at that moment, partially brought on by her sexual exuberance.

Mary lay for several moments, trying hard to regain both her composure and a measured heartbeat. This would be one part of the stay she would keep secret from Billy. In many regards, it had been a frustrated sex act but bloody enjoyable, nonetheless.

He may not talk much, but he certainly knows how to use his tongue, she thought.

The visit of Jimmy Rice just after midnight in a silver Peugeot 308 estate was observed by the OP (Observation Post) who requested a plate check on the vehicle. It came back as being registered to a Mr. Liam Murray. The OP's observations were radioed back to Tennent Street. The HMSU team crashed out of the base and moved to a dedicated RV, closer to the target's address in their unmarked cars.

Jimmy was in the house for only a matter of minutes and told Spud to get ready to move within the hour. Jimmy left the house, got back into the car, and exited out of Jamacia Street and out of sight to the OP.

Mary switched on the external light above her front door, a signal suggested by Billy once she was aware that her guest's move was imminent. This was also observed and reported. The surveillance team of E4A were already in position and set to take the target once he was mobile. The HMSU team would loosely follow E4A and the target waiting for an opportunity to intercept and arrest Declan Spud Swan.

At 12:45 am, a silver BMW estate pulled into Jamacia Street, closely observed by the OP. It stopped outside the home of Mary Sweeney. A large, bald man about 17 stone and wearing blue jeans and a black leather jacket approached the house. He appeared to rap on the door then immediately returned to the car, getting into the front passenger seat. The door to the property opened, and a man positively identified as Declan Spud Swan exited and made his way to the car, getting into the rear seat.

The OP relayed these actions to the teams on the ground and gave a detailed description of the vehicle, its registration, and its three occupants.

The target vehicle travelled along Jamacia Street toward Alliance Avenue. The first of the E4A team acknowledged the call and observed the vehicle's movements through its static position, not reacting to the vehicle. The area was boxed off, and until the target vehicle broke through the controlled box, callsigns didn't need to react directly to it.

Onus on Truths

Nick Burns was in command of the operation and was in the lead HMSU vehicle. All the other callsigns remained on radio silence, allowing the E4A team to control and relay all calls. It was expected that Spud would be taken out of the country by crossing the land border into the Republic of Ireland. Nick was determined this wasn't going to happen on his watch and was looking for the first opportunity to intercept the vehicle and apprehend Spud.

The vehicle continued out onto the A55, heading toward Lisburn and eventually taking the A1 South bound. It was here that Nick decided the teams would close in and effect the stop on the quiet A1 carriageway between Hillsborough and the Dromore exit.

One of the surveillance vehicles overtook the target vehicle as they went through Hillsborough with the intention of putting a block at the exit point for Dromore. Another callsign stopped traffic from entering the A1 at Hillsborough leaving the three HMSU vehicles to continue the pursuit unhindered. Victor 1 (V1) the lead vehicle, had the task of getting in front of the target vehicle and gradually slowing, bringing the target vehicle to a halt. At the same time, V2, the command vehicle would come alongside and indicate for the vehicle to stop. The third callsign, V3, would then close up to the rear of the target car with all three callsigns effectively boxing the target car in and bringing it to a halt.

V1 got into position in front of the target while leaving sufficient space for the target not to suspect anything untoward, at least until V2 was able to get alongside, quickly followed by V3.

Nick would have considered all the risks for carrying out this manoeuvre, waying up the threat to his men, as it had the potential to go very wrong. It was effectively going to be a hard stop on the carriageway.

V1, from his forward position, reduced his speed from 70 mph gradually back down to 40 mph.

The men in the BMW now had the car of V1 in sight and were gaining on it at speed, but the driver wasn't really paying attention to the road behind him as he closed in on V1, which had now slowed even further.

The driver of the BMW shouted, "Bloody hell!" and immediately went to pull out to overtake but was shocked to see yet another vehicle, V2, come level with him. At the same time, V3 had closed to within a few meters of the target. The road was void of any other traffic, something Nick was grateful for.

The target's vehicle was being slowed down considerably, but Spud demanded the driver ram the rear of V1 in the hope of sufficiently opening the gap so they could escape through. The impact on the rear of V1 jolted the vehicle forward but not enough to gain the desired gap.

V2 broadsided the target's vehicle, forcing it up tight against the hard shoulder and the grass embankment to its nearside. V2 was positioned at a 50-degree angle, with its front left bumper up tight against the wheel arch of the BMW. Nick was already out of the vehicle and pointing his G3 rifle at the driver through the window. The occupants of V1 and V3 had also alighted, and using the cover of their vehicles, approached the BMW from both directions.

The front seat passenger and Spud exited the vehicle and started running up the embankment. The passenger was later identified as Micky Devlin from County Cavan and a prominent member of the South Armagh Brigade PIRA. Holding an AKM assault rifle, he turned back toward the vehicles and fired it from the hip. Due to the severity of the slope, as he pointed the weapon toward V2 he had miscalculated the angle of arc and a burst of automatic gunfire ripped through the BMW, hitting the driver of the vehicle several times.

Although Nick was forward of the driver's door, a round had ricocheted and struck Nick in the thigh. No sooner had Devlin fired his burst that the men of HMSU opened up with their G3's, hitting Devlin several times in the chest and legs, killing him instantly. The embankment acted like a bullet catcher, like those seen at shooting ranges, catching the bullets on impact. At least those that hadn't hit the targeted man.

Spud slipped on the bank and had slid back down a few feet before regaining his balance and starting his ascent to the top, seeking his escape. As he came level with the body of Devlin, a member of the HMSU assault team shouted, "He's going for the AK!" and opened fire, hitting Spud several times in the back and head. The lifeless body of Declan Spud Swan slid back down the embankment, coming to rest at the side of the BMW.

Nick was treated at the scene for his flesh wound, whilst shouting orders for his men to secure the area and call for emergency services to treat the driver of the BMW. The driver received two rounds to his body, one to his stomach, which entered through his side and was causing severe blood loss. The team provided first aid, applying a field dressing from their medical pack to help stem the flow of blood. The second round penetrated through the left elbow, causing his forearm to dangle limp, resulting in an un-stable fracture which the team managed to splint and stabilize.

Mary woke the next morning half-expecting to hear the news that a leading republican had been arrested by the Army or Police. There was nothing being reported on the television so Mary thought he must have gotten away. Mary went to work as normal at the Sinn Fein office, but on her arrival, she was shocked to see it was already a hive of activity. Normally she was one of the first to arrive, but not this morning: Rice, O'Kane, McGinn, Connolly, and Andrews were already in the small conference room and actively engaged in conversation. As she entered, the room descended into utter silence, with O'Kane closing the open door to the room. Mary went to the small kitchenette and put on the coffee machine before going to her desk at the front of the office. Whatever was happening, it was clearly important and something she might be able to glean for Billy.

Mary started to think maybe this had something to do with the late-night exodus of her guest. She reflected on her position, not only in the Sinn Fein office, but the amenableness with which she had facilitated accommodation for a stranger and allowed her house to be used for a cache; surely, she wasn't under any suspicion. She started to feel a little apprehensive but knew she needed to remain calm and not overreact, as it was probably something totally unrelated.

Mary made coffee and took a tray with five cups and the percolator into the conference room. It was important to act normal and go about her business as usual. When she approached the door, Frankie opened it, and as she entered, he winked at her and said, "Good morning, Mary." She took solace from his wink and relaxed slightly. The fact that a meeting was taking place suggested that something important was being discussed.

Chapter 28

Billy: Breaking News

Billy arrived at the office just before eight in the morning and noticed the boss was already seated at his desk, which was unusual, as he always went for a run before coming into the office, arriving sometime after nine. Billy went directly to the armoury and placed his weapons and ammunition on his allocated racks, ready for the weekly check and inspection. He was approached by a collator who stated, "Wee Fern had come up trumps again, with Declan Swan being taken out last night by HMSU. Oh, by the way the boss wants to see you and Mac in his office."

On entering the office, the boss asked both men to be seated.

"Great result last night, three members of the same ASU from South Armagh were intercepted on the A1 in the early hours of this morning, hence the reason it hasn't hit the news just yet. Declan Swan, along with Micky Devlin, were killed at the scene, as well as a third man, Sean Feeney, who was hit with two rounds from Devlin's own gun by mistake but survived. He will probably be pissing into a bag the rest of his days. The phone hasn't stopped this morning, and our good friend, Nick Burns, from the HMSU took one in the leg but it isn't serious.

"The Headquarters are delighted by the result but have expressed concern over Wee Fern's security. It might be wise to conduct a reverse contact and get her in to cover the event and assess her security. I know she is good, but bloody hell, she has been sailing close to the wind recently and we still have the Cache in her house to consider. The headquarters are desperate for a post operation report so that they can back brief Jeffery, the security service advisor, on any ramifications or repercussions that could result from this. "Sinn Fein will already be planning their strategy on how to maximise the propaganda and take advantage of any political fallout that may occur. They will try and claim that a 'Shoot to Kill' policy is still adopted by the British in Ireland. Guys, until we have the Who, What, Where, When and Why, the headquarters will be on my back. So, let's get all the answers and pronto."

Billy and Mac left the bosses office, went immediately to the Ops Room and planned a meeting for Mary to be conducted the following morning. Due to the nature of her involvement prior to the HMSU actions, it was decided that she be put through a CS (Counter Surveillance) route prior to pick up. This was designed to highlight if she was being followed by PIRA or under any suspicion. If, for any reason, the team became suspicious of one or more individuals, then Mary would be allowed to finish her route without a pickup being completed. She would walk through a series of choke points and turns that would identify any hostiles tailing her. If everything went to plan, then she would be picked up as normal and brought into one of the debriefing locations for a chat. The team needed to deploy to insert the drawing pin on the gate post which Mary would see when she got home from work. She would telephone the detachment and be informed of the route she was to take the following day. By lunch time, the pin was in place and the news had broken about the shooting and arrest of a terrorist suspect on the A1.

Mary arrived home and was met by Bridget as she opened the front door. "There was a strange bloke who stopped at your back gate this morning. I thought he was trying to get in but you must have had your snib on because he just moved on," she said.

"Where were you?" asked Mary.

"In my bathroom, I just happened to look out and seen him near your gate."

"Strange," said Mary with a shrug off her shoulders. "Do you want a coffee?"

"Why not?" she replied, and the two girls entered Mary's house.

Mary took an empty milk carton out into the yard and, opening the gate as if looking up and down the alleyway, noticed the pin on the gatepost. When she returned to the house, Bridget asked her if she heard the news about the three boys that got shot by the cops last night. Mary had by now heard and made a play of sympathy, though she did feel a certain amount of sadness for the man who she had bedded only hours before he was killed.

Mary noticed Bridget was looking brighter and more care had been taken in her appearance. Mary asked if she was dating someone, but Bridget was quite coy and only smiled. Mary took this as a yes and moved on.

That evening, Mary visited Jamie at the Shamrock but made a call to the detachment on route. Mac was the duty operator and therefore was able to take her call on the dedicated Agent line within its soundproof booth, following the preamble and the obvious security questions to ensure she wasn't under duress or forced to make the call. Her designated Counter Surveillance route was given for the following day. Each Agent had their own designated CS route but they were seldom used, unless in cases like this, when there was the potential of suspicion falling onto the Agent following a failed operation.

Mac explained she needed to be extremely careful, as Frankie and Co would be conducting their own investigation as to why or how Spud was taken out. The last thing they needed was for her to be under any form of suspicion. Mary was happy with the arrangements and hung up.

Chapter 29

Everyone is suspect

Liam (Weeping Willow) was parked outside the Sinn Fein office whilst Frankie and Co were inside, being grilled over the revelations of the previous evening's events. The meeting lasted well over an hour, with Frankie re-emerging and getting into Liam's car.

"I need you to take me over to Jamacia Street, I've a woman I need to see."

Liam looked puzzled and stated, "You know I have a living to make and I'm sitting here on my ass losing money waiting on you."

"You'll be compensated for what you're doing, this is RA business fella. There is a tout in our midst, and I intend to find him."

"I thought you found him in Sean Pearse, so what's changed?"

"Last night is what changed. Someone else touted on the job and I need to find them. Anyone who had anything to do with the job will have to be questioned and that includes you, sonny Jim. Now take me to Jamacia Street, drop me off, and I'll speak with you later."

Liam dropped Frankie at the corner of Alliance Avenue and Jamacia Street. Frankie asked Liam to go to Ian Bradley's flat in Divis and tell him Frankie wanted to use his place again in a few days' time. This was the same flat Liam had previously gone into the entrance of and seen the bath full of water. This was thought-provoking, and Liam had a very uneasy feeling about the whole affair.

Liam had been present at the home of Mary Sweeney, along with Jimmy Rice last night. This was clearly to do with the job and was why he was going to be questioned. Liam was due to meet with his handling team in a few days' time, so he would bring up his concerns then. Liam informed Ian Bradley, and he could see the poor man

Onus on Truths

didn't have an option but just accepted his flat was to be used again as a torture chamber. Liam wondered if he would be questioned here and whether he was to be the orchestrator of his own demise.

Liam had been dropping off a fare on Edna Drive when he noticed Billy walking along Edna drive before being picked up in a Blue VW Estate, a vehicle Liam recognised as one that was normally used during his own pick up and drop off when meeting Billy.

What was Billy doing in the area? where was he going or coming from? Christ, he thought, *my life is complicated enough without this.* There could be numerous reasons for Billy's presence but none that made sense to Liam at that moment.

Liam decided to wait a few hours but would telephone Billy to move his prearranged meeting to tomorrow, considering the Divis flat and potential questioning. Liam made the call to the detachment but was told he couldn't be met, as other pressing engagements (Mary's meeting) would need to take priority. Liam wasn't happy but was told the following day would be suitable and that any issues or concerns he had could be addressed then.

Frankie contacted Liam and told him to be home that evening, as he and a few boys wanted to discuss recent events, and Liam would be part of the plans that were to be discussed. *Just another level of anxiety to cope with,* thought Liam. Later that evening, when Liam saw the combi van belonging to Pinkie and Perky pull up outside his door, he became so stressed. Liam wondered at what point he started to feel the pressure of the work he was doing on behalf of her majesty's government, because he had become a complete wreck. The level of paranoia he was now suffering from was frightening.

Roslyn was once again banished to the kitchen whilst Frankie and the boys had a chat. The eavesdropping microphones were picking up everything that was being said and listened to by the lads monitoring the devices.

The Murray Family holiday in Donegal had been the perfect opportunity to get the CME (covert method of entry) team to pick the locks and insert several listening devices in the house. Suspicion had been increasing for a while concerning Liam's actual involvement. He wasn't telling his handling team all that he was involved in and was conveniently leaving information out from his observations for the detachment. Something had changed with Liam, so the team was being particularly careful in the way they handled him.

Chapter 30

Mary: Suspicion Calls

Mary left her place of work and went directly into the city centre to commence her Counter Surveillance route before meeting with Billy and Mac. An extended team had been deployed on the operation, and unknown to Mary, she was followed by the detachment from the moment she left the Sinn Fein office down to just short of her start point.

Once the surveillance team were satisfied she wasn't being followed, they joined the remainder of the team on the ground, taking up positions at various stages along her route. Mary was checked through a series of choke points before an eventual clearance was given. Mary was led her off route to a vehicle in a carpark where Billy was waiting. Mary got into his vehicle and protected by a cover team, was led out of the area to a debriefing location on the East of the city.

Mary was her usual relaxed self and was unfazed by her recent experience and the subsequent killings. A full debrief was conducted with all the relevant details being extracted concerning Spud and his stay with Mary. Mary had little to pass concerning the man himself and opted to leave out the sexual experience she had shared with him. She was now more aware of who he was and knew he was a bad individual who was responsible for so much hurt to others. She passed on information concerning the meeting the previous day at the Sinn Fein office with the usual suspects and her belief that something was in the planning, possibly a retaliation for the murders of the Armagh ASU members.

If there was to be any reprisal for the Armagh ASU, then the potential for the Cache in Mary's kitchen to be used was a real possibility. During the debrief, Mary went through the night's events, stating that Jimmy Rice, accompanied by Liam Murray, had visited her house shortly before Spud was picked up. Once again, further validation had been obtained concerning Liam and his involvement. Liam was due to be met the following day, and Billy and Mac were interested to see what part he claimed to have been involved in. Mary was dropped back into the city centre to continue with her cover story.

Chapter 31

Loyalist feud

Billy was sitting in the Ops room, writing up his notes and preparing to brief the boss on the MISR's from his routine meeting with Wee Fern. The telephone rang, and it was from Norman McAteer, who was now the Intelligence Warrant Officer of the recently renamed Royal Irish Regiment, the former having replaced all UDR battalions back in 1992. Norman had retained good links with the detachment from his days working with Davy and the MRF. Norman stated that a member of the public had turned up at the gate of Palace Barracks asking to speak with someone from Military Intelligence.

There was a laid down procedure for dealing with such incidents, and it was published in all Guardrooms. Norman was the first port of call, and being his usual diligent self, got the man into a secluded and secure area away from the main gate. This reduced any risk to the individual of compromise. Norman had already got the personal details and passed the name over to Billy.

Billy, accompanied by another Handler, 'Roy,' went to see the individual, always conscious that many an Intelligence nuisance turned up at SF (Security Force) bases and talked the biggest load of drivel. However, it still had to be handled professionally.

Billy and Roy were shown into a room and introduced by Norman to Gary McBurney. Norman left the room and went about his normal business, stating when the team was done, he would return and escort Gary back out of the camp.

Gary recited what had happened to his brother and named all the individuals involved.

The process of establishing why someone would pass on the information, or in his case, inform on paramilitary members, needed careful analytical research. For example, what was his motivation for coming forward? Did he have some ideology or philosophy on how he could make the world a better place? Or because he believed it was the right thing to do? Most common would be to obtain some sort of financial benefit.

None of these applied to Gary McBurney, it was simply revenge that motivated him. The Police had failed in getting him the justice he desired and believed he deserved. It wasn't entirely the Police's fault, getting the evidence to prosecute was always going to be difficult in a community who were repressed and under the control of would-be tyrants or oppressors. He wanted to hurt them and bring down their castle.

Gary told all that he knew about organised crime and paramilitary activity in his area, of which he was extremely knowledgeable, but most of what he was saying was already known by the security services because of the network of Agents already working for SB. Nonetheless, he would still be a valuable asset to have as a eyes and ears Agent. He didn't trust the Police and stated that was his reasoning for coming to the Military, and he would do whatever it took to put those so-called loyalists behind bars.

The detachment wasn't overly concerned about criminal activity. Its primary function was the collection of intelligence on the paramilitary's terrorist-related crimes. Ideally, before the event occurred, in order to preserve life and property. Although during its collection, any such activity would be passed to the police.

Gary had a close affiliation with several members of the UDA, one of which was his cousin, Marty Spence. The beating of Jim McBurney was not well received within the community, and the lack of justice had presented Gary with many an offer of retribution. Jim himself had been a member of the UDA, and so in the eyes of his attackers, a viable target in the first place. What started as a stupid quarrel in the bar had now escalated to a potential feud between the two paramilitary groups. The Unit decided to at least continue to meet with Gary McBurney, Codenamed: 'Walnut.'

Chapter 32

Micky: Tout Rumours

Micky Crawford, or Big Oak, had been met on numerous occasions by the handling team, and despite several warnings concerning his gambling habits he was still being reckless and not adhering to the advice given. Much of his reporting was of a historical nature, and despite great efforts by the team, he wasn't progressing very well. His extra-curricular activities were still a concern to the detachment, but this was exasperated by a call to the boss from Paul Millar, the head of TCG Belfast, stating that Micky Crawford was suspected of being a tout.

This information was received from a Special Branch Agent and was considered reliable. Apparently, the disparity between his work commitments and spending in the bookies was what had caused the initial suspicions. Closer scrutiny had confirmed he couldn't possibly have that amount of surplus cash to spend. The concern for the detachment and, in particular, Billy and Mac, was that although they had cleared some of his debt, they believed it was in a controlled manner to avoid such a predicament from occurring. Big Oak's lifestyle hadn't changed significantly within the local community, however, since employed as an Agent, he had drawn unwanted attention from some quarters. This was likely due to his finances not being sensitively handled.

Billy had thought he had achieved this by limiting only payments that could be explained without drawing the attention of immediate family and friends. However due to his stupidity in reborrowing money from the loan shark, he'd made himself look flush and consequently drew unnecessary attention to himself. It never occurred to him that the loan shark he paid back would have connections within PIRA, and instead of paying the money back slowly, and in small amounts, he'd decided to hand over the £5,000 in one go, only to ask for it back a short time later. The road to hell is paved with good intentions, but his habit of gambling just got the better of him. Questions may have been asked as to where he got the £5,000 in the first place, a situation Billy was uncomfortable with. Hindsight is a wonderful thing, and Billy wished he had drip fed the money, so as not to have created this predicament.

Micky Crawford had just become the number one priority for the detachment, with an emergency meeting being arranged. His situation had become extremely serious, with the potential of his body being found on an isolated border road, hands tied, and with two bullet holes in the back of his head. The Unit hadn't lost an agent before, and they didn't intend to start now. PS (Protective surveillance) was always planned into all operations to help protect the operators and the Agent whilst on the ground. But because Big Oak was thought to have come under the suspicion of his colleagues by his own actions, it would not be unexpected for the terrorist organization to conduct its own inquiries and surveillance on that individual. Equally, the Unit still had its own suspicions concerning his loyalty and motivations, particularly because he was a relevantly new Agent and his trustworthiness was still in question.

A mobile route was given to the Agent to follow with various stops incorporated into it. The route included both quiet and busy areas to highlight any hostile surveillance. Having carried out his own anti-surveillance on route, the team shadowed his progress before eventually linking up with Big Oak and leading him away to a secure location.

The meeting was a heated affair, which resulted in Big Oak being punched and knocked back into his chair, having become aggressive and swearing at the team. As he was being berated about his actions, he'd jumped out of his chair, as if to attack the team. Mac reacting swiftly, and determining Big Oak's action as threatening, threw a cracking right hand onto the jaw of Big Oak. This was so uncharacteristic of Mac, but all members of the Unit were trained to be fast and explosive in their actions to any form of threat. It just wasn't expected to be with an Agent. Big Oak never retaliated but rather knew he was outnumbered, deciding one dig to the jaw was enough to suppress his enthusiasm for a fight. He was taught a valuable lesson in mutual respect by the handling team.

It was explained to Big Oak that his lack of security and spending had already gotten him noticed by PIRA, and the chances of him being picked up by their security team for questioning was a real possibility. He was quite unperturbed by these revelations.

"I've been through it before when they stood me down, so bring it on."

This was a clear act of bravado, so it was pointed out to him that this was much more serious, because they now suspected him of being a tout.

"Your spending through gambling shows a total disregard for all the effort and security measures we have put in place to protect you. If you don't take this seriously, we won't be able to protect you and you will be killed."

It was decided that he wouldn't be met again, or at least not until this had blown over, because if he was under suspicion, then his movements would be monitored by PIRA's security team. It was Billy and Mac's aspirations to get Big Oak fully integrated back into the ranks of PIRA, but unless he changed his ways, it would never happen. The meeting ended with Big Oak once again promising to do the right thing, but at least he did acknowledge he had borrowed against his outstanding loan. The operation to return him to the city took place without incident.

As with every Agent meeting, the handling team briefed the boss at its conclusion, highlighting the intelligence gained. The boss would then determine the level of security classification to go on each MISR. The protection of the Agent's identity was paramount, so a single subject could have several levels, with information being omitted from the report to enable maximum distribution. Only those with top level clearance would see the report in its entirety.

Billy and Mac briefed the boss on the meeting, opting to ignore the right hand thrown by Mac to the Jaw of Big Oak. It was hoped that Weeping Willow would forewarn the detachment if Big Oak was under suspicion, but then, why he hadn't already done so was a question that still needed answered.

Chapter 33

Liam: Close watch

The meeting with Liam took place back at the detachments compound within its debriefing suite. It would normally have taken place at one of its OCP's, but the boss wanted to watch and listen in on the debrief from the monitoring room. Prior to the meeting taking place, Billy and Mac viewed the transcript from Liam's home and were therefore already privileged to the conversation between Liam, Pinkie, Perky, and Frankie Connolly.

Liam appeared quite nervous and raised his concerns regarding his level of involvement with Frankie. It became apparent that it was Frankie he was more concerned about. Frankie's lack of forbearance when it came to other people, even though they were close associates of his, held no water because in Liam's words, "He'd Nutt me just as quick as a complete stranger, the man is a psychopath."

He stated he was concerned for his own safety, as he was to be questioned over the killings of the Armagh ASU.

Billy immediately bounced on this by asking, "Why, what involvement did you have in that?"

Liam looked stunned and tried to gather his thoughts, then said, "I took Jimmy Rice over to Mary Sweeney's house."

"But what has that to do with the Armagh ASU, Liam?"

Liam realised he had messed up and tried to back track but Billy wasn't letting it go. "I'll ask you again Liam, what has Mary Sweeny's house got to do with the Armagh ASU?"

Liam stated, "I think it was being used as a safe house, and I think I know who was staying there. Look…. Jimmy told me Spud Swan was in there, I swear, I never saw him, I stayed in the car."

Onus on Truths

"Were you at the house at any other time Liam?"

"No, I swear."

Billy now had the confirmation he wanted because they already knew he had delivered Spud to the house. They were also aware that the exchange had taken place outside the Lagan Valley Hospital on the same night, curtesy of the wounded terrorist, Sean Feeney. Again, this was a classic case of Liam trying to distance himself from any real involvement, thinking only of self-preservation. Liam was asked to bring the team up to speed with his activities since they last met.

Liam reported on his visit to Jamacia Street on the night of the Armagh ASU killings. Liam stated that Jimmy Rice had called him at around 11:30 pm and asked Liam to take him to Jamacia Street. He said that Jimmy went into the house of Mary Sweeney but was only there for a matter of minutes before returning to the car. He took Jimmy back home and was back in his own house by 12:30 am, having completed a last run into the city for late customers.

Liam was asked if anyone else was present in the house at the time, apart from Mary Sweeney, of course. Liam stated he wasn't aware and hadn't seen anyone else. He mentioned he knew Mary Sweeney through his wife, Roslyn, but not well. In fact, he had taken Frankie to her and Sean Pearse's house during his investigation into Sean a while back. He recognised Mary might be more important than he had previously thought and maybe should have mentioned her during previous debriefs. Then again, Billy or Mac never seemed to ask much about her.

Was it Mary that Frankie went to see when he dropped him off the other morning? No, it couldn't have, been because he remembered seeing her in the front office of Sinn Fein when Frankie and Co were there. So, who was he seeing? Then he remembered that was the same morning he'd seen Billy walking along Edna Drive.

Liam asked Billy why he was on Edna Drive the other morning, as he had seen him. Billy knew he had been spotted by him because a member of the cover team had radioed his presence on the road at the time, with Billy choosing to ignore it and continue with his own pickup.

Billy explained he was conducting a recce for future routes and potential stops that Liam could use when meeting with his handling team. It was all in the continued development and security for his protection.

Liam appeared satisfied with the explanation. Billy had just been conducting the reverse contact for Mary at the time, and he remembered seeing a woman gawping out the bathroom window of the neighbour's house whilst he was at the back of Mary's.

Liam informed Billy about dropping Frankie near Jamacia Street, as he said he needed to see a woman. Liam explained he went to Divis to the home of Ian Bradley to inform him of Frankie's intention to use the flat in the coming days. He further explained that the PAC (Provisional Army Council) of PIRA had instructed Frankie to interview all suspects connected to the Armagh ASU incident, of which Liam was one.

Liam was told by Billy that it was procedure and he had nothing to worry about, and if he continued to deny all that was put to him, then no harm would be inflicted. The IRA would need a confession for the PAC to sanction punishment.

Liam sarcastically stated, "That's easy for you to say, you're not the one being grilled by Frankie."

"We will protect you at all costs, remember you're not the only one being questioned, there will be others, including Jimmy Rice. The circle of knowledge on this thing is much bigger than you think. For example, that woman Mary Sweeney and others within the Armagh Brigade would all have known something." So, he continued by saying, "if you are telling the truth," Billy meant the whole truth, "Then your involvement would not be a concern to the PAC. However, if you had more of an input and not telling us, then it would be impossible for us to protect you."

Liam came clean by declaring he had indeed been involved in the pickup of Declan Swan. Two vehicles had been involved in the pickup, his and another belonging to Syd Collins, which was a black Audi. Jimmy Rice, accompanied by Liam, were in one vehicle, and an unknown male was with Syd in the other. They went to the Lagan Valley Hospital grounds around midnight and were met by boys from Armagh, one of which was Micky Devlin in a dark coloured Land Rover. There were two other vehicles he suspected were possibly linked to the operation and in the grounds, but he couldn't be sure. Swan was transferred into his car and Syd cleared the route back into the city and Jamacia Street.

Syd Collins was a bouncer and worked weekends on the door of the Shamrock Arms. When asked for description of the other bloke, he stated the man never got out of the car, but looked heavy set, with a mop of dark curly hair and large sideburns. By the vague description, he could have been describing Wurzel Gummidge. Going by this revelation, he was indeed a potential suspect and was more involved than previously stated. It was explained, despite his paranoia, that he didn't do anything wrong, so therefore he had nothing to worry about. He was still reprimanded for withholding information from Billy and Mac.

Billy restated, "Liam, if you deny everything they put to you, then you will survive the questioning, as the PAC need a confession to punish."

It was obvious this didn't fill Liam with confidence, but he simply accepted the advice given.

Chapter 34

Bridget and Frankie

Mary awakened to the sound of a car pulling up outside her house. On pulling back the bedroom curtains, she could see it was Liam Murray, but he was alone and stationary in the car.

What's he waiting for? she thought.

A few seconds later, Frankie Connolly exited the home of Bridget Pearse.

What the frig, the stale smoke that afternoon in the kitchen. It was Frankie Connolly. How could she? He was the one that pointed the finger at Sean for being a tout.

Mary couldn't wait to get round to Bridget's to find out what she was playing at, but first, she needed to get ready for work, so it would have to wait. Mary watched as Frankie got into the car and exited the street.

Mary arrived at work just before eight, and Barry McGinn was waiting outside the door as she walked up.

"What's up," she asked. "Why are you waiting outside?"

"Seamus is in Dublin today, and I can't get in, but you, my girl, have a key, I believe."

Mary opened the door and turned off the alarm before heading into the small kitchenette to put the coffee machine on, closely followed by Barry. Barry then took Mary by the arm, not in a rough way but with a gentle grip, turned her toward him and said, "Mary love, Frankie wants a word with you, but don't worry it's just procedure. Everyone who had anything to do with your guest the other week is being questioned."

Onus on Truths

"Christ Barry, what has that got to do with me, he came, stayed, and left again, that's all I know."

"I know, I know, but someone said something because he was wacked on the A1 when he left your house, so it stands to reason he wants to speak with you."

"Well fuck you and all the rest of you because it was you lot that put him with me in the first place and now you think I touted, fuck you."

"Relax Mary, like I said, it's procedure, he just needs to eliminate you from his inquiries.'

"Don't ever ask me to do anything for you again." She hesitated before continuing, "You can tell Jimmy Rice I want a word with him, too."

She had just stopped herself in time, as she was about to say, *and you can get the fucking weapons out of my house as well,* but didn't know if Barry was privileged to that information. Mary was shaking with both rage and nerves but tried to stay calm.

"When is this likely to happen? Because I'm here most days, so he can come and ask whatever he likes."

"Not here Mary, people come in and out all the time, so, it will be somewhere of his choosing, I'm afraid."

Mary's first thought was to get in touch with Billy and get his advice. Something else which would have to wait until later. *Maybe I'll have something to say to Frankie myself, sneaking out of a dead RA man's house at seven in the morning. How would that be seen by Kieran and Co?* thought Mary.

Barry left Mary to open shop and left the building just as other staff members arrived in for work. Mary's morning was consumed with thoughts of being questioned, and she couldn't wait to get away from the office.

On leaving the office, she walked a route she'd been given by Billy several years back. It was a CS route. it was only ever used when she felt threatened or was in fear of compromise. She hoped that she herself wasn't under any form of surveillance by the security team of

PIRA. She wanted to make the call to Billy but wanted to make sure she wasn't being followed first. She made a series of stops along her route, checking all the time and using the reflection of shop windows to watch for figures stopping or changing direction when she halted. She entered a supermarket via the front only to exit via the rear to try and identify any hostile surveillance. Nothing was obvious to her, so she stopped at a phone box and made the call to Billy.

Mary was reassured of her importance to PIRA, and Billy agreed with Barry's assessment that it was simply procedure and she only needed to stick to her cover story. It was tried and tested. Anything she did over the period was natural and fit in with her routine. That's what the cover story was for, her protection, so if she stuck to it, then everything would be fine. Frankie would have nothing on her, absolutely nothing, so she needed to stay calm and deny everything, as he would try and twist things. Just stick to the story and deny.

Billy was having a busy time with two of his main Agents being in the firing line, the same advice being given to each. Well, at least similar, but it needed to be cleverly managed, as both agents using the same tact and conscious uniformity might raise its own suspicions with Frankie. Added to the mix was the concern over Micky Crawford and his predicament. Although not providing nearly as good intelligence as the others, he was still a CHIS and therefore needed protection, nonetheless.

Mary was brave and couldn't have survived as long as she had if she had not been cunning by demonstrating the skill to deceive and evade detection. If the Agents were named after animals, then she would have been named FOX.

Chapter 35

The Guilty Four

Gary, or 'Walnut,' had been reporting on the movements and activities of the 'Guilty Four' as he liked to describe them. He would spend time at the Braziers Arms just to be antagonistic. He was warned by his handling team, Billy and Roy, not to be so aggressive in his methods, as it could end badly for him. He was totally belligerent and loudmouthed whenever in the UVF members presence.

He had become a problem to the Unit because it had a duty of care for him, but his actions were making it extremely difficult for them. His name was mentioned by Paul Millar from TCG as someone who was being targeted by the UVF because of his outspoken condemnation of them. The threat was real, with talk of him being Nutted and placed in a dustbin.

Unknown to Billy, Gary had been conducting his own surveillance on the Guilty Four. He had been intercepted by a police patrol car acting suspicious outside the home of Bobby Weir. Gary was brought in again by Billy to emphasise the point that his one-man crusade wasn't acceptable and would lead to his death if he persisted with it. Gathering information on either of the two loyalist groups was what was needed to gain arrests and subsequent prosecution, but this wasn't the way to do it.

Walnut was threatened with being stood down as an Agent and categorised as an Intelligence nuisance. In a matter of a few weeks, Gary McBurney had managed to cause a major feud between the once closely aligned groups under the CLMC of the UVF and UDA. The fallout was a result of a UVF member, Bobby Weir, being found bludgeoned to death in an alleyway just a few streets away from the Braziers Arms. A cardboard sign left on his body stated, "Jim Mac was one of our own." It was believed to be a clear indication that the UDA had taken reprisal action for the death of one of their volunteers, which resulted in the UVF targeting a relative of Gary McBurney, Marty Spence.

Marty had just exited the main entrance of the Connswater Shopping Centre, carrying a brown paper bag with drinks he had just purchased from the wine lodge. A black saloon car, which had been stolen earlier in the day from the Kings Road area, drove in front of Marty. The passenger window was lowered and an Uzi submachine gun was levelled at him with a rapid burst of gunfire. Marty Spence was hit several times, with the bag of Buckfast wine exploding and sending the contents of the shattered bottles in all directions. Marty's body slumped to the ground, dead, in a pool of cheap wine and blood.

Within 24 hours, the home of Tucker Wright was sprayed by bullets, and a petrol bomb was thrown against his front door. These tit for tat attacks would have continued had it not been for the Police and the forensic team finding a black marker pen which was found near the crime scene with DNA from Gary McBurney. He was subsequently arrested and charged with murder.

Military Intelligence were quick to distance themselves from any association with Gary McBurney, who they described as a 'Lone Wolf.'

Tensions had not been so high between the loyalist groups since the feud of 1974-75 when bad blood originated from the Ulster Workers Council Strike, when both sides were originally in cooperation in support of the strike. It was pressure from the striking men's wives that ignited the feud. With the men not working and money being tight, the wives saw their men folk drinking away what little money they had in the pubs. Through this pressure, the leaders of both groups shut down all the pubs except one pub affiliated to the UVF on the Shankill Road. A second bar tried to reopen and members of the UDA visited it with the intention of closing it down.

Onus on Truths

A man by the name of Joe Shaw was shot and killed following an altercation at the pub. This led to several deaths over this period between the two groups. This feud rumbled on into 1976, with mostly members of the UDA being killed before an agreement was reached and an uneasy truce established.

Gary McBurney had tried to blame the UDA for the killing, hoping it would cause a feud like that of the seventies. But despite his incarceration, he still promised to get the remaining three of the UVF killers as he was led away from court.

Chapter 36

Interrogation

"Liam, I need you to pick up Syd Collins and bring him to Divis. I need you to make sure he gets in the flat. He's at the Shamrock and expecting you," said Frankie.

Liam went straight over to the bar and found Syd waiting at the door dressed for a night's bouncing in a white shirt, black trousers, and a black bomber-style jacket. As Liam arrived, he parked the car at the curb directly outside the bar and Syd climbed into the passenger seat. Syd appeared relaxed and unfazed by the summons and looking across at Liam, said, "Let's do this and get it over with."

Liam thought to himself how relaxed Syd was with the whole affair, showing no signs of panic. It was as if he had been through it all before. The two men drove in silence, with Liam being slightly unnerved as he took the odd glance toward Syd, who was sat back in his seat, idlily looking out the window.

Syd turned to Liam and asked, "Who's at the flat waiting for me?"

Liam was hesitant and wasn't sure if he could or should say but decided to come clean, because after all Syd was not trying to avoid the inevitable. "I believe Frankie, along with Pinkie and Perky are already there."

"I take it you don't call them Pinkie and Perky to their faces?"

"You're kidding right," said Liam. "I want to keep my head on my shoulders."

Syd turned back and continued looking out at the darkening sky over the city. It had just occurred to Liam that he hadn't phoned Billy about what was about to happen to Syd. Once he was excused, he would get to a phone box and report in the details.

When they arrived at the block of flats, Liam took his time and locked the car before following behind Syd as they made their way up the ramped walkway toward the flat of Ian Bradley. The door to the flat was open as Syd made his way through the entrance, closely watched by Liam. No sooner had he entered the hall that Pinkie and Perky came from either side of the hall. Pinkie came from the bathroom and Perky from the kitchen, and they set upon him ramming his head against the wall before administrating several punches and placing a sack over his head. He kicked and struggled against the two brutes and was giving a decent account of himself but was eventually overwhelmed as he was dragged along the hall into the back room and shoved down into a chair.

He was quickly secured with plastic cuffs by the hands and legs to the chair. It all happened so fast, but then there was a total silence over the room. The sack offered no view at all, with only speckles of light cascading through, but the strong smell of a potent cigarette smoke was wafting through the fabric with ease and getting into his nostrils as he desperately tried to regulate his breathing.

The room must have been sparsely furnished because the slightest noise or movement seemed to reverberate off the walls. He recognised the sound of a tape recorder button being pressed. Then he heard a voice for the first time.

"So, here we are." It was the voice of Frankie Connolly and no mistaking. He was told he was being questioned on the grounds of being suspected as a tout.

"What we have here is a tout bastard who jeopardised our operations. A traitor and brit lover who has betrayed his community, family, and fellow republicans. But before long, you will give a full confession, because if you don't, you will never see your family again. We can do this the easy way or the hard way, that's entirely up to you and how well you cooperate."

The hessian sack was ripped off his head, and as he had already envisaged, the room was totally empty except for the chair he was seated in and a small coffee table which had a series of instruments such as pliers, a claw hammer, and even a cheese slice, all of which he immediately recognised as torture tools. If the equipment on the table were props and designed with the intention to scare him, then they certainly had the desired effect. His heart rate had increased to the extent that he thought, at any moment, his heart would pop right out of his chest.

There was a large, plastic decorator's sheet covering much of the floor around the seat. He was facing the wall with '70s style retro wallpaper of large, yellow and green flowers. The wallpaper hurt his eyes more than the single hanging light bulb from the ceiling as his eyes adjusted to the room. Heavy, cheap, green velvet curtains were drawn closed. These were too long for the window, with the bottom of the curtain lying on the floor in a heap. As he tried to take in the room and its surroundings, he caught sight of Pinkie and Perky standing with their backs to the wall.

"I swear to God, I know nothing about botched operations, I had nothing to do with any of this and I'm no fucking tout."

"Well maybe a little persuasion might just jog your memory." With that, Frankie nodded to Pinkie and he walked over, punching him hard on the side of the jaw. Blood splattered from his mouth, spraying the plastic sheet. He wasn't sure if he had lost any teeth with the punch, but it certainly loosened one or two. The rusty metallic taste of blood was sickening and made him feel queasy.

"Has that refreshed your memory?"

His head was spinning, and trying to speak whilst spitting blood, he stated, "I really don't know what you want me to say because I've done nothing wrong."

"Listen here you fucker, you were driving the car on the night Spud was collected from Lagan Valley. You knew the plan. You told the brit bastards everything, so let's get this over with and confess."

The beatings continued and the verbal bombardment was relentless. His routine and movements over the previous months were completely dissected. The interrogation lasted for several hours but without a confession being obtained. Frankie moved in close to the bloodied, semi-conscious body and said in a low but calm voice, "OK, we need to get you looked at. Syd, can you drive Liam in his car down to the Mater hospital so he can be fixed up. Perky untie him." Frankie then said, "Sorry kid, but you were a suspect and it had to be done. Tell Roslyn you were dragged from your taxi and beaten."

Liam attempted to raise his head, which felt too heavy for his battered and broken body, then spluttered the words, "Fuck You Frankie."

As Syd drove Liam to the hospital, he said, "At least you're in the clear now, I went through it several weeks back and my ribs are still recovering. Everyone gets it. At the end of the day someone must pay, so just be grateful Frankie believes you, because the alternative isn't good my friend."

"That fucker, Pinkie, broke my nose." Liam laughed out loud but didn't know if it was out of nervousness or relief whilst simultaneously crying out in pain saying, "Couldn't he just have taken my word for it?"

Both men laughed. Syd dropped Liam at the entrance to the A&E department and told him he would park the car in the side street and the keys would be in the wheel arch. Liam entered the hospital, badly bruised, and battered, but thankful to be alive.

Chapter 37

Mary & Bridget

Mary visited Bridget at her home for a coffee and a catch up, but more importantly, she wanted the low down on Frankie Connolly leaving the house earlier that morning. So as not to be over eager for the gossip, she made small talk and discussed having another night out at the Shamrock.

"Can we make it a non-karaoke night, as I don't want to hear Jamie singing his Elvis numbers."

Both girls laughed, with Mary saying, "My Jamie is a great wee singer, and whilst we are on the subject of men, did I see Frankie Connolly leave your house this morning?"

"Why, you're a nosy bitch Mary Sweeney, but yes, you did."

"Well tell all girl, I want the juicy details."

"Nothing much to tell, ever since Sean went inside, rest his soul, he started coming round. At first, it was more like an interrogation about Sean, but after his death it was more keeping me up to date and bringing the odd envelope with cash to help me out."

"Holy Mother of God Bridget, it was probably Frankie who had him killed. If I didn't know better, he could have done it just to get into your pants. He's that sort of man, pure evil. You know his reputation. If he could get Sean out of the way, then he stood a better chance with you. The envelopes wouldn't have been sanctioned by PIRA, particularly with them accusing Sean of being a tout, and before you start, I know they had no evidence against him but killed him anyway. Christ Bridget just be careful, that's all I'm saying, he's dangerous."

"Mary, he explained his involvement in all of that, and he said Sean was killed over a dispute on the wing."

"Surely you don't buy that Bridget, do you?"

"No, of course not, but can we just leave it please? Mary, I'm no fool so don't go treating me as one, I know what I'm doing. Its sex, plain and simple. I'm not a Nun, and I'm not going to behave like one either."

Mary agreed to drop the subject and moved onto other matters, namely her relationship with Jamie, the blue-eyed, Elvis Presley wannabe. "Like you said Bridget, its sex, plain and simple."

Both girls laughed. The two girls opened a bottle of wine and had a few drinks. In Mary's mind, there were many ways to skin a cat, and Bridget wasn't great at holding her drink, so maybe if she squeezed, perhaps there would be more juice.

By the time the second bottle of wine was downed, Mary staggered out of Bridget's house for the extremely short journey home next door. It was just starting to get dark, but she managed to make it to the front door without falling over the two-foot-high hedge that bordered the two properties. Having had two attempts at putting the key into the lock, both without success before dropping the keys on the floor, she giggled to herself and bent to retrieve them. As she steadied herself and tried yet again to insert the key for the third time, she felt a hand rest on the small of her back.

She was startled by the sudden touch and turned round to face Jamie, who was standing behind her. She giggled again as she realised it was her wannabe-Elvis lover and laughed out loud, saying, "Uh huh huh," in an Elvis-mocking tone.

She was happy to see him, hugged him, said are you here to "Love me tender," and laughed again.

"Christ you're well gone tonight, Mary, give me the keys and get inside before you fall down."

They never made it past the hallway with Mary ripping frantically at Jamie's clothes whilst leaning back against the banister rail, her knee pressed high into Jamie's groin. Jamie, using both hands whilst still in a full kissing embrace, raised her skirt and pulled down her pants. They adjusted their position onto the lower level of the stairs, which enabled Mary to shake free from her pants, allowing her to open her legs. Jamie knelt on the bottom stair pulling her toward him so he could penetrate deep inside her. They had frantic sex on the stairs, with Mary being exuberantly noisy, so much so she thought she heard Bridget banging on the wall. Eventually, they made it up to the bedroom for a slightly less frantic but equally enjoyable session.

Mary woke to the noise of Jamie plundering the kitchen cupboards, trying to locate cups for the freshly made pot of tea he had just brewed. Mary made her way down the stairs to the kitchen only to see Jamie reaching under the cooker with his hand.

Mary, on seeing this, shouted "Jamie, what are you doing?" Jamie jumped up and his heart felt like it was going to pop right out of his chest with the sudden shock of the raised voice.

"Fuck Mary, you scared the life out of me there, I dropped the fucking teaspoon and it went under the cooker, Christ what's wrong with you woman?"

Mary apologised, "Sorry I didn't mean to shout, don't know what came over me. Sorry, just seeing you down on the floor scared me, sorry."

Mary desperately wanted to change the subject and quickly. The thought of him pulling out the cooker could have led him to discovering the hide.

"Just leave it Jamie, I have plenty of other teaspoons and I'll get it later when I wash the floor."

In an attempt to change the subject, she asked, "Was I that drunk last night because I remember making love in the hall but not a great recollection much after that and I've got friggin' carpet burns on my ass."

Jamie laughed and stated, "Frig your ass, you should see my knees." They both laughed and drank their tea.

Jamie left the house, and Mary thought, now it was Bridget's turn to be peeping out the window, watching Jamie walking away from her

Onus on Truths

neighbour's house early in the morning. Mary thought about the previous night and more about her conversation with Bridget and not the carpet burns on her backside. Something wasn't quite right about the relationship between Bridget and Frankie Connolly, but whenever she tried to probe, Bridget just evaded the questions or changed the subject.

Yes, Mary thought, *something is not right.*

Considering Connolly's reputation and his involvement, and knowing Bridget the way she did, something didn't fit. *Maybe Bridget is involved in PIRA business, surely not, but what else could it be, it just didn't add up.* Mary finished her second cup of over-stewed tea before taking a shower and getting dressed for work.

Bridget was never far from her mind, but then again, neither was Connolly, and she would be seeing him soon enough according to Barry McGinn.

Chapter 38

Liam's Recovery

Liam's recovery was progressing well, and he was convalescing at home. Three broken ribs, the loss of two teeth, and a broken nose was the result of the interrogation, and whilst the ribs were an extremely slow-healing process, much of the bruising had diminished. The tall tale of being pulled out of the taxi was not believed by the police but more importantly for him, not by Roslyn.

During his overnight stay at the Mater hospital, the medical staff had packed his nose with gauze to help reset it. The following morning, he woke up feeling quite ill and had the terrible feeling of wanting to be sick. He was also having difficulty breathing. He kept trying to cough up a load of phlegm that seemed to have gathered at the back of his throat, but every time he coughed, his nose and ribs hurt like hell. The Nurse was encouraging him to spit it out so to speak, so he gave one big effort and a massive string of phlegm came out of his mouth, dangling in front of his chin. Liam took hold of it and pulled to free it from his mouth, and in doing so, yanked his head backwards before letting out an almighty scream. The nurse threw her hands in the air and shouted at Liam to stop. There was a look of shock on her face and she immediately stopped him in his tracks, as it was the gauze that had slipped down his throat and was causing the coughing reflux. They had to remove the gauze and repack his nose. Yuk… Liam recalled it as the most horrendous procedure. The removal of clotted, congealed, concentrated blood being forced back up through his nose had felt liked his head was being ripped out from the inside.

Onus on Truths

The police had interviewed Liam at the Mater hospital that night, but Liam couldn't identify any of his assailants or remember where the incident had occurred. No further action was taken. However, Roslyn was having none of it and immediately got onto Frankie, lambasting him over what she said was his doing. Of course, Frankie denied having anything to do with it and said he was looking for the perpetrators, and when they got them, he would make them pay for their actions and Liam would have his justice.

Life in the Murray household was not pleasant; Roslyn continuously ranting and raving about Liam's involvement with Frankie and for the first time openly acknowledging and stating his work for PIRA would either get him killed or imprisoned, and then what would she and Shane do? Shane was at an age whereby he was questioning his mum on his dad's affiliation with his uncle Frankie. As rumours of his involvement being common knowledge. Shane himself rapidly approaching school leaving age.

Liam waited until Roslyn was out of the house and decided to use the house phone to phone Billy. Liam was furious about being interrogated and half-expected the detachment to know he was being taken. It was pointed out to Liam that had he telephoned on the night, as he was meant too, then maybe, just maybe, he would have been saved from the interrogation, but equally importantly, the culprits responsible could have been arrested at the scene.

A telephone debrief of Weeping Willow was conducted, with all the relevant details being noted. Liam believing, he wasn't going to be active for a while but was instructed to keep the detachment informed of any future dealing with Frankie and Co. The positive spin put to Liam was the fact he had survived the ordeal and was now not deemed responsible for the leaks within PIRA. He was still warned about future actions and the need to keep the detachment informed at the earliest convenience.

Also, from a security standpoint, whilst it was appreciated him getting in touch, the use of the home telephone was not in his best interests. It was pointed out that PIRA could have people employed within British Telcom who could not only intercept his calls but see what numbers he had been dialling. His security was paramount, and it was simple lapses of security like this that could get him killed. For example, Roslyn had always been suspicious of his actions but put them down as Frankie and PIRA business.

A cover story must be believed by the family and needs to be checkable. More cover stories have probably been pulled to pieces by jealous wives than anyone else. Roslyn having access to the telephone bill could raise such suspicions with unidentified numbers listed. Billy felt it didn't do any harm just to remind Liam of these small but important points.

Chapter 39

A Spy in the House

Jamie entered the small room to the rear of the bar and was told to take a seat directly facing Frankie, who was seated at the other end of the table. Pinkie was seated in the far corner of the room on an old bar stool. The light from the skylight window was shining brightly into his eyes. Jamie adjusted the seat to avoid the direct sun rays and tiny speckles of dust illuminated by the rays. Jamie started by saying, "I haven't got long, as I need to open up in twenty minutes so can we get on with this?"

"No problem, Jamie, I just need a few minutes of your time, so it won't take long. Now then, how's it going with wee Mary Sweeney, is everything progressing well?"

"Yeah, great, I only see her a few times a week, if I'm lucky, but everything's fine."

"What about the wee matter of information, is she producing any pillow talk of interest?"

"No, nothing I feel is threatening to us. She seems the real deal. Although she did mention you and Bridget Pearse being an item, which she finds worrying. She clearly doesn't trust you and thinks you have an alternative motive for being with Bridget. Then again, that was drink talking, and she's probably just looking out for her friend."

"Jamie don't worry about me; I have my reasons so we will leave it there. What about guests, did she mention that?"

"I don't understand, what do you mean guests?"

"Nothing, it doesn't matter, just keep your eyes and ears open for me."

"Listen Frankie, I like the girl, and I honestly don't think she is a threat, and from what we have previously discussed, she's a good asset for PIRA. She has never discussed any RA business in front of me. Your girl is clean, but I will continue to observe her. If there is anything, then you will be the first to know."

"Thanks Jamie, oh by the way, can we get a pint?"

"It's not quite opening time yet, but I'm sure I could manage that."

Frankie said, "I wouldn't want the peelers raiding the pub."

Both men laughed, with Jamie stating, "No problem come back through to the main bar."

Frankie was being pressured not to interrogate Mary by Jimmy Rice and Seamus because of her past record; they didn't want to lose such a good asset, but they needed to know if she was clean, and Frankie having Jamie watch her felt it was a better way of handling things. He didn't see the need for an interrogation, although he would have no issue in torturing a woman, and it wouldn't be the first time PIRA had done so.

Many a female had been tortured at the hands of PIRA for allegedly informing or simply fraternizing with known RUC or Army personnel, *Jean McConville being one such female who was shown no mercy. A mother of ten was taken from her Belfast home, murdered, and buried in the bog lands of County Louth.* So, Frankie and PIRA were capable of anything.

Jamie felt bad about touting on Mary, but he really didn't think PIRA and Frankie had anything to worry about. He thought back to when he first met Mary and how Frankie had approached him about getting alongside her. A strange tactic, as the RA liked to use women to spy on the men, not the other way round. It would be easier for the women, but Jamie didn't have an issue, as he liked her and she was pleasing on the eye. He knew she had been married before, but it was a long time back and he knew it didn't last long.

Their first encounter was in the Shamrock Arms, and in fairness, she'd had a few drinks and was in good form. It was the night of the karaoke. He remembered how they had a lock in at the end of the evening and a bit of a behind the doors sing song. She ended up staying the night above the bar in his flat. The following morning, he half-expected her to gather up her clothes and try to sneak out, never to be seen again. On the contrary, she'd seemed quite relaxed and stayed for coffee before going home. He asked if he could see her again, of which she was more than happy with. The longer he was in the relationship, the harder it became, and he dreaded if she ever found out that he was spying on her.

Chapter 40

Frankie, I Want Names

Bridget had been acting strange since the drinks with Mary, and despite numerous attempts to talk, she seemed to be avoiding her. This left Mary wondering if she had done something to upset her, but too much wine had been consumed by the girls, and Mary's memory after the first bottle was quite hazy. Had she said something to upset her? Well, if she had, then she had no recollection of it now. Maybe her criticism of Bridget and Frankie was deemed a step too far. Whatever it was, Bridget was keeping her distance.

Flip, it just occurred to her: Maybe Frankie had said something to Bridget about Mary. Mary thought about confronting Bridget to determine what, if anything, was the issue for the avoidance. As she was about to go round and confront her, she noticed Frankie walking up to the front door of Bridget's house. He was on foot and alone. Mary decided it would have to wait for another day.

Bridget had telephoned Frankie and asked him round for a drink, of which he was only too happy to oblige. He arrived and noticed Mary standing at her window. He waved and continued up the path to the front door of Bridget's house.

Bridget was dressed in a tightly fitted pencil skirt and white blouse through which her black-laced bra was clearly visible. She showed him into the lounge, and immediately, Frankie could tell she had already consumed at least two glasses of wine going by the contents of the bottle on the coffee table. It was early evening, with the room being illuminated by a small but ambient table lamp in the corner. Songs by the Supremes was playing on the Hifi, making it feel like a relaxed and pleasant environment.

Onus on Truths

Bridget poured Frankie a glass of Harp beer from one of the two cans next to her wine bottle. She had another four safely stored in the fridge from the six pack she had purchased earlier in the day. Frankie took the glass gracefully and sat down on the floral settee. Bridget wasn't normally as direct, but the whole-body language and seductive manner was welcomed.

Frankie could already sense his testosterone levels rising. If Bridget was trying to get him horny, then it was working. Bridget sat in the chair facing Frankie, and in doing so, was exposing the top of the stockings and her inner thighs. It was a restricted exposure, as the skirt by nature was hampering her from over revealing her matching black pants. It was enough to ensure she had his undivided attention.

They both enjoyed several drinks, with Frankie polishing off all six cans generously provided before tucking into a bottle of twenty-year-old single malt Bush Mills whiskey which Bridget said Sean had been keeping for their 30th anniversary. The statement appeared to have absolutely no impact on Frankie whatsoever as he poured a glass. Bridget stated, "I guess it doesn't matter anymore, so there's no point in keeping it."

"I guess not," came the response from Frankie.

Bridget looked at Frankie, and she could see he had neither empathy or remorse, and it saddened her. Bridget moved over to the settee beside Frankie whilst swirling the contents of her lipstick-rimmed wine glass. Frankie could smell her almost-intoxicating cheap perfume, overpowering his senses.

"Why don't we retire upstairs and get more comfortable?" Bridget suggested. Frankie wasn't slow on the uptake, as the menace of a bulge in his trousers was fighting its own battle for freedom.

Once in the bedroom, Bridget slowly and seductively started to undress, whilst Frankie was frantically kicking off his shoes and trying hard to undo his trousers whilst lying prone on the bed. Bridget wasn't in perfect shape and had started to show signs of middle age but, in her clothes, she was well proportioned and had tremendous breasts. Keeping her high heel shoes on, she slowly undid the zip of the pencil skirt and allowed it to fall to the floor, covering her feet. She stepped out of the skirt, displaying her black stockings, suspender belt, and black laced pants.

Frankie had managed to kick free his trousers and had pulled his shirt over his head, discarding it on the floor. By now, his manhood was free and proud.

Bridget removed her blouse and, holding it in one hand with her arm fully extended, dropped it at her feet. As she made her way onto the bed, she produced a set of pink fluffy handcuffs and said, "Let's have some fun Frankie." The delight on Frankie's face was plain to see, and he retorted "For me or you," with a snigger.

"Oh, you, dear Frankie, I want to be in control."

She proceeded to handcuff Frankie's hands to the wooden slotted headboard, and once he was secure, she returned to a dresser and removed two ties from the top drawer before returning and tying both his feet to the bed end. Bridget straddled Frankie, sitting on top of him and reaching behind her back, manhandling his penis by holding it tight against the fabric of her pants, snug against her ass. "How does that feel?" she asked.

"Fuck Bridget, you're driving me nuts, sit on me before I explode."

"No, I just want to talk a while."

"Fuck talking, suck my dick, I'm going crazy here."

"Frankie, can I ask you a question?"

"What the fuck Bridget, come on stop teasing me and fuck me."

"Oh, I'm going to fuck you Frankie, just not in the way you think."

The shock of the statement and the realisation he was powerless to react sent shivers up his spine.

Bridget was still straddled but reached forward, with her magnificent breasts resting on his chest as she touched and retrieved the kitchen knife from under the pillow. As she retook her seated position, the rock-hard penis was no longer pulsating against her backside.

"Have you lost your desire, dear Frankie?"

"Jesus, mother of God, Bridget, this has gone far enough, it isn't funny anymore."

"Back to my question Frankie, why did you have my husband of almost 30 years killed, you son of a bitch?"

"Christ Bridget, I had nothing to do with that, you've got to believe me."

"You are a lying son of a bitch, you had him killed and you knew he wasn't a tout. Tell me this, Frankie aren't you still hunting for a tout? He was killed on your orders Frankie."

Frankie tried desperately to free himself but couldn't get loose.

"I loved that man and you took him from me, he was loyal to the RA from the early seventies, and he was committed to the republican cause, and that was his reward: to be beaten to death in a prison cell. I couldn't even have an open casket because of the damage you inflicted on him. Who carried out your orders Frankie?"

"Bridget, I don't know anything about that, I swear, but I promise you, I will find out for you."

Bridget took the knife and, using the point, placed it onto his nipple whilst rotating it, causing his nipple to shred into a bloody mess. Frankie screamed in pain, which took even Bridget by surprise. Jumping from him, she rushed to the dresser and grabbed a pair of pants, only to return to the bed and shove them into the mouth of Frankie. Panting heavily, she slowly regained her breath then stated, "Can't have the neighbours hearing us now, can we?" She calmly climbed back on top of Frankie and said, "Now where was I? Oh yes, you were going to tell me why you killed my husband, but it doesn't matter, you can tell him yourself soon enough.

Bridget ran the blade of the knife across his chest from areola to areola leaving a thin red line with blood seeping out and trickling down his chest toward his navel.

"My Sean wasn't even cold in his grave when you came sniffing around me. Did you really think I fancied you? You repulse me, Frankie Connolly. I begged you to protect him and you did nothing.

I have been ostracised by everyone in the community because of you. Mary was right, Sean was an inconvenience to you. When we made out, I felt physically sick, and you know what Frankie? You weren't even that good."

Frankie was squirming, and his face was twisted in pain. Bridget said, "Frankie, who killed my Sean? You know, if you don't tell me, then I will cut off that little thing you call a cock and feed it to you. Big fucking Frankie, king of the nutting squad, you're pathetic."

Frankie was trying desperately to speak but only muffled sounds could be heard. Bridget removed the pants from his mouth and said, "Names, Frankie."

Frankie just pleaded with Bridget, "Please…. Please… no… no…" then in desperation mouthed in almost a whisper, "Barry McGinn."

Bridget replaced the pants and stated, "If you have any last words, then now would be a good time, oh wait, I wouldn't hear you through my pants in your mouth anyway."

Bridget made another cut, this time from the top of his breastbone down toward his stomach. Once again, Frankie made a muffled scream in pain, arching his body into the air with Bridget still straddled across him. He had a distinct mark of a cross etched on his torso. Frankie was in a cold sweat and knew there was a cold, determined look in Bridget's eyes. He had conducted many a torturing session over the years, but this girl had a crazy look about her he had never witnessed. Whenever Frankie looked into his victims' eyes, he always saw fear and hopelessness, but what he was seeing in Bridget's eyes was a determined and unyielding stare. He knew he wasn't getting out of this alive and being gagged only frustrated his attempts of pleading a case of innocence.

Bridget, with tears welling up in her eyes, took the knife by the handle in both hands and placed it over Frankie's heart. Staring into his eyes, she leaned forward, putting her full bodyweight onto the knife. The blade cut into his chest, sinking deep into his heart as she mouthed, "You are a murdering bastard Connolly, rot in hell."

Frankie was wide-eyed as the blade penetrated his body, portraying a look of total fear and hopelessness, a look he had witnessed many times in his life but never expected to be making himself.

Chapter 41

Bridget: The damage is done

Bridget sat on her dressing table stool looking at the blood-soaked body of Frankie Connolly lying on the bed with a large kitchen knife still embedded in his chest. She recalled the chance encounter with another republican prisoner's wife, shortly after Sean's death, when she was informed who was responsible for ordering his murder. The woman's own husband was a trustee serving his sentence on the same wing as Sean. She stated that the murder of Sean had been on the orders of Frankie Connolly. He had secretly ordered it, despite openly declaring that nothing should happen without the PAC ruling. As far as who carried out the summary execution, she didn't know, as everyone was being very tight-lipped about it. Bridget was determined to find out who had committed the murder.

This information was enough for Bridget to set about planning the seduction and murder of the man who'd passed the sentence. It was hard keeping up the subterfuge of like for the man whilst still grieving her loss. Sean had faults, and there were many, but she had loved him. When he hit her, she probably deserved it, or at least that's what she told herself. As she looked back at the body and the knife, she remembered how she had once pulled that very knife on Sean during a drunken argument but fortunately not with the same consequences.

She looked to the ceiling and whispered, "I sent him to hell love." She had lost all recollection of time or how long she had sat there, but she was still in her bra and pants. Her hands and midriff were covered in blood. She shivered and, for the first time, realised she was cold. She walked into the bathroom, undressed, then stood under the shower attachment within the bath and let the hot water warm her shivering body. As she used her hands to smooth over her head and palm the water against her face, a pool of water at her feet turned red as the blood on her body and hands ran clean.

Bridget stepped out of the bath and dried herself before putting on a pair of jeans and one of Sean's old sweaters. She walked back into the bedroom, picked up her skirt and blouse, placed them on a hanger, and returned them to the wardrobe. She never touched any of Frankie's clothing but left them exactly where he had discarded them in his haste to be satisfied. Bridget then went downstairs and cleared away the beer cans and glasses before putting the kettle on.

Having made a cup of instant coffee, she sat at the kitchen table and sipped the piping hot liquid. She never showed or felt any remorse for what she had done and quietly sat, drinking the coffee.

Chapter 42

A Guilty Conscience

Micky Crawford visited the office of Sinn Fein and asked if Kieran O'Kane was present, as he needed a word. Mary was seated at the front desk shifting through the paperwork from the Ard Fheis meeting held over the weekend in Dublin when he entered the office.

The man was dressed in his painters' coveralls and appeared extremely nervous. It just so happened that several members of Sinn Fein were present in the conference room, being brought up to speed by Seamus on the outcome of the Ard Fheis. Although Kieran O'Kane, Jimmy, and Barry were not members of Sinn Fein but rather PIRA, but they were present, nonetheless.

Mary stated that he was busy but asked if there anything she could help him with.

"No, I need to speak with Kieran and now please. Could you go and get him for me, it's important."

Mary got up from her desk and went to the conference room. Knocking on the door before opening it just enough to expose her head into the room, she apologised by saying, "I'm sorry, Kieran, you are wanted urgently in the office. Micky Crawford needs to speak with you. I told him you were busy but he insisted."

"No problem, Mary, I'll be out in a minute."

Mary returned to Micky and relayed the message, telling Micky to take a seat and wait. He didn't have to wait long before Kieran appeared and asked what he wanted. Micky looked in the direction of Mary before turning his attention back to Kieran.

"Could we talk in private, not here?"

Onus on Truths

Kieran stated, "Mary deals with all inquiries in here so it will probably be her that actions whatever you want."

"Not fucking this she won't, now can we speak in private?"

Kieran led Micky into the kitchenette and closed the door. Micky started by stating he knew what people were saying about him, the fact he could be a tout.

"I was a good volunteer who made a mistake."

Kieran interrupted him by saying, "If you are here to try and get reinstated you can piss off."

"No…. and I know I did wrong when I had a fling with Carlin's wife, but it takes two to tango."

"Don't get cute with me Micky, it was another volunteers wife, a volunteer who just happened to be serving time in the H Block."

"I know, I know, but that's not what I have to say… The fucking Brits have tried to recruit me, but I swear I've given them nothing, and I have come straight to you." "Wait… let me get my head around this." Kieran struggled to articulate the words he wanted to say and the questions he was trying hard to formulate, like who, what, where, how, when, and more importantly: why him.

Kieran's mind was racing, His initial thought was, *this is massive, and at a time when secret negotiations between the Brits and the IRA over decommissioning were still being discussed. Whoa, this needs to be exploited and big time. This could be the propaganda coup of the year and divert much of the unwanted attention on the republican movement.*

PIRA used a range of communications and propaganda tools, notably the republican newspaper, An Phoblacht, and already Kieran was thinking along these lines. However, there was still the prospect of an operational exploitation and the chance to take out a British operative. Firstly, Kieran needed to get all the facts surrounding Micky's alleged recruitment attempt.

Mary, who had been listening in the hallway, despite struggling to hear the conversation, did manage to hear enough to know there had been a recruitment attempt by the Brits. Mary recalled how it was her who had given Micky Crawford's name to Billy as a person of interest. She retreated to her desk, carrying on with sorting the paperwork, ensuring a copy of the same was placed in her bag to give to Billy at their next meeting.

Kieran informed Micky that a meeting would be conducted and a full debrief (interrogation) would need to be conducted to obtain all the facts relating to the matter, but in the meantime, not to do anything stupid.

Kieran did ask if Micky had met with the Brits other than the initial approach. He lied and stated he had only ever met them once, after they offered him £10,000, and he was made to walk a route where he was picked up and taken to a house somewhere near the Castlereagh hills. But he was put into the back of a blacked-out van and didn't know exactly were.

Kieran was excited by the prospect of mounting an operation and killing the Brit bastards. Micky was told if he came clean and was totally honest, then maybe, just maybe, he wouldn't end up with a bullet in the Nutt. Micky was informed that someone from internal security would want to speak with him. Kieran give him an address to a retail unit in the Lower Falls Road area for later in the afternoon.

"You're doing the right thing, Micky," and with those parting words, he left the kitchenette and the building.

Chapter 43

Micky Comes Clean

"Micky, thanks for coming in, we appreciate it," said Jimmy. The small room was at the very back of the Unit and had an external door to the rear yard.

"Here's the thing Micky, you have the choice and only you can determine how this goes. You will leave here today either by the way you came in, through the front door, or out the back door and never to be seen again. So, it's very simple really: you come clean, tell us everything we want to know about your Brit friends, and then we decide whether you live or die."

Micky took in his surroundings and noticed the usual suspects present: Pinkie, Perky, Syd Collins, Kieran O'Kane, and Jimmy Rice. In addition to these, a local solicitor, Pat Finnigan, who was known for his sympathetic support to the republican cause, and the man who had represented virtually all the republicans during the time of the interment campaign. He was seated at the rear of the room with a Dictaphone and notepad. There were no torture tools, or at least none that could be seen, but the presence of the solicitor reassured Micky that whilst the solicitor was present, he would not be having his toenails extracted.

Micky told how he had been given a job by the Brit who went by the name of Billy, and although it was a genuine job for which he'd been paid, the offer of follow up work was put to him. He explained that when he turned up to tender for the work at a warehouse at Mullusk, there were four men with long hair in civilian clothing who deliberately exposed weapons, with one of the men setting his pistol on the table before producing a briefcase of money. "There was probably £50,000 in it, and they said it could all be mine, if I would provide information on the RA." I told them I wasn't involved, but they said they knew everything about me and even the money that I owed. They said my access wouldn't matter because I would still be of use to them. I swear to God, they held me against my will and I felt threatened, so I said I would think about it, just to get out of there."

"And did you?" asked Jimmy.

"Did I what?" asked Micky, "Think about it? No, never, I was just glad to get away."

"Did you walk away with a briefcase full of money?"

"Fuck no."

"Then how did you see them again?"

"I told you, they threatened me, they said if I didn't meet them with my answer, then they would spread the word that I was a tout. Which I think they did anyway because people are already talking."

"What I find strange, Micky, is the gossip about you being a tout and spending more than you're making just happens to be when you turn up here pleading a case of no wrong. What else is strange, no bookies around here remember you ever winning large sums of money, but you were still able to pay off £5,000 to that fucker, Pockets McGuire, who you owe a small fortune to. You think the Brits know you, well trust me, we know you better than you know yourself. So, shall we start again? Where did the money come from?"

"They gave me the £5,000 at the meeting and promised more if I worked for them, but like I said, I didn't give them anything, I promise."

Jimmy, who had been standing close to Micky, took a step back and motioned to the heavyweights in the room, mainly Pinkie and Perky, and said, "Get this lying fucker out of here," whilst pointing to the back door.

"Wait…. Wait!" cried Micky, "I seen them once, I told Kieran that earlier, that's when they took me to a house in Castlereagh Hills, it was there they gave me the money, I swear on my mother's grave, it's the truth."

"So, how do you contact them when you need to meet?"

"They gave me a number but I've never used it."

The debrief lasted for several hours, with Micky's life being totally dissected. At the end of the interview, it was decided that Micky would still exit by the rear door but would be staying as a guest of Pinkie in a safe house in Twinbrook until they had a chance to consult with the PAC, the solicitor, and then with operations.

Chapter 44

Bridget

Mary thought she had heard a scream but ignored it, thinking it must have been the kids who were always running up and down the alleyway.

The following morning, she never saw Frankie leave and certainly no taxi had arrived, otherwise she would have heard it. *Dirty stop out,* she thought. *Bridget is playing with fire with that one but hey, I've said my piece.*

Mary still couldn't get her head around what she saw in the creep in the first place. As Mary locked her front door and started to walk down the path, she could hear Bridget's door opening, and Mary, without looking, thought Frankie must be leaving, but it was Bridget's voice that called her. Mary turned to see Bridget standing on the doorstep, dressed in jeans and one of Sean's sweaters. She looked as white as a sheet and asked if Mary had a minute.

"I'm on my way to work Bridget, can it wait until I get home?"

Bridget spoke in a childlike voice and said, "I don't think so, I need your help love."

Mary exited her own path and walked up to Bridget.

"What is it, Bridget?"

"You need to come in."

Mary entered the house and said, "I saw Frankie arrive last night but didn't see him leave this morning, you haven't got him strapped to the bed or something, have you?"" and laughed.

The expression on Bridget's face told Mary that something was seriously wrong.

"Christ what is it Bridget, what's happened? You're frightening me now, what's wrong?"

"I killed the son of a bitch, that's what's wrong. He's up the stairs."

Mary thought, *Christ she shagged him to death, the man had a friggin' heart attack.*

"I put a knife through the fucker's heart. You were right, Mary; he got my Sean killed. Well, he won't be killing anymore, the son of a bitch got what he deserved."

"Holy Mother of God, Bridget, you'll do life for this."

"I don't care, I wanted justice and I got justice."

"Where is he, Bridget?"

"My bedroom, I haven't been up there since last night, but I don't think he's going anywhere."

Mary went up the stairs, almost tiptoeing in case she woke him or something. It was an odd thing to do, but she even creeped along the landing to the open doorway of the bedroom. The naked body of Frankie was still strapped to the bed, with the knife plunged deep into his chest, dried congealed blood around the entry wound and a large blood-stained mass around the body. He was staring at Mary with wide open eyes and blue lips. Mary immediately regretted the joke of him being strapped to the bed.

She returned downstairs where Bridget was sitting at the kitchen table, where she had remained the whole night following her actions, consumed by her own thoughts but no regrets. She was not hunted by demons or tormented by her actions but rather a contentment of sorts. She knew the consequences of her actions, and still, she persisted in committing the act. She planned and executed it exactly as intended. All that remained was for the police to come and arrest her. She had stopped caring. The life she had led following Sean's death was calculated and purely a means to satisfy her desire for revenge, and last night closed that chapter for her. The rest she didn't care about, she simply took solace from knowing Frankie Connolly was dead. Rest in peace, Sean!

Mary first consulted with Jimmy and Kieran, who wanted absolutely nothing to do with what had happened, which Mary found ironic considering how many bodies PIRA managed to make disappear over the years. She then telephoned the police to report the body of Frankie Connolly lying in Bridget's bedroom.

The news was enthusiastically received by the security forces and police alike. The man had been a thorn in their side for many years and always seemed to manage to avoid prosecution despite being linked to dozens of murders himself. It was fitting that he'd suffered an element of torture he himself had inflicted on others. The news was also welcomed by hundreds of his own community, who had endured beatings and his infamous 'Six Pack' shootings.

When the police attended the crime scene, it was deemed, with the best will in the world, Bridget couldn't claim it had been a sex game gone wrong. Not that she had any form of defence or wanted any. Even a Dominatrix who would take the dominant role in BDSM or servitude couldn't explain a knife buried deep in the chest of their sexual partner. Bridget was taken into custody. Mary remained at the property as the police and the forensic team carried out their work. Mary also contacted Billy and told him about the murder.

Billy immediately saw an opportunity to take advantage of the situation. Under the cover of the cordon which had been set up around the house, including the neighbouring properties, an additional four men in white, protective suits entered Bridget's house. They exited via the back door only to enter the kitchen of Mary Sweeney. Billy, Mac, and the two-man team from WIS were able to retrieve the weapons from the hide under Mary's cooker and Jark them.

The hide was indeed an excellent piece of engineering, as previously reported by Mary, with quality concealment. At least her brother Tommy was useful for something. It was a textbook operation, with Mary joking with her handling team about how it was a pleasure to host them in her house instead of them hosting her in a safe house. She even provided tea and biscuits as the team conducted the Jarking. On completion of the work, the team made its way back through Bridget's house, onto the street, and into the white transit van already in situ for their getaway.

The boss was delighted with the operation and telephoned Paul Millar at TCG Belfast, thanking him for his cooperation in securing his teams access to the scene. Billy was congratulated for his quick thinking and for pulling together a successful operation. Once again, Mary had been the star of the show, and high praise was justifiably given.

The body of Frankie Connolly was laid to rest at Milltown cemetery in the republican plot with full PIRA honours and was attended by all the known players from around the country. Seamus did the eulogy and heaped praise on the man like he was some kind of saint, so much so that even those in the congregation looked puzzled, with one woman turning to Mary and asking if she was at the right funeral. For those rank and file of PIRA, it seemed a fitting farewell for a volunteer. A volley of shots had been fired over the open coffin the previous evening by two masked men and posted on the internet.

Roslyn was centre stage of the proceedings, with Liam and Shane by her side. Although visibly upset by the loss of her brother, she was under no illusions that he was malevolent, and she still believed he was responsible for many people's sufferings. Liam, on the other hand, had never liked him, and although not frightened of him, he had adopted a cautious approach when around him. After all, he did have Liam badly beaten. The sad aspect of all of this was that whilst he was rid of one tyrant, there was always another ready to step up as a replacement.

The funeral was followed with drinks at the Shamrock Arms, to which Mary was invited by Roslyn. They did speak, as it was Mary who had been present at Bridget's house on the morning after her brother's death. The whole sordid details of how he met his death were already known, so there was no point in sugar coating the pill. Roslyn found the manner of his death hard to comprehend. Mary did say that Bridget believed Frankie was responsible for Sean's death, and she had been planning it for some time, unknown to Mary.

Chapter 45

Verdict Needed

The meeting had two main points for actioning. The first was to appoint the successor for Frankie, and the second to decide on a course of action for Micky Crawford. Much was made of Frankie's demise, whilst some in the republican movement couldn't comprehend how he thought Bridget Pearse would willingly jump into bed with him. Others knew him as a deviant, who would have got some sort of sick pleasure from sleeping with a dead man's wife and thought it just another level of depravity he would stoop to. An initial thought was one of the Conway twins attempting to take over, but PIRA feared picking one over the other could cause a feud between the brothers, so it was seen as a high-risk strategy and potentially a dangerous manoeuvre. Jimmy Rice was deemed the best successor and although reluctant to take the position, he had already taken the lead role in the questioning of Micky.

Jimmy accepted the role, keeping the twins, Syd Collins, and Liam Murray as his team. Having served a long stretch in H Block and having been a seasoned ASU member, it was time to move up into the very top tier of the organisation and become the head-hunter and enforcer of discipline. Frankie was a big loss, but some of his torture techniques were difficult for even the most hardened to stomach. However, it was Seamus who stated, "What was important now, was finishing the job he had started and find the leak for the Armagh ASU hit." Despite having several reservations, Seamus believed it may have been an Armagh leak, as everyone involved from Belfast had already been questioned and cleared by Frankie.

"With the exception of Mary Sweeney," said Kieran.

"Oh fuck, let's not go there again," said Jimmy. "She is too deeply involved, with fingers in several pies, for her to be a suspect. Frankie had already established she wasn't the leak. For all we know that bitch Bridget Pearse next door could have seen him come and go and reported it. Fuck, it's not like she hadn't got good reason to, we killed her husband for fuck's sake. I'll speak with her, but you're pissing up the wrong tree there. I promise you, if there is a tout out there, I will find them, even if that means starting with everyone in this room. My investigations will be far-reaching and comprehensive."

His words sent shivers up all their spines.

"It's not the Geneva convention here, it's not the Marquis of Queensberry rules, it's now Jimmy Rice's rules."

Seamus interjected, "OK guys, I think you have the right man for the job," and laughed.

"Right, let's turn our attention to Micky Crawford." This part of the meeting got very heated, with Kieran determined to take military action against Micky Crawford's Handlers. He argued for a full-blown operation with every resource at their disposal being used. Seamus and Sinn Fein wanted to exploit it for political gains. Seamus argued for Micky to meet with the Handlers but to expose the whole encounter as the blackmail of a working class catholic by writing their own narrative to suit.

Both factions were poles apart and getting nowhere. A decision was needed and soon. After what seemed an age of arguments and counterarguments, eventually a compromise of sorts was agreed upon. Kieran accepted an agreement to deploy surveillance on Micky and allow him to meet again with his Handlers while following discreetly to observe the Unit's Modus Operandi. It was also discussed to conduct false flagging by giving Micky information to pass that, if exploited, would result in Kieran getting his way and an operation to kill would take place. The only thing everyone was in total agreement on was that Micky should be taken out as well. His release from the Safe House was only to be a stay of execution.

Micky was guarded by members of the security team, who took it in turns to watch over the man. He had already been in their custody for nearly two days and was becoming extremely agitated. He had no contact with anyone on the outside world, and even if he wanted to, he had no means to do so.

Micky regretted going to PIRA and believed he should have had the confidence or conviction to brass out the allegations against him. After all, he didn't think they had any tangible evidence against him in the first place. It was too late now, as he had confessed, and the more he thought about it, the less he could see a successful outcome. Having had the time to reflect, he came to the realisation that as far as the Provos were concerned, he was a "Tout," and touts got nutted. His thoughts turned to Billy and Mac and wondered if they could get him out of this mess. Could he get out of the country with a new identity? First, he would need to get away from his minders and get in contact with Billy.

Liam received a call from Jimmy Rice, telling him to come to a house in Twinbrook. Despite still suffering from his injuries, he made his way to the given address. He was met by Jimmy and shown into the kitchen of the property, where Syd Collins was already present. It was the first he had seen of Syd following his hospital visit.

Syd asked how he was recovering, to which Liam stated he was only in pain when he coughed. "It takes time, Liam, but you'll get there."

"Alright, when you two girls are finished." Both men chuckled and turned to face Jimmy. "Right, we have a tout in the bedroom, and he isn't going anywhere, but he needs round the clock guarding and we are all going to take turns."

Liam was first to complain and state he couldn't do round the clock. "I've a wife and teenage son at home who I never get to see much of as it is. I don't mind doing day shifts but I need to be compensated for the lost revenue from taxiing.'

"You'll be sorted Liam, but I don't expect it to be more than a few days, as there is an Op in the planning to deal with the tout bastard."

Liam was surprised by Jimmy's disclosure, but once again, at least the heat or suspicion wasn't on him. Since his own interrogation and the death of Frankie, he had a newfound belief in his ability as an Agent and PIRA member. He felt more in control and confident but more importantly, he felt trusted by both his PIRA bosses and Handlers alike. He still felt the need to withhold information from his Handlers, having the perception that he could self-protect by distancing himself from certain activities, all this despite being caught out on several occasions.

One such misadventure of his own making was when he'd attended the wedding of Padraic Conway at the Templepatrick Hotel a couple of years back. He was told to produce a list of all the guests following his own disclosure that a couple of OTR's were expected to be in attendance. He was hesitant and kept making excuses of being unable to get a copy.

On the Friday evening before the event, Billy and Mac decided to frequent the hotel in the off chance some of the expected guests could have been staying over. Much to their delight, a large function room had been decorated in preparation for the reception. A comprehensive list of guests detailing the wedding of Mr. & Mrs. Padraic Conway, complete with seating arrangements, was on a metal display stand next to the door of the room. As suspected, a few of the guests using alias profiles were coming across the border to attend.

The detachment knew Liam was more than capable of achieving the list, given his close relationship with the couple. Mac opened the door to the function room and walked around the three sides of an open square table setting and confirmed all the guest names from the small name plates. A mental note of the layout and even the beautiful three-tier cake with its decorative church and iced figures of a Bride and Groom was observed.

Onus on Truths

At the next meeting, Billy raised the issue of the wedding again, and this time Liam did produce a list, which was fairly accurate to Billy and Mac's own observations. However, what took him by surprise was when Billy asked about the day's proceedings and commented on the beautiful cake. Billy was even able to tell him where he was sitting. He believed that he was being watched as proceedings unfolded. It was a bluff, but one that made him sit up and take notice. It didn't do any harm for the CHIS to think the Handlers were always watching him, and therefore the need for him to be honest was essential. The arrest of two PIRA OTR's by the police on the day was an unexpected bonus from the visit and one that could have been missed whilst waiting on Liam to produce the list after the event.

Chapter 46

Parlour visit

Mary was about to leave the office for the day when Kieran O'Kane approached her and asked for a word. Kieran stated that Jimmy had already told her someone would be in touch to get the wee messages out of her kitchen.

"Well, be prepared for a collection very soon."

Mary was only too happy to oblige and hoped that it would be an end to her being a custodian. Although, given she still had a large hole in her kitchen floor, she didn't hold much hope of that being the case.

Mary telephoned Billy and relayed the details of a potential move. She, in return, sought guarantees that nothing would happen in or near her house. Billy gave her the reassurance wanted and told her that no action taken would be attributed to her. Mary mentioned the attendance of Micky Crawford at the Sinn Fein office and asked if they had attempted to recruit him, as she believed that was his reason for being there. Billy stated he remembered Mary mentioning him way back but knew nothing of any recruitment attempt. It was explained it may have been a police operation gone wrong, but either way, she should keep him informed of any developments. Mary told Billy that, following Crawford's visit, a meeting was held at the office with the usual PIRA suspects, including a local Solicitor, Pat Finnigan. From the names given, it was clear to Billy that he must have been interviewed and the presence of the solicitor could only indicate a shit storm was on the horizon.

Billy's analysis of the situation, considering the sensitivities of the broken peace process and issues surrounding decommissioning, was that Sinn Fein would want to conduct a major media propaganda exercise. They would probably promote a public disinformation event in the full view of the press. It was considered that military action by PIRA would be detrimental to Sinn Fein's blueprint or strategy with the British Government.

Billy had tried telephoning Micky as part of his recontact procedure but was unable to get a response. The phone would go directly to voicemail, so no message was left, in case it was being monitored by PIRA. For now, the Agent remained out of contact. Billy wondered if Micky had confessed to PIRA about his involvement with British Intelligence.

Mary, unfortunately, was unable to provide any further clarity on the matter. This was a worrying development, but Billy believed Micky would be unharmed for now. If Sinn Fein were going to go public, then Micky wouldn't be hurt, at least not until after he appeared on the TV. The image of a battered and broken man would only have an adverse effect, and not the desired publicity they craved.

Chapter 47

Safety Measures

Security procedures had been tightened up on each of the Agent's movements and routes considering recent events. Because Liam was driving his own vehicle for the meeting, he used his Counter Surveillance route to ensure he was clear of any IRA surveillance team in the off chance he was under any form of suspicion. The IRA would routinely place members of their active service teams under surveillance just as a safety precaution. He left his home and travelled out onto the A2 Sydenham bypass toward the town of Bangor. He had both an alibi for being where he was and, if seen with his Handler, a solid cover story.

All his movements were monitored by mobile callsigns. Liam continued along his route through a series of choke points to ensure he had not been followed. A short time later, he picked up Billy, who directed him across minor roads to a suitable and secure location, which could not be overseen. Following a radio call informing Billy the area was clear, a quick plate change was completed on Liam's vehicle, with his Taxi sign being removed. A member of the detachment then drove it away to a secure location.

Liam was transferred into the back of a blacked-out vehicle and driven to a Safe House to be debriefed and to cover all the relevant security measures, including his cover story.

Liam updated Billy on the changes following Frankie's murder. He further corroborated what Wee Fern had already reported concerning someone being under suspicion of being a tout but never mentioned who it was by name. He was able to provide the structure changes of the internal security team with Jimmy Rice now at its helm.

Onus on Truths

Once again, Liam had told some truths but not all. He neglected to tell of his babysitting duties for Micky Crawford, although in fairness, he still wasn't aware who he was guarding, but still, he didn't mention the address either. So, whilst Billy was aware a suspected tout was being held in a safe house somewhere in the city, he was still unclear as to who it was and what the location was. If Big Oak was going to be dragged in front of TV cameras, it was hoped either Wee Fern or Weeping Willow would be able to provide a time and place so his movements thereafter could be monitored. It was essential for a surveillance operation to be conducted following the press conference in case a rescue operation was needed to free him.

Liam was not a security risk, but his own insecurities and need for self-preservation led him to always tell half-truths. Although this was a natural, basic instinct for human beings, it appeared Liam was not fully dedicated and loyal to the team. The listening device in his house had not produced anything following the death of Frankie. Meetings were no longer being held there. It was decided the device would be removed at the earliest convenience. Now that Liam was very much an integral part of the internal security team of PIRA, it would be expected he would encounter Micky Crawford, if he was being held, at some point, and it was hoped he would report the matter to Billy. To assist in this, and unknown to Liam, a tracking and listening device were placed on his vehicle as he was being debriefed at the Safe House. If his vehicle was used to transport Micky, then at least any conversations would be monitored.

To date, no information had been forthcoming concerning the exploitation of Micky Crawford by Sinn Fein.

Liam did convey Jimmy Rice's comment about an operation being planned for a tout but knew no further details than that. When questioned as to what sort of operation he meant, political or military, he couldn't say. He didn't even know if the suspected informer was Army or Police. He was instructed to keep his Handler informed of any developments. The need for him to not get personally involved in any punishment or actions in relation to the suspected tout was reiterated. He could not be protected if he knowingly got involved in any action that led to injury or death of another human being. That was why he must report everything.

The meeting was concluded with the reverse procedure to return Liam to his vehicle and subsequent journey back to the city completed.

Billy was told to go to the headquarters and brief the Operations Officer and the security advisor from MI5 on recent developments concerning his cases. It was deemed by the Security Service and the Northern Ireland office that the potential of a political shit storm could hit their desks, considering recent reporting. Each took the view that Sinn Fein were about to cash in on claiming a dirty tricks campaign by the British Government. All this at a time when Sinn Fein were claiming to be working tirelessly to re-establish the peace process, whilst the British Government undermined their efforts by spying and recruiting Agents.

Billy was asked to give his assessment on his recent intelligence reports by Wee Fern and Weeping Willow. Billy was of the view that some sort of exploitation by military means was a real possibility.

The advance warning of a weapons move and the notable absence of Big Oak was causing Billy major concern. The use of the term 'Planned Op' by Jimmy Rice was a strange way to describe a political action to influence Sinn Fein's own narrative. Recent reporting indicated the political wing and the armed wing were not in agreement on many issues. A highly placed Agent within PIRA had already stated many within its ranks were unhappy with Sinn Fein and the soft line of diplomacy being taken. Although happy with the London bombing, they would be happy to return to a full campaign of violence. The fact Sinn Fein hadn't already exploited the situation with Big Oak would suggest they were struggling to impose their influence and gain the leverage needed for a desired result.

The Operations Officer agreed with Billy's analysis of the facts, but still sided with the Security Service and their fear of talks stalling with the Northern Ireland Office should it all go public. The potential damage to the peace process that might be caused due to Big Oak being exposed was uppermost on the security advisor's mind. Strangely though, the same concern did not extend to the possibility of an attempted murder on an operator or CHIS.

The Operations Officer was asked by Billy, "What additional measures were being taken to help locate Big Oak." He was informed every resource at the Units disposal was being utilised. TCG were looking at Special Branch informants for any leads concerning his whereabouts, or for that matter, any other Agents who may be out of contact. The sincerity of the comment gave Billy optimism that a combined endeavour could lead to a positive outcome. Billy asked if any Police informers had gone absent, as they could be blind-sided on this. Billy stated if members of the security team had taken Big Oak somewhere, then it was most likely for interrogation, the Conway twins being at least two of the culprits likely to be connected with his disappearance. He suggested an operation by 14 Int to be mounted on the two brothers. More importantly, Jimmy Rice, being responsible for internal security, would surely have face to face meetings with Big Oak; maybe he should be put under surveillance, as well.

Billy left the headquarters knowing that everything that could be done was, in principle, being done. The one major disappointment was the withholding of information or the lack of endeavour to obtain it by Weeping Willow. It was hoped the listening device placed in his car would reveal something tangible. Not having ever lost a Source/Agent/CHIS, it was unthinkable that it should happen now. The consequences didn't bear thinking about. As far as Billy and Mac were concerned, it was not going to happen on their watch.

Chapter 48

Knock Knock, Who's There?

The knock at the door came just after midnight. Mary, although in bed, wasn't asleep at the time. She had been engrossed in a good book. She got up, and having peered out the bedroom window, couldn't see any vehicles parked at the front. Putting on her dressing gown, she went down the stairs to the front door. She ensured the chain was still on the door and secure in its recess.

Mary opened the door just enough to see who was present.

"Christ Jamie, what the hell, you never said you were coming over tonight."

"I'm sorry Mary, but it's not what you think. Kieran sent me for the wee messages in the kitchen."

"Holy mother of God, not YOU." Mary was lost for words. All this time, and that fucker Jamie was in the RA and she never knew. She was so deep in thought and trying to get her head around it. Even thinking back to when she shouted at him in the kitchen for getting too close to the hide. Had he known the whole time that it was there? She was shaken out of her thoughts by Jamie.

"Mary let me in, for Christ's sake, before the whole street sees me."

Mary undid the chain and opened the door wide enough to let Jamie pass. Jamie walked straight through into the kitchen, but instead of going to the cooker as she expected, he went straight to the back door and unlocked it.

He opened the door, and a man entered who Mary thought looked a bit like Wurzel Gummidge, with a mop of black hair which looked unkempt. He came into the kitchen and closed the door behind him.

"Well, where is it, Mary?" Mary, still in a state of shock, shook her head, unbelieving what she'd heard. *He really didn't know where it was,* she thought. Mary pointed to the cooker, not saying a word. The two men moved the cooker out to gain access. Jamie lifted a teaspoon off the floor before momentarily pausing, then looking at Mary with a sudden realisation of the outburst that had occurred the morning when he dropped it.

The WIS team clearly left it in situ, ensuring they left the Hide exactly as they had found it in case it was a tell-tale sign if tampered with. Mary was unable to prevent the weapons being taken and equally unable to inform Billy of their move, at least for now.

The telephone in the Ops room was picked up by a sleepy operator who was bedded down in the makeshift bedspace. He looked at the wall clock above the large mapping board and it read 02:15am. It was the WIS monitoring team informing him that a device had been triggered. The call was relayed immediately to the boss and the Headquarters duty Watchkeeper. The boss decided all the members of the detachment be called in for a planning meeting and potential deployment.

Jamie had asked the man, who he addressed as Skipp, to place the tartan blanket he had brought into the house and lay it out on the floor of the kitchen. Jamie then removed all the weapons from the Hide. Three AK-47's, a Walther pistol, and ammunition were removed and placed in the blanket. Mary wanted to confront Jamie concerning his involvement, but now wasn't the time. Mary knew better than to ask where the weapons were going but mentioned she hadn't seen a car outside so asked how they intended to move them. Jamie stated they would leave through the back door and be picked up at the end of the alleyway. Jamie commented on how impressed he was by the construction of the hide. He replaced the cover on the now empty hide before moving the cooker back in place.

Mary was still having difficulty comprehending the revelation that Jamie was involved. It had never occurred to her, although she knew he was well known and the bar was used from time to time for PIRA meetings, but it just never entered her mind. What else didn't she know about him?

The two men took their nicely wrapped bundle of weaponry and exited out through the back door and into the night, leaving Mary opened-mouthed and holding a teaspoon.

Billy had been living in one of the Units OCP's with other members of the detachment. It was always policy to have weapons at home for their personal protection. The amount of weaponry and ammunition each operator had at the house could have held off the rebels in Jadotville. The phone on the bedside table rang, and Billy became instantly awake and alert. This was something he had perfected over years of military training. It was the Duty Operator informing him of the boss's decision to rally the troops. No sooner had he got up, he heard the other members of the house rushing around, getting their gear together. Once in the car, he switched on the covert radio, placed his miniature earpiece in, and reported to the Ops Room that he was mobile to Hardcase (a code name for a secure location). The compounds of all the Unit detachments were always located in a secluded part of either Police or Army barracks. It was impossible not to stand out when in or around the camps, as all the operators had longer than average hair, were often unshaven, and drove large cars in and out of these bases.

Billy could hear the other callsigns from the other houses complete their radio checks and make their way to the compound. The journey for Billy took about 30 minutes to complete. He had to make certain that he carried out anti-surveillance to ensure no one was following him from the house. The journey to the detachment passed very quickly with his mind running over the pending operation and thinking about what part he would have to play within it. He was hoping the boss didn't want him to remain in the Ops Room, controlling things on the ground. Although it was vital to the smooth running of the operation, every operator wanted to be at the sharp end on the ground, dealing with the CHIS and the bombs and bullets. As with all operations, his heart was racing and adrenaline was pumping through his veins, yet he was busting at the gut to get going.

The Duty Operator who had received the call was busy prepping the briefing boards and maps needed for the job, tracing the weapons' movements and calculating routes to and from the operations area all being part of his task. Driving into the compound, Billy could see several other members of the detachment were already busy in the stores and armoury, prepping vehicles and weapons for the operation ahead. Despite all the activity, it was still not 5:00am. The night sky had just given way to the first signs of daybreak. However, the detachment was full of activity and couldn't have been more awake.

Preparations complete, everyone was called into the Ops room for briefing by the boss. There was still no certainty of deployment, as the boss liked to remind everyone, The Unit was an Intelligence Collection Agency, not exploitation. They leave that sort of stuff for the boys from the Regiment."

It was not a search and destroy mission but rather a need to establish if Big Oak was the intended target. If so, then once located, they would need to be ready to extract him from his captures following the assault by the SAS or HMSU.

Billy interjected by stating, "This is bigger than that boss, something bigger is going down here. That size arsenal of weapons is not for one man to be nutted. More weapons from elsewhere may also be getting gathered. There is a major operation being planned here, and we still don't know who or what the target is."

The telephone in the secure booth rang, making everyone in the room go silent and turn their attention to the booth. These were the dedicated telephone lines for the Agents. The Duty Operator entered the booth, closing the door behind him, making it secure and silent. He picked up the phone and, after a short moment, indicated for Billy to come to the booth.

It was Mary, she had decided to leave early for work to place the call. It was close to 7:30 am and she half-expected to be leaving a message for Billy not speaking directly to him. She conveyed the information about the weapons move and her relief to no longer be in possession of them. She passed on the names of Jamie O'Connor and Skipp but was unable to provide his real identity. From the description provided and following research by one of the collators on the intelligence database, they identified him as Stephen 'Skipp' McBride.

McBride had served time on the mainland for his part of an ASU who were arrested in a safe house whilst conducting reconnaissance for a bombing campaign in Oxford. They had bomb-making equipment at the house at the time of their arrest. McBride served ten of the eighteen-year sentence before being transferred back to Belfast to serve the remainder of his time. He was released just over two years ago and was an active member of the Belfast Brigade PIRA.

Going by the description given by Liam at the time of the Armagh operation, he was also involved in the transportation of Declan Swan.

It was vital for Mary to keep the office informed of any movement in and out of the Sinn Fein office today and report any suspicious activity, meaning anything out of the normal routine. As always, she promised to do her bit and hung up the phone.

Attention was back on the Ops Room and the assembled operators there. The boss was canvassing the floor for thoughts and ideas on how to proceed. Despite being the boss and in overall control, open dialogue within the detachment was always welcome, and as he always said, no one individual had the monopoly on good ideas. 14 Int were already deployed on the ground but had waited until first light to do so. The secure/secret phone on the Ops desk rang, it was the WIS team, providing an update on the weapons. The cache was still somewhere within the Ardoyne, but none of the main players under surveillance had moved.

Onus on Truths

The HMSU strike team, under the command of TCG Belfast, were on standby to strike once the weapons could be positively identified at a location. It was looking more and more likely they weren't going to deploy. The boss was constantly on the telephone to the Headquarters, and in particular, the Operations Officer, whilst the rest of the detachment retired to the bar/kitchen to consume the bacon and egg rolls prepared by the detachment admin staff.

Just after 9:00 am, a further call was received from Paul Millar at TCG. A strike had been conducted on a house in Butler Street. The HMSU confirmed two males and a female were in the house at the time. The HMSU team stealthily approached the property, determining the back door would be the main point of entry. A team provided cover of the front entrance as the second team quietly approached the rear of the property. On the command of the team leader, a breach of the back door was achieved, with stun grenades being thrown into the kitchen through an open window whilst simultaneously kicking in the kitchen door before the team entered. The ear-piercing and deafening noise caused total confusion and disorientation for the occupants. A female was standing next to a kitchen table, which had a tartan blanket spread out, the weapons on display. She was wearing a pair of latex gloves and holding a pistol in her right hand. Once the effects of sudden deafness and blindness from the stun grenades had subsided, the female turned in the direction of the large black mass of enforcers coming through the door.

The shout by the point man of, "Police stand still!" reverberated around the room.

The female, still facing the rear door, was still holding and pointing the pistol in the entry team's direction. She wasn't given a second warning; the lead man fired his G3 rifle, hitting her squarely in the chest with two rounds. She was catapulted backwards, dropping the pistol as she hit the cooker with tremendous force before sliding down to the floor, leaving large, crimson streaks of blood smeared on the white, enamel surface. Stepping over the body, the team continued with their search and clearance by moving from the kitchen into the main hall. The first man into the hall encountered Skipp McBride halfway along the hallway, caught in the dilemma of which way to run in search of an escape route. He was unarmed and disorientated, but for reasons best known to himself, attempted to run directly at the team instead of lying down on the floor as instructed. He was met by two heavy set HMSU officers and the butt of a G3 rifle to the forehead, which rendered him prone on the floor. He was quickly restrained and cuffed.

The search of the house continued with a cautious but meticulous examination from room to room. It was in the back bedroom of this two-bedroom house that Jamie O'Connor was found cowering in the bottom of an old, outmoded wardrobe. He had made a feeble attempt to cover himself with clothing in his struggle to evade capture. He was promptly arrested and taken into custody.

It was a great result for the security forces, with two active ASU members in custody and a female ASU member killed in possession of a pistol. The female, Martina McIntyre, was also a member of the Oxford ASU and had served time on the mainland, although she was later released and returned to the province. She had remained an active and loyal member of PIRA and had been wanted by the security services for a long time. Belfast was a safer place today than yesterday, with someone having had a reprieve on their life due to the planned PIRA operation being thwarted.

The success of the operation was down to excellent cooperation between the various specialist units. The news was received with utter delight back at the detachment, another couple of faces on the montage board receiving an X through them. It was a victory, but there were a lot more terrorists on the streets who needed to answer for the atrocities they had committed.

Attention was turned back to the detachment's priority: that of Micky Crawford. There was still no information of his whereabouts or indeed his wellbeing. Focus needed to be centred on establishing his reasoning for being out of contact. There were differing opinions in the detachment concerning his plight. Some were of the opinion he was just out of contact by his own volition. Maybe Mary had got his reason for being at the Sinn Fein offices wrong. He wasn't due to be met for another week, so maybe Billy was being oversensitive about it. After all, Liam had been taken, interrogated, and survived. The other element of doubt was the lack of information from Weeping Willow as to the identity of the tout being held.

Mary was disappointed to hear it was Jamie O'Connor that had been arrested for the weapons cache but relieved he hadn't been shot and killed at the property. However, as for Martina, she was a ruthless, cold-hearted bitch, and as far as Mary was concerned, it was no loss.

Mary thought, *now I have someone else other than Tommy to visit at the Maze. He would no doubt keep everyone in prison entertained with his renditions of Elvis Ballad's. If she could think of a song fitting for Jamie to sing, it would be 'Jail House Rock.'*

She would also have to visit Bridget at some point at HMP Magilligan Prison, County Londonderry.

Chapter 49

Caught Out

Liam was due to meet with Billy in just over two hours and was looking forward to discussing the recent developments in his access. However, whilst taxiing, he happened to hit a speed ramp outside the grounds of St. Mary's school and dislodge his exhaust. He took the car to a small garage just off the Falls Road in the hope of getting a quick repair. He believed it would only take a few minutes, therefore was still expecting to get to his meet with Billy on time.

The vehicle was put up on the ramp, and to his horror, the owner, a man by the name of Seamus pointed out a tracking device concealed between the exhaust and body of the vehicle. Liam was furious and immediately pointed the finger of blame at Billy and Mac. After gathering his thoughts, he went to a phone box to telephone the detachment and stated he had car trouble and wouldn't be able to make the meeting but asked for it to be rescheduled. He never mentioned the tracker, as he wanted time to figure out what needed to be done. He felt betrayed and was becoming hostile to the extent of belligerence and wanting revenge. All these years, and this was how he was being treated.

They were spying on the spy, for Christ's sake.

He knew he hadn't always been truthful, but it was only to protect himself. He had passed lifesaving information time and time again. The more he thought about it, the angrier he became. What else were they up to?

Following the find, he decided to have the car searched and was horrified to discover the listening device inside the dashboard. He wondered if any incriminating conversations had been overheard that could be exploited and used against him. The magnitude of betrayal he was feeling was enormous.

Fuck you Billy, he thought, *I'll show you.*

Liam, having thought through his options, went to Jimmy Rice, told him of the findings and explained it must have been because of his association with Frankie Connolly that the police were targeting him, and somehow, whoever they were had gained access to his vehicle to place the devices. He asked Jimmy what he should do. Jimmy needed to consult with Kieran and company but assured Liam he had nothing to worry about, and he had done the right thing coming forward. Liam thought he didn't really have a choice, as Seamus, the mechanic, had already seen the devices, so not reporting it would have been a red flag. Whatever the outcome, he decided, Billy had brought it on himself.

As the peace process had ultimately broken down, and the London Docklands bombing had signalled an end to much of the negotiations, everyone at the PAC meeting decided, much to the delight of Kieran O'Kane, though not to Sinn Fein, that Belfast Brigade PIRA could plan and conduct a military operation against the Brits. What it needed now was a good plan and a crack team to conduct it. Jimmy was asked by Kieran to make his team available to carry out the mission. After much discussion, including the new revelation of the listening device in Liam Murray's car, various options could be exploited. Should they use the listening devices to set up whoever planted them or should the tout in custody be used to set up the Brit Handlers? It was decided the latter be done; therefore, Micky Crawford was brought to a meeting and told the only way for him not to be nutted for his crimes against PIRA was to play a part in an abduction of his Handler.

Chapter 50

Burning Ash: No regrets

Barra O'Neil, or 'Burning Ash', was in the process of locking up the Snooker Hall when he noticed Kieran O'Kane across the road talking to two men. He approached just as the men were walking away. He asked Kieran if he could have a word. Barra, a habitual smoker, no sooner had thrown his butt on the ground that he lit up another cigarette. Kieran smiled at Barra, and before Barra could continue, offered his condolences for the loss of his daughter.

"You're not looking too bright Barra, what's wrong, are you OK?"

Barra responded, "Not really Kieran, I was diagnosed with terminal lung cancer shortly after we buried our Kathleen."

"Jesus that's terrible Barra, so sorry to hear that."

"Listen Kieran, that's the reason I want to talk to you, you know it was the Brits that killed my little girl." He went on to recite what had happened, even though Kieran was aware of the incident because it had caused major riots on the streets for several nights.

Young Kathleen had been coming home from school and making her way to the Snooker Hall to meet her dad. As she was crossing the road, she was struck by an Army armoured land rover as it sped out of the Springfield Road Police Station on route to an incident. At least, that was the reason given to the family at the time.

"I've never gotten over it, and I now know I never will, because I'll be joining her soon enough."

"So sorry to hear that Barra, what can I do for you?"

Onus on Truths

"Well, it's more about what I can do for you. I don't care anymore, and I want revenge on the Brits that did that to my little girl."

Barra started to explain about the recruitment of him as an Agent. He was expected to spy on the lads who used the snooker hall. Kieran stopped him and stated he was going to need to speak about this in private and not on the street. He suggested they meet at another time and place, which needed to be decided, then they could thrash it out together.

Christ, Kieran thought, *is the whole of Belfast touts?*

Kieran had the discussion with Barry and Jimmy before deciding to get Barra in for a chat.

At the meeting, Barra came clean and told them everything about how he was approached in the Snooker Hall by two men who stated they were conducting research into the demographic trend of the city and the economic impact of the Troubles on local businesses. They stated it was a yearlong study and wanted to conduct a series of interviews with him during that period.

"They always arrived when I was least busy and therefore able to converse with them. It was always cordial and I never saw any harm in it." Barra couldn't recall how the subject had changed from demographics to local personalities, but at some stage and over the course of several months of interviews, he was cultivated and accepted their request to report on people who frequented the place. Barra continued by stating how plausible they were, and he never for a minute thought they were Military Intelligence until it was too late. But now, he just wanted revenge and didn't care about the consequences from PIRA or the Brits for being a tout. He stated he could arrange to meet with the Brits and hurt them for what they did.

Kieran was of two minds as to what should happen to Barra O'Neil. In one aspect, he was a tout and needed sorting. On the other, the man had suffered the death of his daughter and then been diagnosed with cancer. Kieran felt sympathy for all of thirty seconds before concluding that the bastard needed sorting, but the question

Hamilton Spiers

was how to exploit the situation. This just added another dimension to their options for exploitation.

The death of Barra O'Neil's daughter was tragic, and the condemnation was swift, followed by PIRA orchestrated riots. There were no such condemnations or riots following the death of a soldier stationed in the Springfield Road Police Station on the 25 May, 1971. Sergeant Michael Willets, a 27-year-old member of the Parachute Regiment was on duty in the main reception area of the police station. A suitcase containing a 30lb blast bomb was thrown into the reception area. The room had several civilians sitting inside, including two young children. On seeing the bomb, Sergeant Willets realised what was about to happen. In the words of the song by Harvey Andrews, 'He knew the bomb had seconds and not minutes on the fuse'. He thrust the children into a corner and used his body as a shield to protect them and their parents. He was killed instantly but saved the lives of the civilians. He paid the ultimate sacrifice. Sergeant Willets received the George Cross posthumously for his heroism in saving their lives.

Chapter 51

Time to Act

Billy received the telephone call from the Agent requesting an emergency meet. He stated he had vital intelligence to pass that was of life and death importance. It was great the Agent was back in contact with the office and willing to meet. The operation was planned for later that afternoon. It allowed time for the other members of the detachment to complete the ongoing meet of another detachment Agent and be available for Billy's operation.

Barra O'Neil had been taken to a safe house until a decision was made on a course of action. Having already received the blessing from the PAC for military action to take place, Kieran felt that having another tout just strengthened his case for exploitation. The only dilemma was who to use to expose the Brits, Barra O'Neil or Micky Crawford? A plan was decided upon, with a team of five being assembled at the safe house.

Liam was in the lounge when he heard a female voice at the front door talking to Kieran. For a moment, he thought he recognised the voice. He went to the window and glanced out as he heard the door close and saw the back of the woman walking away from the house, pushing a pram. His attention was brought back to the room as Kieran entered and instructed Liam and Syd to commandeer a vehicle. They were told to ideally get a people carrier, which would have the seats removed for easy access. It would be used as a getaway car. Pinkie was instructed to get a transit van, then both vehicles were to be taken to Mulligan's scrap yard and prepared for the operation. Jimmy Rice was to source three longs (AK-47's), two shorts (pistols), and four walkie-talkies. The assembled team, having received their instructions, were despatched to obtain the equipment. Who or what the target might be was not divulged to the team. They had been told to report back to Kieran once everything was in place. Kieran was determined to lead this Op and was equally determined for it to end in someone's death.

Liam was in a difficult predicament. On one hand, he needed to tell Billy of the intended Op, but on the other, he was still furious at being bugged. He still had a nagging doubt it could have been the police who had planted the devices. Kieran never named or gave any indication who the operation was being conducted against, so maybe it was totally unrelated to a tout. There were still too many loose ends. So, in the end, he decided he should wait until more details were known before informing Billy.

The procurement of the vehicle was easy enough. A family from the Cavehill area gave up the ownership of their Renault Espace people carrier with a little encouragement from Liam and Syd Collins. They drove it to the scrap yard as instructed.

The Espace, along with a white transit van, were parked inside a large, corrugated workshop and left with Patrick Mulligan. Micky was told he would be taken to a secure location to make a telephone call to his Handler and arrange the meet. He would state he had life or death information and needed to see him urgently. Once he knew where the meeting was to take place, an operation would be mounted to abduct the Handler by Micky pulling a gun on him. Once he was in the vehicle and had the Handler under control, he was to get him to follow a white transit van to a designated location. Once there, the team would drag the Brit from the car and Nutt him. It was all very simple really.

"Do as you are instructed and you're off the hook. If he has back-up, then there will be another team in wait to take them out when they arrive on the scene. All that's left is to make the call."

Micky was told to get ready to go.

Barra O'Neil was told he needed to make a telephone call to his Handler asking to meet as well. Although he hadn't met in a long time, the call would be welcomed. Barra was told to state he had life or death information to pass and needed to meet urgently. He was told he would have his revenge on the Brit and would be given a pistol with which to do it. He was informed if he was really determined to go through with it, then he should shoot him once inside the car. He would then be picked up by the getaway car. Barra was then led back to his room.

Pinkie knocked on the bedroom door and stated it was time to make the call. The man exited the room and was halted at the top of the landing, where a hessian bag was placed over his head.

"It's a safety measure to protect the safe house, you can take it off soon enough," said Pinkie.

The Agent walked behind Pinkie with his hands on his shoulders as they went down the stairs to the kitchen. The house was quiet and appeared void of any people. He was taken to the back door and told he needed to get out to the car via the alleyway, where someone was waiting for him to make the call, which needed to be recorded. He was also informed that the person in the car would give him the pistol for the operation. He was taken through the back gate and ushered along the alleyway. He could just make out the sound of a vehicle's engine ticking over as he moved along the alleyway. With his head bent toward the ground, he was able to have a limited view of his feet through the slackly secured sack on his head as he shuffled along the wet cobbled pathway. He walked past and over discarded rubbish and dog droppings which he was trying hard to avoid stepping in. It took all his concentration to navigate along the narrow gap of the alleyway whilst maintaining a hold of Pinkie's shoulders. Suddenly, Pinkie stopped abruptly, with the Agent bumping into his back. He no longer had a grip on Pinkie's shoulders. He reached out, feeling for the shoulders once supporting his forward movement but felt nothing but an abyss. There was a noise of what appeared to be approaching feet. Suddenly, the hessian sack was removed from his head and he froze, looking in disbelief at the two figures in balaclavas directly in front of him whilst trying to figure out where they had come from. It mattered not, both figures were pointing pistols at him. A voice from behind the balaclava spoke in an authoritative voice stating, "Barra O'Neil, in the name of the Irish Republican Army, you are hereby sentenced to death."

The Agent was shot at point blank range in the head. The two men turned, exited the alleyway, and made their escape in the Combi Van which had been parked at the end of the alleyway with its engine ticking over. Pinkie came back out of the rear yard, where he had retreated, too. He entered the alleyway, stepping over the body, making his way back to the safe house.

The knock on the bedroom door was answered by Micky. The voice on the other side said, "It's time to go and make that call."

The Agent left the bedroom and was escorted out from the house to a waiting car.

He was driven to another part of the city, where he was accommodated, fed, and prepared for the operation ahead. The telephone call was placed to the detachment, detailing the importance of meeting with lifesaving information that needed to be passed. A walking route Codenamed 'The Embankment' was given to the Agent, which was familiar to him. This information was passed to Kieran O'Kane, covering the route in its entirety and its likely pick-up points.

The ASU assembled at the new location, as the original safe house was deemed too close to the killing of the Agent that morning. A female in her late 30's was already in the house, and Kieran was able to brief her prior to the other members' arrival. As soon as Jimmy arrived with all the weaponry and equipment for the operation, the female was issued with a walkie-talkie, with Jimmy carrying out a radio check before she left the house. The news hadn't yet reported the body found in the alleyway. Kieran hoped it would break soon, as most of the security force's attention would be drawn away from the Markets and Ormeau Road area to focus on the killing.

Padraic Conway and Syd Collins arrived together, both having been freshly showered, dressed, and forensically cleansed. Padar was already in situ, having brought Micky to the new location. The only member of the team still to arrive was Liam Murray. Time was of the upmost importance, and for the operation to work, detail planning needed to be thrashed out now. Ideally, it would have been better to have a few days to work on the plan, but the importance placed on the meet meant it needed to be actioned right away.

Kieran stated he wasn't waiting any longer for Liam, and he could be briefed by Jimmy on his part later. Detailed tasks were given to each member with Micky, being separated from the meeting, having already been told of his involvement. Syd Collins was given the task as driver of the transit van, which was to intercept the Handler's car. It was stressed the importance to trap the vehicle in so the attack on the Brit could be executed. Kieran was to be the Passenger of the van and would take on the responsibility of killing the Brit. Pinkie and Perky were to be in the rear of the van, and their role was to protect Kieran but also to take out any cover teams the Handler had deployed on the ground. Each of the three would have AK-47's, with Kieran having a pistol.

Jimmy was to follow the Agent along with the female and keep Kieran informed of his progress. Several positions along the Agent's route had been earmarked as RV Points. It was decided as soon as the Agent entered the vehicle, the attack needed to begin. It was to be fast and explosive, ensuring the death of the Handler. The issue of weapons, balaclavas, clothing, and gloves were given to each man. The briefing of the death squad was just finishing when Liam arrived and apologised for his lateness, stating he had been down to Dublin Airport that morning and had done everything in his power to get back on time, but roadworks on the A1 sent him on a long diversion around Newry. Kieran interjected and said, "Alright, forget it, we're done here, Jimmy will brief you and just make sure you get there on time, OK."

"Where on time?" asked Liam.

"Jimmy, speak to him for fuck's sake."

Liam was instructed to go and pick up the car from Mulligan's scrap yard and then pick Jimmy up and take him to the city centre. He was issued with a walkie-talkie and told, when the time came, he would be instructed to pick up the lads.

"Yeah, but what's going down Jimmy? I'm in the dark here."

"Just get the fucking car and I'll brief you on route."

As Liam was heading to the Scrapyard, the news on the radio reported a body had been shot and dumped in an alleyway in the Twinbrook area. Liam stopped at the phone box and telephoned the detachment. He reported he believed a tout had been executed. He further stated that a planned Op was being carried out but he wasn't aware of the circumstances yet. He knew he was going into the city centre but would try and telephone again once he became better informed.

Billy had already deployed out on the ground when Liam telephoned, with the duty operator taking the call. No sooner had Liam hung up when the line rang again. This time, it was Mary, stating she had heard the news about the killing, believing it must have been Micky Crawford. She also believed something was in the pipeline, as everyone at the Sinn Fein offices were acting strange, with closed door sessions combined with the absence of Kieran and Jimmy, who would normally have been involved.

The duty operator reported to the boss that both Weeping Willow and Little Fern had reported they believed an operation was in the planning but didn't have any further details yet. The team on the ground was warned to be extra vigilant. It was decided to wait for Weeping Willow to get back in touch, as he would be best placed to report.

Billy and the team knew of the killing but without confirmation as to who it was, the operation needed to continue believing the worst case: a no show of the Agent. Although the focus had been on Micky Crawford, it could have been anyone killed, including a Police informant.

Liam picked Jimmy up and was directed to the Markets area. He continued to pump Jimmy for information. Jimmy explained Liam's role, once radioed by either himself or Kieran, was to enter the Ormeau Road and effect the pickup. It would become evident where the boys would be, and he was to ensure they got away from the area, as the van was to be abandoned. He was not told the target but knew it was to be a hit on the military. Liam was desperately trying to remember if there was a barracks or similar target on the Ormeau Road but couldn't think of any viable targets.

Jimmy went to hand Liam a pistol to go with the walkie-talkie but was rebutted with Liam saying, "What the fuck Jimmy, if I'm only driving, I don't need that."

"It's in case it gets mucky, you might need it."

Liam refused to take it off Jimmy, stating, "I've never even used one." Jimmy exited the vehicle and walked to the end of the street, taking up a position with views along the lower Ormeau Road.

The transit van stopped, and the Agent alighted the rear of the vehicle before it moved off. The Agent was left in the street, turning both ways in the attempt to orientate himself to the ground. He made one final pat on his pocket to ensure the pistol was there and secure. He identified St. Malachy's Church behind him. He then walked along Henrietta Street toward the Lower Ormeau Road. He checked his watch and was satisfied he was on time. As he approached the Lower Ormeau Road, he noticed a Renault Espace people carrier parked at the side of the road with its engine running but no driver. As he turned onto the Ormeau Road, he could see Jimmy Rice lurking in a doorway of a shop as he passed.

The road was busy, with fairly heavy traffic and lots of pedestrians. A female pushing a pram was paying a little too much attention to him as he crossed over to the left side of the road. She was leaning down toward the pram but appeared to be looking at him while seemingly talking to a baby.

Liam got back into the car, totally out of breath, having just returned from the nearby telephone box. He had phoned the detachment, and in a state of panic told the duty operator that "It's happening now on the Ormeau Road. I can't talk, I've got to go," and hung up.

Jimmy was reporting the progress of the Agent as he walked his route, with additional commentary coming from the female. Kieran's voice would come on the air, but he was selective when he spoke so as not to jam up the airways.

Billy heard the first reported sighting of the Big Oak as he made progress on his route. The radio signal was weak and intermittent between the team and the Ops Room, so one of the callsigns suggested the team change their channel from the Unit's main radio base station to a car-to-car relay system in order to have better communications for the pickup. This meant they would be briefly out of contact with their Ops Room and the duty operator during the pick-up phase of the operation. All callsigns acknowledged and changed channels.

A warning was given of a man some 100 meters behind the Agent, who appeared to be lurking yet was focused on the road ahead. The cover team did another sweep of the road, but the individual in question was no longer holding down the position in the doorway. There were numerous people on the road and trying to differentiate between friend or foe was difficult.

Following the call from Weeping Willow, the duty operator tried to establish comms with the team but had to opt for trying to get Billy on his mobile to get him to abort the operation, as it was a setup.

As Big Oak walked toward the end of the street, the words of Kieran were still uppermost in his mind.

"Be confident and stay focused, it will all be over soon enough."

The last few days had been a living hell, with the constant threat of being 'Nutted' hanging over him. During his captivity, he'd tried numerous times to get along with his minders, hoping for leniency, but calls through the locked door got no response, there was no interaction between them. The only way out of this mess was to do as he was told and comply.

Onus on Truths

*How did it get to this poin*t, he pondered, *and how could I have been so foolish?* His Handler had always emphasised the importance of his cover story and the need to be security aware. 'Loose talk kills,' was always a phrase used by his handling team. He now realised he had panicked because of stupid rumours, but if he was honest, his compulsion to gamble is what had caused his demise.

The sound of his heart beating in his chest like a Lambeg drum was causing his anxiety levels to rocket. He could not see any way out of this. Did the Duty Operator suspect something was up when he made the call? Did he pick up on his nervousness? The call itself seemed to come as a relief for the handling team. During his detention, he'd overheard something about a killing to take place. Little did he know that at the time he was making the call, the killing was already in the execution phase. Then again, his call had been scripted for him by Kieran.

His work for British Military Intelligence was to be short lived. Even if he managed to capture his Handler, he would be a wanted man by the security forces. This was a no-win situation. He thought hard about which was the better of the two evils. He could always escape to the safe haven of the South or be whisked away with a new identity to England by the Brits. He decided it was the Brit who would die. Afterall, Kieran promised him redemption.

He had been handed the pistol, which he took without checking and placed into his coat pocket, but his constant patting of his coat ensuring its presence was unnerving him. He kept thinking to himself over and over again, *Just get Billy to follow the white van, that's all I need to do.*

The further he got along his route, the more nervous he became. He was constantly on the lookout for any cars that could be watching him but couldn't identify any. As he reached the Sean Graham bookmakers, he almost had a compulsion to enter. He looked up at the shop sign before turning back to see a car pull up beside him.

The final clearance was given to Billy to conduct the pickup.

Liam had been listening to the progress but still wasn't totally aware of who or what the target was. Kieran radioed, telling his team he was moving closer, as the traffic was heavy and the Agent was already halfway up his route. Just then, Jimmy came up on the walkie-talkie telling them that a silver VW Estate had just pulled up alongside the Agent.

Big Oak immediately recognised Billy as the driver who was waving through the passenger door window toward him. He instinctively raised his own hand in acknowledgement, realising he was at the point of no return. He could feel the blood drain from his face, and he became lightheaded as he opened the car door to get in.

Billy looked at him, and he could see from Billy's expression, he was questioning his demeanour. Micky panicked and immediately went for the pistol. He could see Billy asking him something, but he was so transfixed on getting the pistol out that he never heard the words. He felt the blow to the side of his head and stars appeared in front of his eyes as his head banged against the door frame.

The sound of a mobile phone going off could be heard as he screamed out in pain before seeing the butt of a pistol hitting him squarely on the forehead and then nothing but blackness.

Kieran acknowledged the call from Jimmy and told Syd to get the boot down.

"I can't, look at the traffic."

"Fuck the traffic, overtake we can't miss this."

Syd pulled the van's steering wheel hard right and accelerated, overtaking all the traffic in the left lane. Pinkie and Perky were thrown about like rag dolls in the back before being catapulted to the back of the vehicle on impact of the van colliding with the Handler's car.

Following the collision of the two vehicles, Kieran screamed at Syd to come round to his side of the van and make sure the tout didn't get out of the car. At the same time, he climbed out onto the footwell and turned his body so he could engage the occupants of the car.

Syd grabbing his AK-47, exited the van, and moved round to the front of the vehicle. He could see a car come to a halt directly in front of him and two men dressed in civilian clothes exiting with machine guns. He fired his AK-47 toward them, but he could see he never hit his intended targets. The returned fire was much more accurate and conclusive. Syd Collins lay dead on the road.

Kieran heard the burst of fire and the thud of Syd Collins's body being catapulted against the front of the van. The impact made Kieran lose his grip, but he quickly regained his balance whilst searching the interior of the car for his targets through the windscreen. He pointed his pistol in the direction of the vehicle, more in expectation than judgement, and fired indiscriminately into the car. He tried to gain a better view from his position of the potential carnage he hoped he had caused. In doing so, he gave Billy a partial view of his torso and head.

As if in slow motion, the windscreen was giving way to tiny projectiles, which stuck his body and head. He felt the impact on his upper body and was in freefall when further rounds from Billy's pistol struck his head, ending his time on earth.

Having got back to their feet in the rear of the van, the Conway twins could hear the rounds reverberating around them. Pinkie pulled up the shutter door as Perky jumped down, looking to engage the Brit cover team. By the time he had scanned the street, the two members of the cover team were already approaching the rear of the van.

Perky, hearing a cry of, "Army!" turned in the direction of the voice, raising his AK-47. Before he had the chance of firing the weapon and endangering the lives of the numerous civilians, the operator fired his pistol with two well aimed shots, killing him.

Pinkie was engaged before he had a chance of exiting the vehicle. Unfortunately, the contraction following the bullet's impact caused him to involuntary squeeze the trigger of his rifle, resulting in bullets hitting neighbouring buildings.

Jimmy Rice, at the outset of the exchange of gunfire, was already running in the opposite direction and radioing Liam to get mobile and rescue the ASU.

Liam, who was totally unsighted to the main event unfolding, put the car in gear and, at speed, came onto the Ormeau Road, narrowly missing a panic-stricken woman who was franticly trying to push a pram across the road. For a split second, he thought he recognised the women but was too engrossed in his pursuit to give it any more thought.

As he approached the scene, it resembled a traffic accident devoid of witnesses. Liam could just make out a motionless body in a seated position against the inner wall of the van. Liam came to a halt as two men in civilian clothing and wearing baseball caps with ARMY in large letters across the front turned in his direction.

Liam panicked, and in doing so, slipped his gear. In his haste to correctly select reverse, he carelessly selected a forward gear, shooting forward toward the Army operator. Identifying the action as aggressive and believing this to be a follow up attack, the operator fired two shots into the vehicle, hitting Liam in the chest. As he was losing consciousness and struggling for breath, he thought he saw Mac moving up the side of the van as his head came to rest on the steering wheel.

Chapter 52

The aftermath

Jimmy Rice watched as the events unfolded from the safety of a doorway further down the road. He struggled to comprehend the furiousness and skillset of the under-cover soldiers and how accurate they had been in the killing of the ASU. His men had come up against an extremely well-trained elite force. All that was left for him to do was to get out of there before further security forces and police turned up. The only solace he could take from this was he was pretty sure the tout and Handler had been killed. The objective of the mission had been achieved but at a high price.

The death of five ASU members would send shockwaves through the republican community. *Christ, the repercussions from this are going to be enormous,* he thought.

The female surveillance pram pusher, Kira Duffy, was only too grateful the idiot in the Renault Espace never took her out in her haste to get away from the area.

As she made her way back from the Ormeau Road, she vowed never to get involved in anything like that again. She was told she was only following a man and needed to report on his progress, she certainly didn't expect to be mixed up in a shootout at the O.K. Corral. She was shaking uncontrollably and fighting back tears before being totally overcome with emotion. She had to sit down on a doorstep in University Street and weep uncontrollably.

Chapter 53

Post Op reaction

The cordon went in around the contact site with the QRF securing the scene. The body was removed from the car and placed into a body bag on the footpath. Mac was standing at the side of the car. His HK-53 was slung by his side, his hands covered in blood. He watched intently as the paramedics worked in the cramped confines of the vehicle.

The recovery team of mechanics from the Unit's headquarters arrived to recover CT2's vehicle on a flatbed as the rounds that impacted had hit the radiator, rendering the vehicle immobile.

Weapons had been recovered and bagged as the crowds reappeared from their safe havens to leer and shout abuse at the soldiers and police keeping them at bay.

The four men in balaclavas were arranged in body bags and placed in the back of a mortuary van. Two paramedics were at the side of the Espace carrying out CPR on Liam. The mortuary men lifted the body bag off the pavement when Mac stopped them and said, "His name is Micky Crawford." He then turned his attention back to the car and said to the medic, "How's Billy doing?"

The medic, without looking up, said to Mac, "Its touch and go."

A helicopter landed on the grounds of Ormeau Park, and Billy was flown to the military wing of Musgrave Park hospital, where Army surgeons were waiting to operate in the bid to save his life. Liam Murray was taken to Royal Victoria Hospital by the ambulance crew escorted by police, also in critical condition.

Chapter 54

24 hours earlier

"I don't care Jimmy, both touts must die, and before you start, I know the circumstances with the daughter, and I feel for him, but he's a tout."

Jimmy retorted, "Kieran, I understand, but the dilemma is, who is best sorted to set up the Brit? For what it's worth, it must be Micky Crawford because he has operational experience and he can handle a gun."

"Does it fuckin matter? There won't be any bullets in it anyway."

"It will matter if he points the fuckin' wrong end at him."

Both men argued back and forward and debated the pros and cons of the situation. The deciding factor was the reduced chance of anything going wrong if Micky went, as Barra O'Neil wasn't even sure if he would recognise the Handler who would pick him up.

"So, it's decided then, Micky Crawford it is."

Kieran laid out the plan, explaining Barra needed to be taken out of the safe house and nutted. As soon as it was done, the safe house needed to be binned and the team move back to the Ardoyne before the place became a cluster of cops. It was also decided that Syd and Perky would do the nutting but needed to get back in time for the Op. Kieran said to Jimmy, "I'm leading this to ensure we get the Brit and that tout Crawford."

Chapter 55

Fake News

Mary was watching the small TV in the Sinn Fein Office as the news broke. The news team reports showed the aftermath of the incident from their vantage point on the roof of broadcasting house. Their reporters were quickly on the scene, trying desperately to fashion their own narrative and headlines. It was reported that undercover soldiers thought to be the SAS had intercepted an armed gang in the process of conducting a robbery on Sean Graham Bookmakers, putting members of the public in danger, who were caught up in the crossfire. It further reported that two men in a car had been engaged, with one being killed and one airlifted to hospital, both thought to be undercover soldiers.

Another civilian in a silver Renault Espace was caught up in the crossfire, whose condition was still unknown. Four members of the gang were believed to have been killed. It was reported as the bloodiest day in Belfast since the breakdown of the negotiations between Sinn Fein and the British Government.

Mary was desperate to phone the detachment and get an update but had to remain in the office at the request of Seamus and Barry.

Jimmy Rice arrived at the Sinn Fein office in an agitated state. He went straight into the kitchenette and downed a pint of water without taking a breath. Seamus and Barry came rushing out to meet him. Mary had come out behind them and was surprised when she wasn't asked to leave the vicinity. This was a new acceptance level and one she knew would please Billy.

Jimmy ran through the operation, highlighting the swiftness of the Brit teams and the ease with which they'd wasted the ASU. He kept heaping credit on the Brits action until Seamus stated he needed to get a grip and slow down before he hyperventilated. Jimmy explained it was obvious they should never have gone after them in that way, but Kieran had been insistent and look what it got him.

Seamus knew the political fallout of the operation would be massive. He stressed the importance to regroup and lick their wounds.

"Right then, you need to get your cover story in place Jimmy." He then turned to Mary and said, "Jimmy was with you this afternoon, helping to rearrange the office OK.?"

"Yeah sure," said Mary, accepting this as further validation of her worth to them. Mary, deciding to take a risk but being careful to choose her words prudently asked, "Which volunteers did we lose today?" All three men turned their heads in her direction. By using the term "We," she was portraying empathy for their dead comrades and hoping to ingratiate herself with her bosses. It seemed to have the desired effect, with Jimmy telling her the names of Kieran, the Conway twins, Syd Collins, and Liam Murray, although he was still alive when taken away in an ambulance, but it didn't look good. The tout, Micky Crawford, had died in the Brits car.

Mary tried not to look shocked, but she had believed Micky Crawford had been killed that morning in an alleyway in Twinbrook. *If it wasn't Micky, then who was it?* she thought. Mary didn't dare ask who the man in Twinbrook was for fear of being seen to be too inquisitive. She had survived this long right under the noses of PIRA and Sinn Fein, so she needed to remain close to them but not be over keen, which could raise their suspicions. After all, she had a brother and a boyfriend both serving time in the H Block for the cause. She felt her position was secure, but she still needed to be cautious.

Mary walked past them and put fresh coffee on, then asked if there was anything she could do to help.

"Thanks Mary, but we just need to get this storm behind us. You will probably have to deal with the numerous calls and enquiries coming into the office with this. In fact, you can come with me when I visit the families of the dead volunteers," said Seamus.

Chapter 56

The Detachment

The detachment was coming to terms with the day's events, which wasn't helped by the ridiculous reporting by the News Channels of the incident. To lose an Agent was devastating, but to also have an operator in critical condition and still in an operating theatre was overwhelming. The reports indicated a team of surgeons were working frantically to save his life.

Mac had just finished being debriefed by the powers that be, including the legal advisor from the Military. The telephone call received from Micky Crawford requesting the meeting was received with relief that he hadn't been 'Nutted.' But despite the best efforts of Weeping Willow to forewarn his Handlers, the decision to change radio channels at the precise moment the duty operator was trying to warn them was a tragic set of circumstances made all the worse when Billy was unable to answer his phone resulting in the injuries to Billy and Weeping Willow.

Mac knew the inquiry into the incident would be a long and painful ordeal for the Unit. Individual training records would be securitised. Endless interviews under caution and the call from the Liberals and Sinn Fein asking why they couldn't simply arrest the terrorists—the old argument of the Army's "Shoot to Kill" policy raising its head again, regardless of who the perpetrators were. Military weapons would be handed over for forensic analysis and every assistance would be given by the security forces administrators to assist the authorities trying to lay blame at the Units door. Of course, ignoring that PIRA had set out on this murderous campaign in the first place. No such inquiry would be conducted into PIRA.

No filing cabinets getting ripped apart to check PIRA shooting records or whether individuals had been up to date with their mandatory training tests. Mac laughed to himself and thought, *Oh how the world is so ill divided.*

The call was received from Musgrave Park Hospital stating Billy was out of theatre. He was still critical but stable and in an induced coma. The surgeons stated the trauma suffered required his body to repair itself and strengthen, giving him a much better chance of survival. A member of the Unit was dispatched to the hospital to provide additional security, given the sensitive nature of the Unit and its personnel.

Liam Murray was placed under police guard as a terrorist suspect but was also critical but stable, having suffered a collapsed lung and a gunshot wound to the shoulder. Everything possible was being done for both casualties. The evening news had also reported the death of Barra O'Neil, the owner of a Snooker Hall on the Springfield Road.

An IRA statement was released, confirming Barra O'Neil had confessed to being an Agent for the Crown and was executed. The news channels reported on the recent death of his daughter, killed by a British Army vehicle near his place of work—a narrative of confusion for many. Why would a man work for the Security Forces having had a daughter killed by them? It didn't seem to make sense. It was a public relations stunt that may have backfired on PIRA.

The deaths of Big Oak and Burning Ash, tragic as they were, had been a direct result of betrayal and deceit. Both had confessed and tried to harm their Handlers. Although in the case of Burning Ash, the detachment wasn't aware of the path of betrayal he was undertaking.

An emergency meeting was held at the Police headquarters at the All-Source Intelligence Cell, termed so because it brought together all intelligence organisations. Much was made of any collaborate information or the lack of it that may have been reported prior to the attack taking place.

It was deemed that most of the police assets knew nothing of the attack. Moreover, much of everyone's attention was on the shooting in Twinbrook earlier in the morning, an assumption Kieran did get right. No vehicles had been reported stolen in the previous 48 hours, or at least none that weren't accounted for.

Despite Weeping Willow's involvement in the operation, everything was being done to assist in reducing the litigation against him. The case was put to the police that he wasn't armed, and although there was a walkie-talkie near the vehicle, which could have been dragged out when the medical teams extracted him from the vehicle, it could have just as easily been discarded or dropped by one of the occupants from the van. In essence, Liam Murray had stolen a car and had panicked resulting in a DOC (Decent Ordinary Criminal) getting caught up in a firefight and getting shot, a measure which any good lawyer could argue. Of course, the NIO (Northern Ireland Office) would compensate him for his injuries. If nothing else, the bosses endeavour brought much laughter to a very serious meeting.

Weeping Willow took one for the cause and survived, that would go down well in the PIRA ranks. If he was to survive and the latest prognosis was good, he would be a good asset to have. The boss left the meeting having done everything in his power to safeguard Weeping Willow.

Chapter 57

Mary's Rise in status

Seamus and Mary left the offices of Sinn Fein and went to the homes of the fallen volunteers. The seventy-year-old woman and mother of the twins took the news extremely badly, sat in a geriatric chair with an oxygen bottle next to her side for her COPD (Chronic obstructive pulmonary disease) condition. She held her rosary beads in one hand, rotating each bead between finger and thumb. She didn't appreciate the visit of Sinn Fein and stated, "The lord will judge my boys but you will have to answer to the Lord for sending them to their death."

The wife of Padraic was also in attendance, and it was a visit and duty Seamus was glad to get over. The promise of a fitting farewell held no favour for either the mother or wife.

The second visit was to Jean O'Kane, who appeared totally apathetic to his manufactured sympathy. She believed if the leader of Sinn Fein could benefit from the death of her husband, he would milk it for all it was worth. Kieran was a volunteer who lived and died for the republican cause but wasn't a fan of Sinn Fein and its pursuit of a United Ireland by adopting dialogue rather than the arms struggle.

Syd Collins was a single man who had been in and out of so many relationships over the years, there wasn't anyone Seamus felt he needed to pay his condolences to.

Roslyn Murray and Shane were at the hospital, waiting at her husband and Fathers' bedside and praying hard for his recovery. Mary told Seamus she would pay Roslyn a visit later, because knowing Roslyn the way she did, she believed sympathies would be better received coming from her rather than the head of Sinn Fein. She further stated, he'd had enough anger directed at him already today, so he should leave it to her.

Seamus told Mary how he was very taken with her and her devotion to Sinn Fein and PIRA. So much so, he suggested the position of Sinn Fein councillor would be offered to her, such was the level of trust he had in her.

This was a dream move for Mary and Military Intelligence. Her level of access would be second to none. Mary would be privileged to all Sinn Fein matters and would get to attend all high-level meetings. Mary's reporting would be invaluable to the British Government when Sinn Fein got back around the negotiations table proper. This development and advancement in Mary's access would be received with utter euphoria back at the detachment, an enormous positive following the recent devastating events inflicted on the detachment.

Mary did visit Roslyn, as suggested, and found the poor woman in a terrible state. Roslyn told Mary that if Liam pulled through and survived, then she would kill him. Mary thought it a very typical Irish thing to say but understood exactly what she meant. Roslyn reminded Mary of their previous conversation about Liam's involvement and the likelihood that he would either end up killed or in the H Block.

Mary tried desperately to keep Roslyn's spirits up by declaring he would survive, and if he got prison time then they could go together, as her boyfriend Jamie was already there. Roslyn said, "Oh, Mary, I'm sorry love, I forgot your fella was in."

"Well, it's not that serious between us, but I guess it would be rude not to visit," she said with a laugh.

Roslyn was grateful for the visit from Mary as well as the offer to have Shane over to stay with her if needed, to give Roslyn time to visit the hospital. Although Roslyn stated he was old enough to look after himself but appreciated the offer anyway. Mary used the visit to try and establish what, if anything, Roslyn knew about Liam's involvement in the ambush attempt. As it was, Roslyn knew he had an early taxi run to Dublin Airport on that morning but he hadn't come home afterwards. Mary left the house, but not before promising to stay in touch.

The fallout of the attack was being felt right across the republican movement, with the PAC demanding a meeting to discuss the post operational report, or better termed, a meeting to get a fall guy for it going so badly wrong. In the opinion of the PAC, it was a hastily organised operation without proper planning and preparation. A development that was unexpected and totally blindsided the PAC was the declaration by Jimmy that Liam Murray was under investigation by himself, as the only member of the ASU to survive the attack and for suspicious actions during the operation itself. Apart from being the only survivor, there was his refusal to take the pistol. He was also conspicuous by his brief absence of the radio, missing several calls on the walkie-talkie, which resulted in Jimmy back tracking and seeing the car void of its driver, although the radio was eventually answered by Liam, stating he had to take a quick nervous toilet break. It was further explained his personal car had been fitted by a tracker and listening device, which were probably placed there to capture conversations with RA members and knowingly by him. The information received by the mechanic indicated it was a well concealed job, which would having taken a significant amount of time to install. So, the question of where and when it took place was important. The speed and reaction of the SAS boys to the attack would suggest they were pre-warned.

This was received with a certain amount of scepticism but was somewhat plausible and needed further investigation. Regardless, Liam Murray was in hospital and in a coma. It would be some time before he could be interrogated.

The news of Jimmy's suspicions was received back at the Sinn Fein office with disbelief. The analyses of Liam Murray's involvement with PIRA were being dissected, operation by operation, any possible compromises being exposed. It was as if they were trying extremely hard to make a narrative fit.

Jimmy remembered Liam had been present at the interrogation of Malachy Tweed with Frankie but not at the nutting. Mind you, the police did raid the cottage hours after his departure. Then he'd helped Jimmy with housing Declan Swan. He was aware of his presence at Mary Sweeny's house and could have reported it to his Handlers. Finally, he turned up late at the safe house for the operation against Micky Crawford. Where was he? Could he have been meeting with his Handlers and telling them of the vehicles being used on the intended operation. Suddenly, it didn't seem so far-fetched. All this, including what Jimmy had already told the PAC about his suspicions, all added up to Liam Murray being a tout.

The opportunity of exploitation for the devices on Liam's car had passed because of his involvement in the operation. It didn't hold the same authority, as he could no longer be considered a poor, hard-working catholic preyed upon by the Brits when he was involved in the operation to kill them. Mary was approached by Jimmy whilst at her desk, who asked about her previous contacts with Liam Murray and whether she had any suspicions whenever he visited her with Frankie. Mary explained she had no interaction with him on any of those occasions, as he always remained in the car. It became evident to Mary that Liam was being suspected, and this was a concern for Mary. She had offered up Liam's name to Billy, as she had done with Micky Crawford. She was now aware of Crawford being a tout, but the revelation that Liam was also, played heavy on her conscience. Although Liam had been working as an Agent long before she mentioned his name, this was unknown by her. It became evident around the office that Liam was under suspicion and Mary knew she should mention this to Billy.

Her next call to the detachment was greeted by Mac, and he informed her that the attack had been on the Unit and that Billy was a casualty. Mary was shocked by this revelation and clearly displayed empathy concerning Billy. Mary took it as an attack on her team and her Handler, but more importantly her friend, and she was clearly shaken. She relayed the suspicions of PIRA concerning Liam Murray and knew she wouldn't get any acknowledgement from Mac whether Liam was or wasn't an Agent. What she did say however was, "If he was working for you, then you need to do something, because he will be interrogated and that's if he survives in the first place, considering his condition." She also informed Mac of her promotion within Sinn Fein and her newfound status as a Sinn Fein councillor, which Mac was thrilled about.

It was a remarkable achievement, which everyone at the detachment and headquarters were delighted about. It was deemed testament to the philosophy of the Unit's belief that if you capture their heart, then you steal their soul. More importantly, it demonstrated the theory behind the onion ring as being correct. Mary, when recruited was on the outer fringes of the ring, but over the years, her access had steadily increased to a point where she was now at the very centre of the onion.

Liam's progress had been slower but still bloody impressive. Both produced intelligence reporting on both the military and the political wings of PIRA. Mary's information about Liam was a major concern. Mac briefed the boss on the developments and the suspicions of PIRA concerning Weeping Willow. It was decided, following a call to the headquarters, that a meeting was to take place with the Operations Officer and the Security Service Advisor, Jeffery from MI5. It was starting to look like a relocation would be needed or at least planned for.

The rise in status for Mary was extremely well received by MI5, with a consideration of Mary being transferred and coming under MI5's jurisdiction. This would mean a new Handler from 'Box' taking over the casework for Wee Fern. Mac believed Box would pull rank on this, and in the chain of command, Billy and himself could end up losing control of their star asset.

Mary's promotion and future employment was secondary, as the pressing matter now was the safety of Weeping Willow. He was vulnerable, and if Jimmy Rice had already decided on his guilt, then being in the Royal Victoria Hospital could expose him to an assassination attempt.

Paul Millar at TCG Belfast was called and warned of PIRA suspicions to make sure the police guard on the ward protecting Liam Murray was made aware of this to likewise ensure increased vigilance.

Liam was eventually taken off the ventilator and appeared to be making good progress. Although agitated and confused to begin with, the doctors checked he hadn't suffered any form of brain damage from being in the coma. Of course, as soon as he was considered compos mentis he was charged with his part in the attempted murder of a soldier (Billy).

Word had got back to Jimmy that Liam Murray was awake but under police guard. Jimmy had convinced himself that Liam was the tout he had promised to hunt out when given the job of internal security. His biggest problem was the need to recruit new volunteers to his team. He had managed to bring in two boys from the Ballymurphy ASU, but internal securities retention stats seemed to curtail his efforts to get the volunteers to come forward. The loss of the complete team wasn't exactly a good recruitment advertisement. A hit on the bedridden ailing patient would be problematic and complex in both planning and execution, but Jimmy was still keen to undertake this regardless, partly to deflect criticism of their failed assassination attempt on the British Military Intelligence Officer. The philosophy of PIRA was the military had to stay lucky all the time and PIRA only needed to get lucky once in their dirty tactics war.

The security on the ward had been doubled until the police considered Liam to be well enough for transfer into custody. Behind the scenes, talks were taking place between the Unit and MI5 to consider contingency plans for the resettlement of the Agent and his family should corroboration be received of any threat to his life. He had survived one interrogation, but the chances of doing so again considering the inferred evidence against him was slim.

***

Dickie Garland had just finished his shift in the ICU (Intensive Care Unit) at the hospital. He met with Jimmy Rice to update him on an increased protection placed on Liam Murray. A second police officer had been added to the guard force. Dickie had been reporting back to Jimmy ever since Liam was admitted to the ward. Jimmy believed if the additional protection wasn't validation of his guilt, then he didn't know what was.

Dickie was quizzed on the hospital security, staff shift changes, and more importantly as far as Jimmy was concerned, the work pattern for the police protection.

PIRA had volunteers who worked for the security company, so ensuring secure access was virtually guaranteed. The Royal Victoria Hospital dated back to the 1700's and was built on the grounds of the old Belfast lunatic asylum.

Right-thinking people in Northern Ireland would tell you the lunatics simply moved over to the other side of the city, took up residence in Stormont, and now run the country.

The Royal still had a network of old tunnels and caverns which were situated below the main wards. These were ventilated by disused plenum system of large fans, which blew clean, warm and humidified air along a tunnel and through the wards. These networks of tunnels were considered a good route to gain admittance to Murray. A diversionary plan was needed if they were to ensure access to the patient. Dickie was asked to provide medical clothing, such as scrubs and shoes sufficient for two volunteers. A sketch plan was handed over by Dickie, detailing the tunnel layout and the servicing lifts leading to ICU.

Accompanied by a conscious security guard, a recce was conducted of the tunnel network and grounds stopping short of using the service lifts for fear of being compromised. The lifts exited directly outside the ICU and would be held by a member of the security staff to ensure a quick getaway.

It was agreed Dickie would ensure access into the ward, which had hydraulic doors controlled from the inside. Dickie would exit just

Onus on Truths

as the ASU hit team exited the lift and approached the door. The ASU members, being dressed in medical clothing would not raise any suspicions. Timing would be essential for the smooth running and execution of the plan. It needed to be soon, as the target was gaining strength and would be transferred back into police custody, thus losing the opportunity for the kill.

Mary was helping the new receptionist settle in following her own promotion when Dickie Garland entered the office with a large parcel wrapped in brown paper and tied with string. He asked for Jimmy but was informed he wasn't in the offices. He asked if the parcel could be passed as a matter of urgency. Mary took the parcel into the kitchenette, setting it on the bench. Her inquisitive nature got the better of her, so she untied the parcel and had a quick look at its contents. The medical clothing set the alarm bells ringing, and she knew it could only mean one thing, and that was making Roslyn Murray a widow and Shane fatherless.

Christ, she thought, *does the level of depravity of these monsters know no bounds?*

The call to the detachment was once again received by Mac, and the disclosure that some sort of attempt was being planned on Liam Murray's life was extremely worrying. Mary didn't know who was to be involved or when it was likely to happen, but the parcel had been delivered and was expected urgently.

The boss, having been briefed by Mac, telephoned Paul Millar and warned him of the potential hit on Liam. Paul explained he had already doubled up on security at the ward following his previous call. The boss questioned the rationale behind such a move, as this only increased the suspicion by PIRA that Liam Murray was more important than first thought. Affectively, the actions had made him a target.

Following the call to Paul Millar, the boss contacted the top surgeon at Musgrave military hospital and asked if a patient in Liam's condition could be moved. Several conversations were had between surgeons of both hospitals and an agreement of a move was obtained. Liam Murray was to be transferred to the military wing of Musgrave.

Chapter 58

Girls Reunited

The meeting with Mary took place back at the detachment. There was much excitement over her promotion, with the boss wanting to congratulate her personally. The suspected planned attack on Liam was discussed, with an exhaustive debrief being conducted to try and ascertain by who and how the attack may take place.

Mary was disappointed she hadn't gained any further information but hoped if she told Jimmy of her intention to visit Liam by accompanying Roslyn, then maybe she would gain an insight into how the information was received. If he discouraged her or stated a better time to go, then it might just give an indication as to when it was likely to be executed. As always, Mary promised to do her utmost to obtain the information. She had managed to convey the name of Dickie Garland to the team as the person who worked within the ICU at the Royal.

The boss remained present throughout the debrief, and once Mac had finished documenting the salient points from the meeting, it was the boss's turn to address Mary with a proposition. He stated there was a special guest who would like to chat with Mary concerning her newfound status within Sinn Fein. The door to the debriefing suite opened, and Jill entered the room.

Mary turned to see her old Handler and friend and was overcome with emotion. The two girls embraced each other, presenting a real display of affection and warmth. The two girls were left alone to catch up, with Jill establishing the framework for future meetings between the two.

There would be a slow handover between Military Intelligence and MI5, with Jill flying into Northern Ireland to co-host the meeting for Mary. It was clear the direction for Mary was going to be led by the team from Box. Mary's access going forward was deemed to be extremely important and would be focused on political issues. Mary was happy with the new arrangements and comfortable, as she'd had several Handlers during her long and successful spying career. At least, it was with someone she already knew.

Chapter 59

Operation Transfer

The operation to move Liam Murray from the Royal was quickly arranged to ensure his safe passage between the two hospitals. The work pattern for Dickie Garland was obtained to ensure his absence from the ward and any possible compromise to the transfer. In the early hours of the morning, Liam, sedated and still connected to a monitor, was transferred to a waiting ambulance. A team from the detachment provided a discreet but heavily armed escort for the short distance between hospitals. Simultaneously, the police arrived at the home of Roslyn Murray, informing her that her husband was under threat from PIRA and that she and her son needed to come with them.

Roslyn was in total shock. She was told to bring any important documents with her, mainly bank cards, chequebooks, and passports.

It was expected that word would get back to Jimmy first thing the following morning once Dickie Garland turned up for work, although he would be arrested anyway for his part in the planning of the operation by supplying material or goods in support of PIRA operations. The home of Jimmy Rice would be searched in the hope the medical clothing would be recovered and therefore implicate him in the operation. Regardless, all suspicions would been confirmed once Liam was transferred and the notable absence of his family was discovered.

Work had been taking place in the background, with the resettlement team on the mainland obtaining temporary accommodation for the Murray Family, along with new identity documents from the security service for their new life abroad. The transition would be difficult, but neither of them had any real family ties left to be concerned about. It was one thing for Liam to go, as he knew the consequences of being caught was punishable by death. But the turmoil Roslyn would endure combined with the stigma she would feel was going to be extremely challenging for the resettlement team. This was a life changing and defining moment in their lives. Life would not nor could not ever be the same again.

Roslyn hastily packed a few small grip bags with personal possessions. She was still in a state of shock. She left it to the last possible minute to wake Shane out of his night sleep to get ready for the unknown. Shane was not a child; it would be a devastating blow to learn his father was a tout and he was going on the run. He had done nothing wrong yet would have to leave all his friends behind. The street was deserted, and no obvious twitching of curtains was taking place. A male and female police team accompanied Roslyn and Shane to RAF Aldergrove and a secluded house at the rear of serving soldiers living quarters. The house was nicely furnished, Roslyn was told it would be her temporary home until Liam was fit enough to join her.

Roslyn was visited the following day by members of the resettlement team, who introduced themselves as Bob and Kathy. They explained that Liam had been working for British Military Intelligence for a very long period and in that time, had saved countless lives with his information. The unfortunate circumstance he now found himself in was just extremely bad luck and unavoidable. They stated Roslyn, Liam, and Shane would be taken and settled somewhere safe to start a new life away from the bigoted thugs of the paramilitaries.

Chapter 60

Wakey Wakey

Liam opened his eyes and tried to adjust to the bright lights above his head. The humming sound of the faulty fluorescent tube and the bleeps of a monitor next to his bed were the only sounds in the quiet ward. Something was different, the smell and décor all seemed new to him. He must have been moved to a different room, which in his mind was positive, this surely meant he was getting better. He heard footsteps getting closer, but they stopped as they reached the curtain which was enclosing his bedspace. Liam waited but no one appeared. "Hello?" he said as the curtain was pulled back to reveal Mac standing in the opened gap. Liam was confused and was trying to make sense of his presence when he became even more confused by the appearance of a doctor dressed in a military uniform with a stethoscope around his neck.

"Good morning, Mr Murray," said the doctor. "I trust you slept well?" The doctor checked Liam whilst Mac waited outside the curtain. Once finished, Mac entered and set on a chair beside the bed. It was explained to Liam that PIRA had planned to execute him and that was the reason he was moved.

"Am I in England?" he asked.

Mac laughed and stated he wasn't and that he had been transferred to Musgrave for his own safety.

"What about Roslyn and Shane?" he asked.

"They are safe and away from harm," he was told.

He started to well up, tears starting to form as he contemplated his future. Liam couldn't comprehend why he was being suspected of being a tout. Mac covered the events of the ambush attempt and the death of the ASU members. He also told Liam about Billy and the death of Micky Crawford. It all started to make sense to him now. Liam tried to explain his part, and how he'd tried to warn the detachment but didn't know what or who the attack was against.

After a long and frank conversation and knowing his family was safe, Liam had accepted his situation and the consequences of his life as an Agent. He would be well looked after, with enough money to start over and live a comfortable life. Just where that was still needed to be decided.

Billy had remained in a coma for two weeks, and during that time, his body had become strong enough to be moved to the neuro recovery ward. The consultant treating him informed his wife Abby that because of post traumatic amnesia (PTA) there could be difficult times ahead. It was explained he may not remember the incident, as his brain would be confused, and he may have long term problems both physically and psychologically. The first face Billy saw was that of his wife. He immediately recognised her but was confused as to the circumstances of him being there.

As the days passed, his memories became less fragmented, and slowly, he was able to put the pieces together. He would later describe it as reading a good novel with twists and plots that only by reading it a second or third time did it really make any sense. When he was considered well enough for visitors, Mac and the boss spent some time bringing him up to speed on the incident and the ongoing media tempest of lies and propaganda vended by Sinn Fein. The disappearance of Liam Murray, 'Traitor and Tout', by the British Secret Service was a front-page headline of the An Phoblacht newspaper.

Billy had made a great recovery, and one of the last visitors to the ward to see him was Liam Murray. Liam was being discharged into the custody of the resettlement team for his reunion with his family and relocation to England. He was destined for a better life, free from terrorism and the hope or expectation of a better life for his son away from Belfast. His service, and more importantly, his access into PIRA would be hard to replace.

Billy made a full recovery from his injuries and returned to active service. He was awarded the Queens Gallantry Medal (QGM) by her Majesty Queen Elizabeth II at Buckingham Palace, accompanied by his wife and two sons. The Queen, who was extremely knowledgeable and totally acquainted with the Northern Ireland situation, remarked how proud she was of all achievements by her Armed Forces and the work done by her undercover soldiers in their fight against terrorism. When asked for Billy's opinion, he stated:

"They haven't gone away you know."

The End

Death Rattle

Epilogue

"Take cover!" was the shout from the gate sentry at Green Village, a private contractor's compound in the east of Kabul. The Ex Gurkha-soldier turned back toward the advancing truck, laden with its thousand-pound bomb. Raising his rifle and taking aim through his iron sight, ensuring it was aligned on the driver. The ex-soldier could see the whites of the eyes of the Taliban suicide bomber as he steered his instrument of death directly at the gate. With a shout of, "Insh allah!" he crashed through the main entrance, detonating his deadly load. No sooner had the sentry shouted his warning that the thunderous noise of the explosion rocked the very foundations of the compound. The shock wave from the kinetic force produced by the explosion shattered the windows of the converted shipping containers used by the Afghans for their bazaar shops, showering the occupants with fragments of glass. The impact of the truck demolished the front entrance but was halted within the chicane which had been designed specifically for the purpose of channelling or stopping such a breach. The detonation managed to blow in the inner gate, thus compromising the internal security of the compound.

The six personnel on duty never stood a chance as the ball of fire rose high into the sky, turning into a gigantic black cloud of smoke and debris which descended as a dark, blanketed mass, covering the compound and temporary blocking out the sun. The force of the blast catapulted the ex-Gurkha-soldier hired to protect the dignitaries within into the blast wall, killing him instantly. The carnage caused by the truck and its lethal cargo left a 25-metre crater in the ground.

Billy was settling into his new surroundings, having just landed at Hamid Karzai International Airport a few hours earlier, when the explosion knocked him off his feet as he was putting away his clothes into his wooden wardrobe, which landed on top of him. Shaking himself free and wrestling with the pile of shirts he had just manage to place on hangers, he grabbed his rifle and body armour and immediately ran for the corridor. He was quickly joined by other contractors as they quickly made their way to the entrance of the building.

"Welcome to Afghanistan," came a voice from behind him.

"The shelter's fifty meters to the left!" another voice shouted.

The sound of Kalashnikovs could be heard as the compound security were exchanging gunfire with the twenty Taliban fighters now rushing in the exposed entrance. Billy turned right away from the safety of the shelter opting to help defend the compound from the would-be attackers. The best form of defence is attack.

He ran past the recreation building and Gym with its over turned sports equipment, crushing glass beneath his feet as he ran. Suddenly, he was knocked off his feet with the sudden impact of a grenade exploding to his right. Twisting his body into the prone fire position, he brought his rifle up to aim whilst looking over the sight and barrel in search of a target or targets. A Taliban fighter armed with an AK-47 was closing in quickly on him. He was instantly recognisable, dressed in typical Afghan 'perahan tunban' (Baggy top and bottoms) with a turban. Billy took aim and, with his rifle on semi-automatic mode, fired a short burst of 2-3 rounds, hitting the fighter in the centre of his chest rig. One of the rounds ricocheted off the magazines within the rig and struck the fighter in the throat with the other rounds penetrating his rig and chest cavity. The fighter fell to his knees, arms dangling by his side as if he was ready to start to pray to Allah. Billy was transfixed on the body in front of him, still in the upright position but clearly dead.

People don't die kneeling up except in the movies, thought Billy.

The shout of, "Target right!" and a volley of shots brought Billy back to his senses, and he instinctively rolled out of the prone position he had previously adopted to seek a more secure location, somewhere that could provide both cover from view and fire. He found it in the form of a small fountain and water feature located in the small communal gardens next to the dining facility.

"Go firm Billy," came the cry of the voice, "The Guardian Angels have it now." As Billy looked up, members of the Blackwater Security Company were running past, but already the sound of gunfire had started to diminish. The voice Billy had heard was now standing next to him.

"Are you going to lay there all day or can we get a beer?"

Billy looked up at the face in front of him, "Mac, good God, I didn't know you were out here!"

"It's my second-year mate. Welcome to New Discovery."

References

AIO. | Assistant Intelligence Officer

CHIS. | Covert Human Intelligence Agent

CT1. | Cover Team One

CT2. | Cover Team Two

FRU. | Force Research Unit

Hardcase. | Secure Military Location

INLA. | Irish National Liberation Army

IO. | Intelligence Officer

MRF. | Military Reaction Force

OCP. | Official Clandestine Premises

OO. | Operations Officer

PAC. | Provisional Army Council

PIRA. | Provisional Irish Republican Army

QRF. | Quick Reaction Force

RSM. | Regimental Sergeant Major

RUC. | Royal Ulster Constabulary

SB. | Special Branch

SRR. | Special Reconnaissance Regiment

Alpha. | Code word for Agent or Target

Box. | Security Service or MI5

HMSU. | Headquarters Mobile Support Unit

Printed in Great Britain
by Amazon